PRICE
OF
LOVE

PRICE OF LOVE

SANDRA ROBINS

PRICE OF LOVE

PAPERBACK ISBN 978-1-7398983-0-4
EBOOK ISBN 978-1-7398983-1-1

*To my **parents**.*
Thank you for your support and vast depths of love.
I love you!

Sarah

The pink neon sign shimmered and flashed. I stood there, paralyzed with fear, even though I knew that I didn't have the luxury of choice. Any choice I had, had vanished two jobs and two loans ago. One thought kept slipping through my mind: *If I do this, my grandmother will be able to stay in a private care home, receiving the best care in town.*

As a child, I lost my parents in a car accident. I only remember them vaguely. My grandmother is all I have left; she raised me on her own, as best as she could, which I am forever grateful for. I was thinking of her, standing on the threshold of a place I would never, ever consider entering of my own free will, not to mention what I was about to do. I must have searched the entire internet until I found a place called *"Lotus Flower"*. I knew from the reviews I could make a lot of money working there; that's why I wanted to do it. It was about the money and about the time—the time my grandmother had left.

Feeling the tension, I pressed the handle, and opened the door. The room was less dingy than I had imagined.

The mild tones reminded me more of a relaxation and massage studio than of a brothel. The young girl at the front desk measured me with her eyes, assessing my qualities. She wore a heavily cut blouse and shorts, and at that moment I regretted not being blessed with bigger boobs.

'May I help you?' she said, sending a sweet corporate smile in my direction.

'I have an appointment with the owner of the premises. I'm looking for a job.' *Phew! I did it.* I wasn't sure how I managed to get the words out of my mouth—the mere thought of what I was about to do made my palms sweat.

'Last door on the left, please knock three times and enter. The boss is waiting for you.'

'Thank you,' I answered and headed hurriedly to the door. If I was going to turn back, this would be the moment to do so. Nevertheless, I knocked three times, and on a polite 'Come in,' I walked through the door.

I was greeted by a man in his 60s, who handed me some documents to fill out as I sat down at the desk opposite him. He looked at me curiously, asking me one simple question, 'Why?'

'Why do I want to work in a place like this? I need money,' I answered truthfully.

'Everyone needs money, but there are other ways to earn it. You seem nice and, no offence, quite innocent. I'm not sure if this place is what you are looking for.' He studied me closely.

'Stand up,' he asked gently. I did so immediately.

'Put your hands up.' I did as he asked.

'Stand on one leg.' Again, I fulfilled his request.

'Good,' he said softly.

He stood up and walked towards me, circling around me like a hawk stalking its prey. I was wrong in thinking that I was dealing with a friendly uncle.

'You are cute,' he murmured. He took a lock of my hair and sniffed it, sending chills down my spine. What am I doing here? Money, I need money! The determination returned.

'Good, very good.' He was still talking to himself. 'Take off your shirt.'

I looked at him in disbelief. He noticed the defiance on my part, because he repeated harshly:

'Take off your shirt and your bra, too,' he added with a glint of amusement in his eyes.

It was good to know that the situation amused him. I, unlike him, was terrified. I had two choices: do what he said or run away. Like a robot, I removed my t-shirt, hesitantly reaching for the clasp of my bra. The clothing landed on the floor. I stood, undressed from the waist up in front of a stranger.

He came up to me, placing a big cold hand on my chest. I shuddered at the foreign touch on my body. A part of my mind protested vigorously, and I had the urge to remove his paw, spit on him and run away. What was I doing? I counted to ten in my head, focussing on my goal. This wouldn't take long. At least, that was my hope.

The man twisted my nipple a little more and began sliding his hand down my pants. Then he sniffed his hand. Frankly speaking, sniffing was an understatement. He inhaled the scent.

The phone rang. The conversation was short and to the point. Only a few remarks like '*yes*', and '*I understand*', as he focused all his attention on me, or rather, on my bare breasts.

'I have the perfect girl for this job. The rate is the same as always.' He grinned at me with his teeth, and he hung up the phone.

'It's your lucky day. Get dressed, I have something better for you. You want to make more than you could here? I'm talking really big money and classy clients.'

I looked at him, having no idea what he was talking about. I reached for my bra and put it on hastily. 'Same as here', he circled with his hand, for added effect, 'But more exclusive.'

The door opened, and an elegant woman entered. Well dressed, about fifty, perhaps older. She looked at me, and a wide grin came to her lips.

'Is that the one?' she motioned at me.

I picked up my shirt in a hurry and put it on.

'I'll take her. She's pretty.'

She placed an envelope on the table, which landed in the man's desk drawer in no time.

The only thing my mind registered was, that I was sold.

* * *

A black limousine was parked in front of the building. Leaning against the car was the driver, who upon seeing us straightened up and opened the door to the luxurious interior.

'There is no need, Marco,' said the lady, 'I know a café at the end of the street, I think we can talk there,' she looked at me expectantly.

I nodded gently, permitting what was to come. We walked on for a while in complete silence. She opened the café door and let me pass.

'What coffee would you like?' she asked politely, looking at me with a smile.

'I'll have a latte,' I mumbled out.

She turned towards the waitress at the counter and ordered. I had a brief moment to look at her. The well-tailored coat seemed very expensive. She wore a pair of flat-front trousers and high-heeled shoes. She was holding a leather briefcase in her hand. The café wasn't busy, they were going to close soon, bearing in mind the late hour of the day. Soon, two aromatic drinks were placed in front of us, and we seated ourselves at the end of the café. I took a sip of my latte and hugged the cup tightly with my hands. To any outsider, we looked like two acquaintances having a cup of coffee. However, I was aware of my situation, and I could not control my hands trembling. I gripped the cup even tighter, finding it hard to act confident with my whole body shaking.

The woman reached into her leather briefcase and handed me a bundle of documents.

'Before we start, you have to sign this. It's a confidentiality agreement.'

She handed me a pen. I looked at her surprised. The hesitation on my face must have been visible, because she started to explain as if she has had this conversation hundreds of times before.

'Signing these papers does not obligate you to work for me. I need to make sure that everything you find out will stay between us. If you decide to work for me, you will be given a contract to sign. Each contract covers six months, and you can either renew it or leave. However, keeping everything you come to know a secret, is binding for the rest of your life.'

I looked at the folder; it sounded like a deal with the devil. I pulled out the papers in one confident motion and read them through to the end.

In a fit of madness, I signed two copies of the document. I left one for myself, putting it in the folder, and I handed the other to the woman.

'I am Suzanne,' she finally introduced herself, 'Most people call me Sue.' She smiled gently, packing her copy into her briefcase. 'Let's get down to specifics. The money you can make with me is huge. Our clients treat the girls with respect. They are rich and influential men or women, depending on your preference. You might need to work at different times of the day. Are you studying?'

I nodded in confirmation and gripped my coffee mug tightly again.

'That's a good thing. I respect girls who have plans in life and are ambitious. If you have a job, you have to take a leave of absence for the duration or give it up altogether. Unfortunately, it is difficult to balance everything, and I know from experience that a "regular" job no longer seems worthwhile in this situation. Every girl works five days a week. All weekends are mandatory. You can choose which days of the week you want to work. Meetings usually consist of dinners, banquets. Your job is to make our clients' time pleasant. Sometimes it is just about providing company at parties; smile, look good and speak as little as possible. More often, it's dining with the client, relaxing and satisfying their needs as much as possible. You know what I mean, don't you? Sometimes you will have to satisfy two customers at once, but don't worry about that for now. Everything, I repeat, everything must take place with your permission. Do you understand?'

'Yes, I think I understand what I'm agreeing to.'

'All right, then. Think about this again,' she said and handed me the latest Samsung, 'I saved my contact number. Please, text me your address when you are ready. My driver will pick you up tomorrow at ten in the morning, and you will meet the other girls. We will then discuss the details of the contract.'

She stood up and hugged me. It took me completely by surprise. She said I was cute, and left.

I sat down wearily in my chair, thinking about what I had just gotten myself into. I could still back out. I probably came off as a total idiot in this meeting. I had so many questions, and I didn't ask a single one. I sipped my already cold coffee, glancing distrustfully at the phone I got from her. After considering the pros and cons, I wrote a text message with my address and sent it off.

* * *

I woke up before my alarm and, even though I had plenty of time, I was almost late for my meeting. I took a shower and thoroughly applied lotion all over my body. My long red hair decided to rebel and curled itself more than usual. After unsuccessful attempts at styling into an elaborate hairstyle, I pinned it up into a loose bun. Everything was going wrong. I spilled coffee on my favourite T-shirt, meaning I had to change into a green blouse, jeans and black suede stilettos. I was used to wearing sneakers every day, so I decided to give myself a boost with sexy shoes.

The driver who came to pick me up turned out to be the same man I had last seen outside Sue's limo. This time he came in a black SUV with tinted windows. I hoped that no one I knew saw me get into it because I didn't want the gossip to start. The driver, named Marco, was very polite to me. However, he was unwilling, or unable to answer most of my questions. Probably, like me, he had signed an agreement to remain silent. The conversation wasn't going too well, so I gave up and decided to use these moments to relax as much as I could. We passed the town where I lived, entering a road between fields with grazing sheep and horses. The wooden fence turned into a grey, high wall of stones; finally, we drove up to a gate with a guard, followed by a gravel road leading to an enormous building. It crossed my mind that it would be difficult to escape from here. The property looked very impressive, like an old mansion with the building arranged in a U-shape. The grey stone glistened in the sunlight. I wondered how many rooms there could be. The building was majestic.

Marco led me into the giant lobby where Sue was waiting. Once again, I was amazed by her beauty. Just like last time, her hair was up in a bun, and she was wearing stiletto heels on her feet.

'I'm glad you are here,' she hugged me gently in greeting, 'First you will meet the girls, and then we will deal with the contract unless you have changed your mind.'

She walked over to the front desk and pressed a button. After a while, girls started approaching me from all directions, introducing themselves. I counted fifteen of them. Each one had a different type of beauty. The last one of them ran down the stairs, and she quickly come up to me.

'She is a redhead! We don't have a ginger one yet,' she said with excitement as if I was some valuable acquisition and not another excuse for a whore.

'I'm Amy! Nice to meet you,' said the petite blonde.

Sue clapped her hands, focusing everyone's attention on her.

'I'd like to invite you for a meeting. It will be on Friday, meaning it's time to arrange the schedule for the weekend.'

'I'm going to have a cigarette,' declared the pretty brunette, 'I need one before I have to listen how to give a blowjob again.'

The rest of the girls laughed, and she started pretending how to give a guy head. The rest burst into even greater laughter.

Sue just rolled her eyes. 'You have seven minutes.' She turned to me and said, 'Come on.'

I followed her into the other wing of the building, and we took our seats in a large room with a massive table in the middle. Amy, the brunette whose only name I remembered, sat down next to me. She handed me coffee in a cup.

'Is it okay with milk?' she asked.

'Yes. Perfect!' At least I had something to keep my hands busy.

'Sugar is over there,' she pointed to a table in the corner of the room, where I spotted coffee in a thermos, sugar, milk and cookies.

The rest of the girls were watching me with evident curiosity. I felt again like it was my first day of school

- silly and foreign. I focused my attention on Sue. She was handing out folders to each of us.

'Inside, you have a schedule. If you have any questions, you know where to find me.'

'I'm going to Greece for a week!' One girl was happy, looking through the contents of the folder.

'Yes, the client has decided to take you with him. If you have any problems, call me. And this time, wear UV sunscreen. I don't want you coming back burnt like last time and looking like one big disaster.'

'Alright,' answered the girl, lowering her gaze while the rest cheerfully started to comment.

'Remember that we have an open show for the gentlemen today,' Sue continued, 'I hope you are ready for tonight. If you decide to stay with us, you can help hand out drinks. That's enough work for your first day,' she said in my direction.

'We gather at the club at eight o'clock and please don't be late. That's all for now.'

The girls started to leave the room obediently.

'Come into my office. We will discuss your contract,' said Sue.

We walked along the corridor to her office, where I sat down at the desk. Documents were waiting for me to sign, and I glanced at the large file of papers.

'Read it first. It has everything you need to know. I'll leave you alone. If you want something stronger, help yourself. The bar is over there,' she smiled, pleased with her own joke.

'I'll check on you in a bit. I'm glad you decided to join us.' She put her hand on my shoulder with encouragement.

I probably looked like I wanted to run away. I focused on the documents, first, typing in basic information on the questionnaire, such as my first name, last name, and place of birth. Then there were a few questions about my preference for music, sports from my girlhood and the present, and whether pole dancing was familiar to me? That's interesting. A few questions about favourite places, dishes, my day-to-day routines. I felt like there was a question that applied to every part my life. Then I moved on to the next part of the survey. It began by questioning whether I was a virgin. And that was the moment when I decided I needed a drink. I poured whiskey into a glass and taking a big sip, smiled at the thought that she must have known, by offering me an alcoholic endorsement, that I would have a hard time. I returned to the questionnaire with the booze in my hand. It got worse with each successive question. Whether I approved anal sex, what toys I enjoyed, what I didn't want to do in bed? Would I allow sexual intercourse in public places, such as the restroom at a restaurant? I took another sip of alcohol. It felt like an emotional rollercoaster. Finally, read the information on the possibility of me getting pregnant. I had no right to seek proof of paternity or ask for alimony. I drank the rest of the alcohol.

This was not an ordinary contract. I didn't expect to be required to sign something like this. I topped up the drink and reviewed my situation. I still needed money. The girls I met did not look worried or upset. Each of them looked immaculate and happy. The contract was for six months, not my whole life, but I knew that nothing would be the same after that. I had no choice. I signed the documents.

* * *

I flitted between the tables with my tray, carefully not to kill myself in the high heels I chose to wear this evening, or should I say, was made to wear. All the girls looked very elegant and defiant, all wearing high heels. I, on the contrary, was working as a waitress tonight. I was dressed in black mini shorts and an open back top. Thanks to the white and black cuffs on my wrists, I was supposed to look more like a waitress. I found myself smiling at the thought. This whole day seemed so surreal. It had only been a few hours since arriving at the residence.

I was walking to the bar when a guy grabbed my arm.

'Honey, can you get me another scotch on the rocks?'

He set the empty glass down on the tray, which I almost dropped. He grabbed my hand so unexpectedly that I flinched slightly. I walked over to the bar and placed my order with the bartender. Apart from a few security guards, he was one of the few men working here. He looked very handsome and had a boyish charm about him. I knew from rumours that he was one hundred percent gay. He knew most of the guests and various facts about their lives - a veritable mine of knowledge.

Some men were frequent guests, but some came only once, as a birthday present or a bachelor party. Everyone was carefully checked, and their names and credit cards were entered into a special database.

After another run between the tables, I began feeling tired. I slumped slightly on a stool at the bar to give my legs a rest, if only for a moment. I don't think I'll ever get used to high heels, I thought bitterly.

'A long night?' the blond guy on the stool next to me asked. 'May I buy you a drink?' He smiled sympathetically.

'I don't think I should drink.' I tried to decline politely. Tonight, I was just a waitress. I didn't have to entertain the guests.

'You should celebrate your first day on the job,' he summoned the bartender.

'How do you know it's my first day? Is it that obvious?' I gasped with a whine and hid my face in my hands.

He began to laugh and said, 'Pour the lady a Prosecco,' he asked the waiter and placed a glass of bubbly in front of me. 'Drink it. It will help you loosen up,' he encouraged.

I took a big gulp and felt the alcohol flowing right into my stomach. I knew I could drink while working here, but not so much that I would get drunk—everything in moderation.

'Shall I tell you a secret?' he asked in a conspiratorial whisper.

'Go ahead!' I answered in a whisper as well.

'You look very professional. I know all the girls, so that's how I know it's your first day. I just wanted to get to know you, to have a drink with you.'

He raised his glass in a gesture of toast. I felt relaxed for the first time in hours.

The lights went out, and the room suddenly filled with darkness. The buzz of conversation quieted down, and the tuneful music was replaced by Rihanna's song Umbrella. I would never choose such a song for my performance. It's not really my thing, but seeing the girl on stage moving to this music made me understand her choice. This song was made for her. Her movements were perfectly in tune with the melody. It was the first time I had ever seen someone dance like that live. She moved lightly and looked seductive and sexy. She had everything that attracted men to places like this and made them pay a lot for an ordinary drink.

I caught a glimpse of the man next to me. Instead of watching the performance, he was watching me with interest. The song came to an end, and the room grew brighter again. Sue was approaching us with a quick step. I stood up and waited for her to tell me to get back to work. She, on the other hand, greeted the blonde-haired man effusively, and they left together. Before he left, he looked at me and said, 'See you later, Sarah.'

I was perplexed because, after all, I hadn't introduced myself to him, and he knew my name anyway. I, on the other hand, had no idea who he was. As time passed, more and more girls were leaving with customers. After a while, only a few guests and bar staff were left. I cleaned up the last glasses. I was glad that the evening had come to an end. At that moment, I only dreamt about going to bed and taking off my shoes. I didn't care if it was my bed or the room I got at the residence.

The blond guy showed up at the bar again. He offered to drive me home. I agreed with a slight hesitation, but I was happy to get to fall asleep in my bed. We went together to the car where Marco was already waiting to take us home. During the trip, I found out that the mysterious guy's name was Alex. Despite being tired, we had a pleasant talk. In front of my house, I hurriedly said goodbye and ran towards the front door. I wanted to fall asleep as soon as possible. It was almost 4 a.m., and I didn't want to look like a zombie the next day.

I woke up around noon to three missed calls from Sue on my company cell phone, as well as a message saying that she doesn't need me today and I would see her again Sunday afternoon. I put the phone back on the table and snuggled back under the covers, falling into a shallow sleep.

The next day, I spent the entire afternoon at my grandma's place. She was having one of those days and didn't recognise me. The disease was progressing, and I couldn't handle it. The only thing I could do for her was to give her the best care I could afford. In the beginning, I reacted with disgust and aggression when I heard about a special clinic for people with progressive dementia. Ironically, I looked at my granny and thought it was a joke. After all, she wasn't that old yet. At the time, I thought this problem only affected much older people. I knew absolutely nothing about this disease doing my best to keep my grandma with me.

It started with small things, like asking about things I'd already bought or hiding objects in odd places. Unfortunately, her dementia progressed rapidly. It got to the point where she didn't recognise me. Even worse, she began acting out aggressively. She thought I was just a stranger trying to rob or kill her. I waited as long as I could before I decided to place her in a specialised institution.

Today she was having a weaker day again. She looked at me like I was an intruder and not her beloved granddaughter. I looked at her, and all I wanted was to become a little girl again and cuddle with my granny. I left her favourite cake on the table and kissed her forehead gently, to which she shooed me away like an intrusive fly, and I left in a hurry. On my way out, I wiped away a flowing tear.

I fell behind in my payments to the clinic. Unfortunately, these services were costly and beyond my financial capabilities. I hoped that working for Sue would change things.

In the hallway, the manager caught up with me.

'Sarah, I'm sorry to have to remind you that you are behind on your payments.'

'Yes, I know. By the end of the week, I will pay off some of the debt, I promise.'

I have to ask Sue for an advance, I noted in my mind.

I saw the relief on the manager's face. I was unable to count the number of times she had asked me about money. The last time she told me directly that I would have to take my grandmother home. At the same time, she knew it was impossible. At that point, I started looking for a quick solution to get the money.

I picked a coffee on the way and strolled around the city. I was doing absolutely everything to avoid going home, where another tough conversation was awaiting me.

When did my life become so complicated? To cover the hole in my budget, I rented one room. My friend's cousin was looking for an apartment, and I was looking for a tenant. At the very first meeting, I liked this boy, who became my best friend.

'Do you think something is wrong with me?' I asked him a question.

We were sitting together in the living room on the sofa.

'You are smart, kind, pretty, slim and red-headed. What could be wrong with you?' Alan looked at me closely, 'What's more, you have a sexy ass. Sexy asses are… sexy!' He patted his thigh lightly for better effect.

I started laughing. The way he said things made them all sound so simple. There was nothing wrong with me. My proportions were kept up, so why were guys running away from me? What the hell was it about me that no one wanted me?

'Maybe I'll dye my hair, and it'll give me a serious look. Maybe I'll go for a nice bronze. Guys like brunettes, ' I thought out loud.

'Don't even dare to touch it, or I'll cut your fingers off. You have the most beautiful, coppery hair colour I've ever seen, and you want to change it? It's perfect. Every guy dreams of having a ginger like you in his bed. Well, maybe not every guy.' he corrected himself hastily. 'Actually, I don't count.' He waved his hand as if he wanted to push away unwanted thoughts.

That's what I loved about him endlessly. He could always lift my spirits, give me good advice in any situation. If only he knew what was on my mind…

I poured us some more wine and gave him a glass. The plan was simple. If we were slightly drunk, it would be easier for me to ask him for a favour. I knew he was the only person I trusted completely. We had just watched a movie, and I couldn't remember a single scene because

I was so stressed. I set the popcorn bowl down on the table and looked at him shyly.

'What's going through that beautiful head?'

He noticed I was up to something. He knew me too well.

'Well, I have a certain problem, and I think you can help me.'

Alan knew my story and supported me as much as he could. I owed him already too, and even if he insisted, I wouldn't take a penny more from him.

'I know how to make a lot of money in a short time, but there is one detail that bothers me.'

'Let it all out,' he said with a bit of amusement.

'My virginity,' I said without thinking.

He raised his hands in protest, 'Oh no, you can forget about it! You'll have to deal with this on your own.'

'Don't leave me like this, please! I know you don't do this with women, but why don't you treat me like an exception?' I looked at him with the most pleading eyes I could afford.

'No way. This is… this is… inappropriate. Don't look at me like that! I'm not going to do it!'

'You just push, and that's it. I don't expect anything else.'

He looked at me like I was an alien, 'Just? Do you know what that means? Where are the butterflies in your stomach? Where are the feelings? You can't treat it that way. That first time should be memorable, magical!' He pressed his hands to his heart with dreamy eyes,

'It should be perfect. And me?' He looked at me reprovingly. 'I'm gay, have you forgotten? No way. It would be easier for you to seduce some naive guy in a club. Wait, what did you say? Why do you want to get rid of your virginity, and why right now?'

'I am twenty-one years old! At this age you can't say it's rushed.'

'Don't change the subject,' he threatened me with his finger, 'I have to pour us some wine. I can't be sober for a conversation like this.'

He went to get another bottle.

I explained to him the proposition I had received. I had to admit, he was not enthusiastic. He sat quietly for a while.

'I'm not going to say that I support what you are going to do, but I am your friend. Friends support each other. Tonight, we're going to find you some horny sucker and solve your problem. It's Saturday night. Go, take a shower. Do all those magical things women do, and we're going to the club. It's hunting time!' he said, pushing me gently toward the bathroom.

I got ready faster than usual. I still had a condom I got from a friend, which I placed safely inside my bra. I was wearing a dress that was far too short. I had bought it once but never wore it: it was hardly suitable for walking on the street, but for the club it was perfect. It barely covered my butt. Before I knew it, we were there. Today the place was unimaginably crowded. Some famous DJ was playing music. We had two shots and a cocktail for courage. Alan took me to the middle of the dance floor, and after a few moments I was already enjoying myself. I discreetly looked around for the perfect guy or at least someone close to it. If I didn't love him, at least let him be handsome. I smiled at the thought of this ridiculous plan. A few guys hung around me during the dance, but none were good enough. After a few tunes, I went to the bar for another drink. Alan had gone to the restroom, so I was alone.

'Where is your friend?' a man queuing next to me asked.

'I think he's lost.' I assessed him from head to toe. He must have been watching me, too. He knew I wasn't alone here.

'My friend owns this club.'

He tried to impress me with cheap talk. I wondered if I should let him off the hook. But I had to admit that he could pass for handsome. All his features were in the perfect place. Unfortunately for me, he was too fancy. I didn't like that kind of man, but it was enough for tonight.

'Would you like to dance?' he offered. We left our glasses, and he told the bartender to keep an eye on them. They seemed to know each other. We danced to two songs. I had to admit, he knew how to move on the dance floor. The dance felt like foreplay. I got goosebumps just thinking about what I was going to do. He gently brushed his hand over my shoulder, his blue eyes with a humorous glint.

'Shall I show you the rest of the club?'

I nodded my head as a sign of agreement.

He grabbed my hand and led me toward the back room. I caught sight of Alan, who's flash of his eyes indicated that he was waiting for me. A door closed behind us with a sign '*Admission for staff only*', and it immediately felt quieter around us. We found ourselves in a small office. The next thing I registered, were his lips on my mouth. I tried to keep up with his pace. It was obvious that he often invited his friends here from the dance floor. I could feel his insistent tongue, as I tried to return the kisses with the same intensity. His hands gently, deliberately roamed my body. When I felt my ass stop against the edge of the desk, I came to my senses. I evidently hadn't drunk enough to do through with it in this way. My partner sensed that I was pulling back gently, and stopped kissing me.

'What's going on? You don't want to?' he looked at me with a lusty gaze.

'It's too fast,' I responded.

The man took a deep, calming breath.

'Okay,' he ran his hands through his hair, ruffling his perfect hairstyle, 'I'm Mick. Can I take you out for coffee?'

I looked at him in disbelief.

'I'm Sarah. I'd love to go for a coffee with you.' I started laughing.

'Mick, man, I need the documents from my desk.'

The door opened, and man walked in. He looked at Mick, then shifted his focus on me. He assessed my dress, which made my legs appear twice as long as they were. Looking into my eyes, he held my gaze until I broke it off. A knowing smile appeared on his lips.

'We're leaving now,' answered Mick, 'We're going dancing.'

Just like last time, he grabbed my hand and pulled me towards the dance floor. That's when it dawned on me.

I waved to Alan that I was okay. I continued dancing for another hour. I noticed that my friend had a few pretty girls hanging around, but he turned them all away. My head was buzzing by the end of the evening, and my feet felt sore from the high heels, but I was having fun and didn't want to go home yet. I'm not sure when I would have the opportunity to go to a party for fun and not for work. By the end, Mick and I exchanged phone numbers so we could arrange that coffee date.

* * *

I made it to the residence in my blue Volkswagen Polo. I hoped it wouldn't break down on the way there. Lately, I've been hearing disturbing sounds from under the hood, and it was yet another thing in my life that needed to be fixed. I parked by the 'For staff only' sign and entered through a side entrance. This was my second time here, and I still felt in awe about the size and luxury of the mansion. I carried a bag, which contains my most necessary things just in case I had to spend the night here. I greeted the girls in a friendly manner and went to my room, which I would temporarily live in. The room was quite big. There was a huge bed in the middle with a bedside table next to it. There a dressing table on the side and two armchairs with a table in the centre.

I put my toiletries in the bathroom adjacent to the room and hung my clothes in the closet.

A few minutes later, Sue knocked on my door and introduced me to the gynaecologist. I was relieved that she was a woman. We had talked earlier about the necessary blood tests to rule out any diseases. I also decided to start taking birth control pills. The doctor took my blood sample, handed me the pills and said goodbye. The results were to be ready the next day by noon, sent by email. After that, I could officially go out with clients. There was only one small detail left to be agreed upon.

I asked Sue about the advance payment because I could no longer pretend that I did not need money urgently. She smiled gently and wrote a check. Seeing the amount, I was slightly surprised.

'That's too much. I haven't earned anything yet.'

'Relax. This is just the beginning,' she laughed, seeing my confusion. 'I told you there is a lot of money at stake. For that, you need at least ten sets of new lingerie, stockings, stilettos, and of course, dresses. Let me ask someone to take you to the boutique and help you pick something. How about Amy? I've seen you get along with her.'

I shouldn't have been surprised. Nothing could escape her attention in this place.

'Tomorrow, after breakfast, the dance instructor will come. You'll take some lessons. You need to learn how to be confident on stage. Stage familiarity is fundamental. You did well last night at the bar, several customers were asking about you.'

Her words gave me confidence. I saw it coming, but I was still surprised. I felt even more disappointed that nothing had worked out from my Saturday hook-up.

'Don't worry. You'll let me know when you're ready.'

* * *

We waited for the instructor in the gym. The pole dancing class was about to start any minute. I could feel the excitement, and even though the girls tried to engage me in conversation, I didn't pay attention to them at all. I didn't like to exercise, especially cardio. I was more the lazy type, but I knew would not go over well here. It was already pointed out in the introduction that I had to be able to move on stage. Dancing on demand is nothing special. I heard a story about one girl who got drunk and decided to dance on the table. She fell off, but thankfully, nothing happened to her. She got over her fears, and only a few bruises appeared. After this incident though, Sue made a fuss. She reprimanded all the girls that you have to know how to handle your drink. It is not forbidden, but getting wasted is prohibited.

I was thinking about my first job. What will the first client be like? Will he be young or old? Will I be able to cope afterwards?

Just as I suspected, I had very weak leg and arm muscles, and struggled to stay on the pole. The other girls were doing it effortlessly. At the time, it didn't look complicated. I agreed with the instructor that I would participate in the class just like the other girls. My goal was not to be discouraged and to train as much as I could. On top of that, he was going to teach me the basics of erotic dancing with props, which meant that there would be no getting around it without regular training.

At that point, I realised how much energy this would take. After my workout, I was tired and hungry. When I got to my room, I found an envelope on my bed containing my test results. The good news was that I was as healthy as a fiddle. I also found iron supplement pills. I was deficient. *'Take one a day'*, I read on the package.

The girls I took the pole dancing class with were eating lunch in the kitchen. I surveyed the fridge. After some consideration, I made myself toast with cheese and ham. Seeing what they were eating, I felt guilty for not choosing vegetables and chicken.

Amy ran into the kitchen. I was amazed at how energetic she was.

'What's good to eat here?' she glanced at our plates, 'Can you make one toast for me? I had a rough night.'

'Night and afternoon,' said the petite blonde.

'Tell me about it,' laughed Amy. 'I'm only going to eat and sleep until tomorrow.'

'We are off tonight. Are you coming with us to the club?' asked one of the girls.

She shook her head in despair, 'I guess I'll skip the lie-in after all. Wake me up early enough so I can get ready. You should come with us too,' she said to me.

'I already promised to meet my friend in the evening.'

'Take him with you,' the girl with blond hair suggested enthusiastically.

'I'll ask him if he wants to.'

'You have to come; you're a member of the team now.'

'Thanks!' I reached for the toast and bit into it. I was lucky to have inherited good genes from my parents, and I didn't put on much weight, regardless of what I ate.'

I called Alan. He liked the idea of going out together. We both loved to dance. Since I got to the residence, I've had hardly any time for him. Even though I gave up my previous job, I was swamped. I visited my grandmother as often as I could, exercised regularly and helped out at the residence.

I was going to meet Alan at the club. The girls and I were taking a cab. The residence was in uproar. It was rare that all the girls could go out together. This time they had asked for a free Saturday evening. Everyone wanted to look perfect.

Amy was sitting on my bed. I browsed through my clothes while she helped me pick out an outfit for the evening. It was already my sixth outfit in a row.

'I liked you best in leather pants and a glossy top. Sexy, but not slutty.'

'Thanks for the honesty.' I sipped my "relaxation" drink, which is what Amy called it. For today, she chose to wear white jeans and a black corset. To me, it looked more like underwear than a t-shirt, but she looked pleased with her choice.

We arrived at the club before eleven, and I followed the girls to the VIP entrance. I saw the envious looks of the people in line. It was the best club in the city, so the number of people queuing was always gigantic. I knew it because not so long ago, I was standing in line myself. Somewhere in the distance, I heard my name. My friend ran up to me and kissed me on the cheek.

I introduced him to Amy, and he kissed her in greeting as well. Sometimes I forgot how direct he could be with women.

'Come with us,' Amy said, next she grabbed him under the arm, and I did the same on the other side. At the entrance, the security guard gave each of us a stamp on our wrist, and we went in.

'I'm a VIP,' Alan rejoiced. 'What a coincidence, this is the same club where we went to last time.'

'Have you been here before? Nice place! We get free drinks here. Let's get something.' Amy dragged us to the bar.

After my third drink, if we were counting the one before the party, my head was buzzing. I was getting drunk fast, so I had to control myself. I was relaxed enough not to care if anyone was looking at me, and let myself be carried away by the music. I jumped and screamed because they had just played Jon Bon Jovi's old hit. *It's My Life*—such a great song to jump and go wild to. I danced out all the stress from the past week.

We were dancing on the lower dance floor of a two--level club. Upstairs I could see tables where we could sit freely without any problems. It was rather impossible to talk over the loud music.

Upstairs I spotted a man who seemed to be looking in my direction. I looked to my side, making sure he wasn't looking at someone next to me. He was looking at me. I probably wouldn't have paid attention to him, but he was in a suit, which looked out of place in here.

On top of that, he wasn't having fun. He was just watching. If I wasn't mistaken, it was the owner of the club—the same guy who surprised my would-be lover and me in the staff office. I tried not to pay attention to him, but it was difficult. My gaze involuntarily fled in his direction.

'Would you like a drink?' Amy shouted over the music.

'Yeah, last one. Let's go' I grabbed her hand, and we started squeezing through the crowd toward the bar. I ordered vodka with cranberry juice. I turned around and saw him again. He was still looking at me. Now I was sure he was watching me.

'What are you looking at?' Amy asked, sipping her vodka cola.

'I think someone is watching me. Right there on the balcony. A guy in a suit.' I pointed discreetly in the direction without turning around.

'Where? I don't see anyone.'

'Right there.' I turned around, and there was an empty space where he stood. He had disappeared. I couldn't tell if I was relieved or disappointed.

'You either imagined it, or maybe you caught his eye, and he's on his way over to you.'

'Your last one,' Alan threatened me, pointing to the drink in my hand. He knew very well that if I drank more, I would end up having a sleepless night with a toilet bowl instead of a pillow.

'I haven't seen you drunk yet,' Niko interjected.

'I see you have met our bartender.'

'Yes,' said Alan shyly, as if asking for permission to make his acquaintance.

'Just please don't try to get information about me from him,' I threatened Niko with my finger.

He just laughed, 'It's too late now. We began our acquaintance talking about you.'

'Well, that's great,' I rolled my eyes. 'Come on, let's dance because the world is starting to spin.'

We got back on the dance floor and danced until the club closed.

I got to my room in the morning. I washed off my makeup which was now on its last legs. It didn't work very well, with the mascara just smearing over my face. I brushed my teeth and changed into my PJ's. I fell asleep immediately, cuddling my head into my pillow.

I woke up to the banging on my door.

'Go away,' I shouted, 'Whoever you are.'

Niko came into the room.

'Get up, sleepyhead. It's already one o'clock, and I brought you a dose of vitamin C, in other words, freshly squeezed orange juice.'

I looked at him suspiciously.

'Alan's concerned?' I asked.

'Your mobile is off, so he sent me to check on you. He asked me to let him know in ten minutes, or he'd be here.'

'Now I have two nannies?' I whined.

'He's your friend. It's natural for him to be worried.'

'Exactly, he's my only friend, so you should know I care about him a lot. Remember that.'

'We just exchanged phone numbers. Perhaps we'll go out for coffee. Now take a bath. Olivia made a big pot of soup for everyone downstairs.'

'Olivia?'

'She can be nice sometimes, but only sometimes…'

I fell on the pillows a few moments later, and I buried myself in the warm quilt. Much later, after a long bath, I finally looked like a human again. I pulled on my leggings and a loose T-shirt with "Every Red is… Beautiful" written on it. I got it from Alan for Christmas last year.

I engulfed a plate of soup in the kitchen. It was delicious. I heard something about watching a movie together in the TV room, and squeezed myself onto the sofa between Amy and Niko. We still had three hours before the next showcase event. Just like last time, I was going to be a waitress.

* * *

Early in the morning, I had a class at the university, and after that, I immediately went to my grandma's. She looked tired and fell asleep pretty quickly. I didn't stay long. Another dance class was waiting for me. This time it was individual. I was preparing a dance routine with a chair. I felt barely alive after that. I thought that the last class was a tough workout. However, this time, I found out I was seriously mistaken. My legs were shaking like jelly an I was sore all over. I dragged myself up the stairs, dreaming of a hot bath. Sue called out for me from downstairs when I had almost made it to the top.

'Is this a joke? I have to go down again?'

'Come quickly! I have good news,' she looked pleased.

'I'm coming, but it is going to take me longer. My legs are killing me.'

'Come on. You'll be strong and fit. Your ass is going to get super lifted.'

'Is there something wrong with my ass?'

She laughed out loud. 'You're so sweaty.'

'I told you, I just had a workout.'

'Training, not swimming'. I made her laugh even more.

What put you in such a good mood?

'You have your first contract.'

'Me? What?' I was speechless. I sat down on the bottom step, 'I'm not ready to… you know.'

'Don't worry about it. It's a different kind of business. You have a dinner date. Here are the restaurant details. He'll meet you there.'

I took the piece of paper from her hands. The name of the restaurant didn't tell me anything.

'Wear a white blouse, black elegant pants and stilettos.'

'Alright. I can't believe this.'

'I can see. You'll give me some feedback when you are back,' she said with such excitement as if we were friends and my dinner wasn't an errand for an expensive escort agency.

'Marco will drive you to the place. Good luck.'

I looked up and said, 'I think I'm going to sit here for a little bit longer.'

After a while, Amy appeared with a plate full of cookies. 'You want one? Why are you sitting like that?' She sat down.

I took the treat off her plate. 'I got my first job.'

'Congratulations!' She was so happy.

'It's going to be an unforgettable night.'

'It's just dinner,' I cooled her enthusiasm.

'Excellent. That's great news, too. You should be getting dressed instead of sitting here.'

'Only if you drag me upstairs.'

Amy kept laughing, but I didn't see anything funny about the situation. I knew that the next day I'd have extremely sore muscles, and I'll barely be able to move. She walked me to my room and I took a quick shower as there wasn't enough time for a bath. The bubbles had to wait until tomorrow. Meanwhile, Amy was snooping around in my closet. Amy herself helped me choose most of my clothes. She had a great sense of what I needed to wear to look good.

'Put this on.' She put the hanger with the little black dress against her body. 'You have great legs, and they need to be shown off.'

'I am to wear black pants, a white blouse and stilettos. Sue's orders.' I tried to comb my long curly hair.

'Then at least let the shoes be red.' She spun around in the middle of the room with a pair of stilettos in her hand.

'There was no question of the colour, so let them be red,' I agreed.

Amy fixed my hair in an elaborate bun. It is a miracle. Taming my hair was no mean feat.

'You should be a hairdresser.' I touched my hair, for which I got a slap on my hand.

'Don't touch it. I haven't sprayed it yet.'

'You have talent,' I convinced her.

'I like to pin up my hair and comb it and even dye it.'

'Go to school or take a course.'

'You really think I could do that?'

'Just look at this beauty on my head. You're made for it.'

'I'll think about it.' She sprayed a lot of hairspray in my hair. 'I'll lend you my red clutch bag. It'll go perfectly with the whole thing. Don't forget the condoms.'

She ran out, only to return with a beautiful soft red leather clutch bag and a whole box of condoms. Not a package, but a box. She stuffed two into the purse and the rest under my bed.

'It's just dinner.' I protested weakly. Besides, no one here knew I was a virgin except Sue.

'Better safe than sorry.' She kissed me some more and said, 'Good luck! And I want to be the first to know the details.'

Marco drove me to the restaurant. As always, he was low-key and reserved.

* * *

As soon as I crossed the restaurant's threshold, the wonderful smells of the food enveloped me. My stomach contracted painfully. I was afraid I wouldn't be able to swallow anything because of my nerves. At the reception desk, I gave my name. The waiter led me to a table. I had arrived first so I took a sip of water.

After a while, the waiter came to my table to take my order. 'Good morning, what can I get you?'

'Thank you, please give us some more time,' said a voice behind my back.

'Of course,' he said and quickly walked away.

As soon as we were left alone, I smiled widely. My mystery man turned out to be the blond guy from my first day in the residence.

'Hello, I should formally introduce myself. I'm Alex.'

'Sarah.' I shook his hand. 'Nice to see you again.'

'Nice to see you, too. What would you like to drink? Prosecco?' He smiled cheekily, subtly reminding me of our first meeting.

'Please.' I let him choose.

'Are you disappointed that it's me?'

'Disappointed? On the contrary. You've intrigued me lately.'

'That was the plan,' he winked at me. At that moment, the tension faded, and we had a lovely time. He told me about his parents, his brother. He asked about dance lessons, my family. I realised how quickly the time passed when they served dessert, and after a while, the meeting ended. It took a few minutes to catch a cab for me. I dreaded saying goodbye. What was I supposed to do? Shake his hand? Kiss him? When the car pulled up, Alex embraced me gently and kissed my cheek.

'Sleep well,' he whispered in my ear.

I got into the cab. He paid the driver for the fare and then stood on the sidewalk until I completely lost sight of him. It was a pleasant evening. I found the man to be funny and charming, and I felt very comfortable in his company. At the same time, I had a feeling that something was going on here that I wasn't aware of.

The next day, right after class, Alan and I went to our favourite burger place. The burgers were huge, made from fresh meat and served in a crispy bun. We visited my granny together. I also told him about dinner the night before. He said I had nothing to worry about. The most important thing was that I had a good time, making me feel reassured by his words.

I met with Alex a few more times. I liked him. I laughed a lot when I was with him. We were at the cinema, and he let me choose a movie. I opted for a comedy. We would both burst out laughing at the same time. We both liked to eat well. He would take me to expensive restaurants that I wouldn't normally be able to afford. Sometimes we would accidentally bump into his friends, and then he would pass me off as his friend. Each time, he kissed me on the cheek to say goodbye and ordered a cab back to the residence. He never tried to kiss me on the lips or touch me. He also never personally came to pick me up. The next day, money was deposited into my account. It felt strange to see it. Alan concluded that the guy must be very lonely. After all, he was paying for companionship. Simple camaraderie. There was no chemistry between us, no attraction. Nothing worth paying so much for.

Alex and I went out to eat again. I bought a roll to feed the ducks in the pond at the park. It was mid--September, and I loved this time of year. Winter was always difficult for me. Cold hands and feet. A nightmare. I exposed my face to the sun and closed my eyes, relishing the warmth of the rays on my skin. I knew he was watching me.

'I need to ask you something,' he began uncertainly.

'I'm all ears.' I didn't move, not wanting to risk him changing his mind and not saying what he came here for. I knew him well enough to know that he was nervous about something today. He just wasn't as relaxed as he always was.

'I'm going to my parents for three days. Will you come with me?'

I opened my eyes and looked at him, surprised.

'Parents? Your parents?'

'Yes. We'll have a lovely weekend. If they ask if we're together, please don't deny it.'

'Is that what you want? You want me to pretend? And if they ask how we both met?'

'We'll say we met at the ice cream parlour.'

'An ice cream parlour? Sweet start to a friendship. Are you suggesting that I'm an ice cream person?' I was staring at the water. 'Okay, that's fine. I'll go with you.'

He happily lifted me in his arms and began to spin in circles with me.

'Put me down, people are watching!'

'Let them watch.'

The people around us were stopping, smiling. They probably thought we made a cute couple—a couple for the next three days.

* * *

I packed everything I could possibly need for a getaway weekend in my suitcase. At Sue's insistence, I even packed a swimsuit. Apparently, there was an indoor pool on-site, and the house was located right next to the beach. I couldn't remember the last time I had been to the seaside. Probably when I was a child. It would be nice to feel the sand beneath my feet again.

I informed my grandma that I was going away for a few days and would get in touch with her as soon as I got back. On the way there, we stopped for lunch. Alex explained that his parents were celebrating their wedding anniversary and were throwing a small party to mark the occasion. I expected it to be some sort of special occasion, as Sue had told me to pack an elegant dress for the evening. The reception was scheduled for the following day. Today, however, we were going to have a casual dinner together. At the very thought of it my stomach turned. Ever since I was a child, I had been taught not to lie. All of my life's principles have been bent upside down lately.

'Eat something. This pasta is delicious.' Alex popped another portion into his mouth. We stopped at a pub just down the road. The decor was simple and inviting, and the food tasted like home.

'I'm nervous. I don't think I'm going to be able to stomach anything.' I glanced at my untouched plate.

'You have nothing to worry about.'

'I can't lie,' I added in a resigned voice.

'I already told them that we met at the ice cream stand. You just have to nod when they ask you about it. Be yourself.'

'What if they know we're lying?'

He covered my hand with his. It was the most intimate moment since we first met. I guess he sensed what I was thinking because he quickly took his hand away and went back to eating his food.

I rummaged around on my plate a bit more and left almost the entire dish untouched. During the journey, I managed to take a nap. I woke up when we arrived. We passed through a wooden gate. It resembled the enclosure of a horse paddock. The sun was reflecting off the stone building. It must have been very old. I always wondered what such houses looked like inside. Alex took our suitcases and led us in. After a while, I heard a dog running on the wooden floor. He ran right up to Alex and started licking him and jumping for joy. Only after a while did he greet me, but not so effusively. From what I could tell, it was some kind of greyhound. He was skinny, and when he stood on two paws, he could lick my face, which he did eagerly.

'Blue! No jumping!' A man walked towards us with a springy step. I guessed it was Alex's father. They didn't look anything alike. He must have taken after his mother.

'He always greets visitors that way. Can't contain his excitement. Hello, I'm George.' He shook my hand.

'Nice to meet you,' I greeted him a little abashed. I was fully aware that I was being judged right now. They must have already made a judgment about my suitability for their son.

'Dad.' The men also shook hands in greeting.

'Is that Alex?' A question came from the hallway.

'Yes, mom, it's me.'

An elegant woman ran up to us and hugged her son tightly in greeting.

'Here you are at last!'

She greeted me, embracing me as she had embraced her son moments before.

'This is Sarah, and this is my mum, Elizabeth.' Alex made the formal introduction.

'Call me Liza, and don't you dare call me anything else,' she laughed teasingly. Looking at her, I had a feeling that she reminded me of someone.

'I have prepared a big room for you. You can leave your suitcases there and go down to the dining room. I will serve dinner in a moment.'

'We'll be there in five minutes. Sarah, come and take out your outfit for tomorrow, or it'll get even more creased.'

'How thoughtful.' His parents smiled at each other.

We made our way up the wooden staircase. The room was enormous.

'We were given the best guest bedroom. I see someone here has assumed that we sleep together. I think we'll fit in somehow, won't we? Do you want to change before we go downstairs?'

'I'd love to use the bathroom.'

'Yeah, sure. The door on the right.' He pointed in the direction with his hand and took care of carrying our luggage.

I disappeared behind the door. A pale, sleepy face glanced at me from the mirror. Taking a nap in the car was not the best idea, but the news about our night together effectively woke me up. I went back to the room to get my makeup bag. Alex was sitting on the bed with his legs stretched out in front of him. He was focused, clicking away on his cell phone. He was slim, and his blond hair was always neatly trimmed.

'Are you ready?' he asked without even glancing at me.

'I'll freshen up my makeup, and we can go.'

'You look fantastic.'

I looked at him with big eyes. This was the first compliment I had heard come from his lips.

'Just one minute, I'll be ready soon, I'll be back before you know it.'

I lied. It took me a little longer than a moment to wash off my makeup and redo it. The decorative mirror covering the whole wall and the jacuzzi tub in the corner of the bathroom didn't escape my attention. *I absolutely must try it out*, I thought excitedly.

When we came downstairs, we found ourselves in a spacious dining room. Right in front of me, through the balcony doors, I could see the garden veranda that made me want to walk on the grass barefooted.

'I'll serve dinner now since we're all here,' said Elizabeth and disappeared behind another door.

I had to admit that the size of this mansion was overwhelming.

In the middle of the dining room, a table was already waiting for us set with plates ready for dinner. I counted the plates quickly. Five. Five place settings. Only now did I look around the room. He was standing by the fireplace, in a careless pose with a glass of whiskey in his hand. He looked exactly as I remembered him. He was staring at me with his brown eyes. I couldn't look away. He was the one who had been watching me at the club recently. It can't be true that the world is so small. If he associates me with Sue's residence, I'll be in trouble, and so will Alex. He probably knew who was partying at his club. I twitched slightly as Alex began to introduce his brother to me. The man only narrowed his eyes at me. He was judging me. I hated that feeling. He didn't say hello, didn't say anything. Even Alex was surprised by his behaviour.

'Please, sit down,' the host invited us to the table.

Alex pushed my chair away from the table and took the seat next to me. His brother sat down opposite me, and he kept looking at me with silent questioning in his eyes.

'Go ahead and eat', the hostess urged us.

'So, how long have you known each other?' Boris, for that, was the name of my persecutor, decided to attack with the power of a torpedo and blast all the cannons.

'Not long. A few weeks,' explained Alex, oblivious to the confrontation.

'It really is not long,' he commented gruffly.

'Time has no meaning. Right, George?' Liza smiled tenderly at her husband.

'We didn't have to know each other long to know that we wanted to be together,' she added.

'That's right, Mom. Thank you.' Alex was happy. He took my hand and intertwined our hands in a sudden surge of affection. I was sure that my face had turned the colour of peonies.

'Did you two know each other the last time I saw you at the club?' Boris tried to provoke me.

'You two know each other?' Elizabeth was surprised.

I had to cut off the conjecture quickly.

'I thought it was you. I was there the other day at the club with some friends. I told you about that. I was going with Alan,' I turned to Alex for rescue.

'Oh, that was when I couldn't go with you,' he lied easily. 'Alan was keeping a good eye on you.' He lifted our entwined hands and kissed my fingers. My embarrassment level tripled. His parents looked at us with tenderness. Unfortunately, Boris did not seem to be fooled, and that did not bode well.

* * *

I wanted to help Elizabeth in the kitchen, but she insisted that she could handle everything herself. We finally got to dessert; she served a delicious fruit tart. Boris apologised to us unexpectedly and left.

'He went to the beach with his dog. He always does that. Don't worry about him.' Elizabeth turned to me.

'Dad, why don't you show me those papers we talked about? Let's get it done today so we can have peace of mind tomorrow.'

'That's a good idea. Let's go to the study.' They both got up from the table.

'Will you be alright?' Alex smiled apologetically at me. 'It won't take long.'

'I'm not going to bite her.' His mother replied, wounded.

'See you later.'

'I'll help with the cleaning,' I offered eagerly as soon as the men left the room.

'Thank you!' Liza gratefully accepted my help. 'The rest of the food needs to be packed and put in the fridge and the dishes need to be put in the dishwasher.'

We started to clean off the table. In the process, she told me funny stories from her sons' lives. Once everything was in place, I went to my room to get a sweater and walked out to the beach. The lower I went down the brick steps, the stronger the gusts of wind became, but not strong enough to make it unpleasant. The wind was rather crisp, the kind that washes away sorrows and worries after a long day at work. I was beginning to envy the people who lived in this beautiful home. As far as the eye could see, the beach was quite empty. Maybe it was a private place with no access for the public? It was weird that no one was around. I reached the sea. I took off my shoes and walked barefoot on the warm sand. The waves made a rhythmic sound. It was a beautiful view. I finally stopped and looked at the sea. Blue came running to me from the side. All wet, he was carrying a ball in his mouth. He left it at my feet and barked to encourage me to play. I threw it to him several times until I was standing face to face with Boris.

'It's a beautiful place,' I confessed quite honestly.

'Yes. My favourite. I like to come back here. It makes you forget.'

'Forget?'

'Relax, I mean, of course.'

'Of course,' I nodded. I took the ball and played with Blue for a while. I could feel him looking at me. I don't know if he wanted to say anything else. He was staying silent. What could such a handsome man want to forget? The wind blew his brown hair. He was standing with his face toward the sea. His lips were tightly pressed together, and he had an impenetrable expression on his face. Rough, though handsome as hell.

'Back then, in your office at the club...' I began hesitantly. Blue had just left me the ball again and ran into the sea himself. He jumped over the rushing waves.

Boris looked at me with interest. He wasn't smiling.

'I wasn't with Alex then,' I said truthfully. 'I don't want you to judge me by what you saw.'

'What did I see?'

'Well, I was there, but your friend turned out to be a gentleman,' I was struggling to explain.

'He didn't shag you? Is that what you mean?' I thought he was joking, but he was pretty serious. He scowled at me with his eyes. I had to get out of there.

'You could put it that way.'

I walked towards the house as fast as I could.

* * *

In the evening I took a shower and changed into shorts and a T-shirt. Satin was not the best choice because my nipples showed through the fabric, which was not an intended effect. Before the trip, I was wondering what to bring to wear for bed. This set seemed casual to me. I was wrong.

Throughout the evening, Alex was charming, and I felt very comfortable in his company. I could say the same about his parents. When bedtime came and we were left alone, I feared it would be awkward. Nothing could be further from the truth. We agreed that I would use the bathroom first. When I came out, he looked at me and my shirt. He smiled, took his toiletries, and disappeared out the door. After a while, I could hear the water running into the tub. I brushed my hair, which made it even more poofy. I slipped under the duvet and fell asleep, despite my desire to wait for my partner. Throughout the evening, Alex was charming, and I felt very comfortable in his company. For a moment, I didn't know where I was. Right next to me, Alex was sleeping peacefully. I didn't want to wake him, but when the mattress moved, he opened his eyes.

'Are you getting up?' he asked sleepily.

'Yes. I wanted to swim in the pool.'

It was just an excuse not to stay in bed any longer. On the other hand, a private pool was really something.

'Alright, then. I'll sleep a little longer,' he snuggled more into his pillow and fell asleep again.

I tried not to make any noise. I changed into a black one-piece. On top, I threw on a summer dress. I took a thick towel from the bathroom. The pool was on the property but not in the same building as the living area.

Green plants in pots stood at the entrance. The room resembled a beach house. I left my dress and towel on the deck chair and walked up to the stepladder. I dipped first one leg, then the other. I wasn't the type of person who jumped into the pool easily. I preferred to take the plunge slowly. The water was cold, perfect for swimming. I hadn't been to the pool in a long time, and I could only swim breaststroke properly. On that day, I pushed myself. At the same time, I was surprised by how much my fitness had improved. In the past, I wouldn't even swim half of what I could swim today. I was about to leave when Boris appeared in the doorway. He took the towel off his hips and put it next to mine. I stopped in the corner to take a break. The room was perfectly silent. Only the towel and dress betrayed my presence. He approached the ladder and, at the last moment, decided to jump in instead of stepping carefully down into the water. I was able to get a good look at what he looked like in swim trunks. His body was slim and tanned. Plus, he swam like a pro.

'Hi,' he greeted me. 'Alex isn't with you?'

'He's asleep. I should go.'

'You don't have to run away.'

In fact, I wanted to run away like a chicken. I didn't like the fact that in his company I didn't know what to say. I was beginning to feel insecure, aware of every movement of my body.

'You haven't seen me swim yet. I don't want to embarrass myself.'

'I promise I won't laugh. I can pretend I don't see anything.' Amused by his own joke, he swam away.

I swam four more lengths. I wanted to prove that his presence did not impress me. As I got out of the pool, I could feel his gaze on me. I didn't hear the water move. He was probably staring at my ass. I wrapped a towel around myself and only then turned toward him.

'Bye. I'll be going.'

'I'll see you at breakfast.'

I dashed to my room as fast as I could. I shouldn't be alone in the same room with him. The way he looked at me sent shivers down my body. I should definitely avoid him for the rest of my stay at his parents' house.

I took a shower to wash the smell of chlorine off my skin. I put on a blue dress and gold sandals. I found Alex in the kitchen as he was cooking something. He had already mentioned about how much he liked doing it.

'Coffee?'

'Yes, please.' He placed a mug of the steaming black drink in front of me.

This was usually my main stimulant in the mornings. Evidently, the swim had worked just as well.

'Milk is in the fridge. Have you been swimming?'

'Yes. This place is amazing.'

'Yeah, it is. Can I make you some toast and scrambled eggs?'

'Yes, please,' I added milk to the coffee and put it in the fridge.

'I'll have some too.' Boris joined us. His hair was wet. He must have taken a shower because he smelled of some cologne. He was wearing a clean white T-shirt and shorts.

'You look like a cook,' he teased his brother.

Alex threatened him with a wooden spoon and smoothed down his apron.

'Do you begrudge your brother his food? Where's mum and dad? Have they already gone to the stables?' He asked with interest, not looking in my direction.

'Yes, they left early because of the party.'

'You have horses?' I asked, a little surprised.

'Mom loves those animals. My parents have their stables outside of town. They have leased some of the stalls.' Alex divided the food into three plates and put them on the table.

'Do you ride horses, Sarah?' Boris asked, carefully pronouncing my name.

'No, unfortunately. I rode maybe twice in my life as a child.'

'Alex should teach you to ride. After all, you two are together.'

My fork hovered over my plate. But Alex laughed and promised to teach me to ride the first chance we get. Then the brothers started talking about the party this evening and the guests. During this verbal exchange, I was able to take a look at them and compare the two, though I didn't know why I was doing so. They differed in appearance. One was a brunette, the other a blonde. They also had completely different temperaments. Alex was cheerful and talked a lot. Boris was generally quiet and looked absent-minded. Nevertheless, I couldn't take my eyes off him when he looked at me.

* * *

The party was going to be in the evening, so we still had the whole day to ourselves. The brothers unanimously decided that we would go to the stables. I was glad to have such a prospect of spending the morning. I had a short phone conversation with my granny and promised to visit her on Monday after class. It was good to hear her voice. She was in a cheerful mood this time, and it made me feel a lot better too.

Alex insisted that I absolutely had to go horse riding. He called his mum to ask about an extra outfit for me.

The journey took us about half an hour. We drove in a new Audi Q8 that belonged to Boris. He drove confidently and fast. I was puzzled by his gaze, which I caught in the rear-view mirror. Next to him sat Alex, unaware of anything. He started talking about a big deal that would bring him a lot of profit in the future. Boris, single-wordily answered. He was not really interested, but he kept meeting my gaze in the mirror. He was like a ticking time bomb. I just didn't know when it would go off.

'I've heard you're opening another club,' Alex asked cheerfully.

'Yes. In a month. I'm looking for a team and a manager. I will not be able to manage it myself, because it will be in another city. Besides, I already run three other clubs, and it is becoming more and more difficult for me to balance all my responsibilities.'

'What about the family business?' Alex asked, seemingly calm.

'I don't want it. I already told you. You're doing fine.'

'But you should be in charge of it.'

'We're brothers. Don't start that again. I don't deserve anything more than you do.'

There was an awkward silence after those remarks. Boris turned up the radio so that his brother would not ask him any more questions.

When the car stopped, I saw the paddock. Delighted, I ran in the direction where I could spot the horses, leaving my companions far behind. I felt like a little girl.

I had loved animals all my life, but horses had always seemed magical to me. I approached the fence. On the other side, several beautiful specimens were strolling peacefully. They walked majestically and proudly.

'Which one do you like best?' Alex, who had already arrived, was curious about my opinion.

'The white one,' I pointed at the horse. Its coat shone beautifully in the sunlight.

'That's Luna, a mare. You are right. She is gorgeous. But I thought you'd choose the chestnut one. It would suit you and your hair. You'd look like an Amazonian on it.'

'It's beautiful too,' I admit. 'They're all beautiful, but I like the white one best.'

'Come and say hello to Luna.'

Alex grabbed my hand and led me to the other side along the fence, closer to the horses.

Boris walked a few meters behind us, not taking his eyes off of us. Alex called out for Luna. I could touch her, feel the texture of her hair and the warmth that radiated from her. The moment seemed magical. She captured my heart the moment I saw her, and when she looked at me from under her long lashes, she stole my soul.

'Boris will keep you safe. I'm going to go find my parents. They're probably cleaning the stalls. I'll be back in a minute.'

'But…' I wanted to protest.

'Luna is his mare. He knows her best,' he pointed at Boris with his head.

The explanation was logical. I chose her myself, so I got myself into this awkward situation. I was supposed to avoid him. That was the plan. I could still back out, lie, find an excuse… but the mare looked so beautiful. I really wanted to ride her.

'You ready?' Boris opened the fence so that I could enter the paddock. I walked to the other side, and he closed the gate. We took a few steps toward Luna.

'I'm getting unsteady on my feet.' Suddenly, I started backing towards the gate.

'Are you afraid? She's a gentle mare.'

I turned back to him, and he walked towards me, bringing her closer.

'Touch her. She can feel that you're afraid. She's just as nervous about it as you are.'

Horses are extremely intelligent creatures. They sense our emotions fear, anger, joy. That is why they are often used to treat emotional or mental disorders. Hippotherapy is extremely helpful.

I touched her snout, and she snuggled into my hand. I could feel clearly what Boris was talking about. All the tension surrounding me that day was slowly disappearing.

'Do you want to feel her heartbeat? It's here.' He touched her side.

I walked over and placed my hand next to his palm. They contrasted sharply. Mine was small and pale, and he was much larger and olive-skinned.

'Here.' He covered my hand with his and moved it to the indicated place.

In fact, I could feel the rhythmic beating of her heart. But what I felt more was the touch of the man's hand on mine. He stood close enough for me to smell his scent. I didn't know what was happening to me… I felt a wave of heat flow through my body.

'How's it going?' Alex was standing just a meter away from us along with his parents.

Confused, I jumped away from the mare and Boris.

'We were just about to put Sarah on the saddle.'

Boris was in full control of the situation. Very professionally, he started to explain what I should do. Several times he assured me that there was nothing to be afraid of. I held on to the saddle. I put my foot in the stirrup as he had shown me earlier. I wanted to pull out, but I did it extremely clumsily. At the next attempt, Boris gave me a little push, so I got on Luna's back. Only with his help, I was able to throw my leg over her back. I sat in the saddle, and the mare moved slightly backwards and forwards. Alex put his thumbs up. Let's hope I didn't look as silly as I felt. I slid my feet into the stirrups.

'Okay, I'm ready,' I said more to myself than to him.

I held the saddle firmly with both hands.

The horse moved slightly ahead, and I trembled on its back.

'I'm going to fall off!' I panicked a little.

'Calm down.'

We walked around the paddock. Boris led Luna slowly and confidently. He held the reins firmly. Every now and again, he would make sure that everything was alright. By the second lap, I began to enjoy the ride. I relaxed a little, for which my instructor praised me. We did five laps in total. When we finished, Boris helped me get down onto the ground. He grabbed me around the waist so I could land gently on my feet. He held his hands on my waist a few seconds longer than was necessary. At least that was the impression I got.

'Thank you.' I looked into his honey eyes.

'Next time, you'll go alone.'

Was he crazy? There wouldn't be the next time, but he couldn't know that. I walked out to Alex behind the fence. My legs were trembling slightly with emotion. I saw Boris adjusting the saddle, and he jumped on it in one smooth motion. He started at a trot and sped up. It was evident that he loved horse riding. He looked manly and wild. Even though I was immersed in a conversation with Alex and his parents, I could see that he was watching me. I could feel his gaze on me every time he approached in my direction.

'He was born in the saddle,' Liza turned and said to me.

'Sorry?' I raised a puzzled look at her.

'I am talking about Boris. He is a great rider.'

'Yes. I can tell.'

Alex put his arm around my waist and pulled me slightly towards him. He clearly didn't like the direction the conversation was going.

'Shall we have some coffee?' he suggested.

'Great idea,' George remarked.

We sat down outside the cafeteria at a wooden table. I was enjoying the September sunshine. This year the weather was exceptionally good. Even though it was the beginning of autumn, it was still warm and pleasant.

'When did you get the idea to keep horses?' I turned to Liza because I already knew from previous conversations that it began with her.

'When I was a little girl, I lived on a farm where we raised horses and cows.'

George grabbed her hand as if to give her encouragement and support.

'That was a long time ago,' she smiled softly. 'After that, I didn't deal with them for many years. George bought me the first one as a present after Boris was born.' Her eyes got glassy when she mentioned it. 'Then it just sort of escalated. We bought another and another,' she laughed, and more wrinkles appeared in the corner of her eyes. 'We were trying to spread the love for animals and horses to our boys. And it worked. They are both excellent riders.'

'Mom!' Alex was outraged.

'Honey, it's true. I have great sons.'

I rose from my seat, 'I'll go and stand by the fence, and maybe I'll get a chance to stroke some horse.'

'We'll be back in15 minutes. I'll come get you,' announced Alex.

I walked towards the horses. I thought about what a happy family they were. They had each other's backs. I envied them. I shouldn't have, but seeing this idealistic way of life, I couldn't accept my fate - an extremely cruel fate. First, I'd lost my parents, and now my grandmother was fading away with each passing day. Tears came to my eyes. I had always been strong. I wanted others to see me that way. Today showed me what my life could have been like if I hadn't lost my parents. I wiped a tear from my cheek.

'Sarah! Watch out! Behind you!' I turned around when I heard Alex's terrifying scream.

Through the tears, my vision was completely blurred. What I saw froze me, and though I should have run, I didn't move. The big black horse was running straight at me. The clatter of hooves was getting closer and closer. There were clouds of dust everywhere. People were shouting that I should run away, but I just stood, paralysed. I couldn't move. Everything was happening so fast. Suddenly, Boris appeared out of nowhere, galloping on Luna. His mare was slower. He had to make a real effort to catch up with the black stallion, but he managed to match the pace. He grabbed the reins of the fleeing horse and jerked it, changing its course. He stopped somewhere away from me.

'Sarah! Are you alright?' Alex ran towards me as fast as he could. I was overwhelmed with emotion, and I burst into tears. He hugged me to his chest, and I stood there crying. Meanwhile, a large group of people had gathered around us. I heard them say that Blue had spooked the horse.

'Come on, let's go.' Boris's voice reached me. 'My parents will unsaddle Luna and take care of the horses. They will sort everything out and join us later.'

This time Alex sat in the back with me and didn't let me out of his embrace the whole way. Just like on the way here, I saw Boris' gaze in the rear-view mirror - this time with a worried expression.

* * *

Delivery trucks filled the driveway at the front of the house. Outside, the confusion was nothing compared to what was happening inside the building. There were service people everywhere. The bottom of the lobby was drowning in a sea of flowers. Two young women with florist logos on their shirts were pinning satin ribbons down the length of the stairs. The caterers ordered for the evening had just pulled up. People passed us in the entrance and disappeared into the kitchen with trays overflowing with food. A young woman in a tight dress was running around with a notebook in her hand. She was giving instructions to all the people around us. It was madness.

'This isn't going to be a small party, is it?' I focused my gaze on the balloons hanging from the ceiling.

'Intimate, only sixty people. Don't worry about that now. Come on, lie down for an hour. Would you like something to drink?'

'Tea, preferably mint tea.'

'I'll see if we have some. Go upstairs. I'll be there in a minute.'

When I entered the room, I washed the smears of mascara off my face. I took off my horse-riding suit. I changed into leggings and a T-shirt. I had brought a pretty tight dress for the evening, so I wanted to feel comfortable for a little bit longer. I brushed my hair and slipped into bed under the duvet. Despite the warm day, I was shaking all over. Probably because of the emotions.

Elizabeth brought me some tea, and she put it right next to the bed, then sat on the edge.

'I'm glad you're alright,' she looked at me sadly. 'Blue was the culprit behind the fuss. That black horse has only been with us a week, and he hasn't had to deal with excited strays before. When Blue started barking at him, he got scared and ran away in a panic. You stood in his way. I'm so sorry.'

'Don't be. I'm all right. I was just a little scared,' I interrupted her. 'I was lucky Boris was there.'

She patted me on the head with a motherly gesture, 'Yes, you were very fortunate. I'll see you at the party.' She stood up, walked a few steps towards the door. She stopped, as if she wanted to add something else, but changed her mind and left.

After a short nap, I felt much better. When I opened my eyes, I saw Alex. He was standing in front of the mirror, his back to me, dressed in his suit pants, buttoning up his white shirt. I had to admit that he looked very handsome.

'What time is it?' I asked sleepily.

'Time for you to start getting dressed.'

I jumped out of bed.

'Are we late?'

'Not yet. You have all the time you need. I have to get some things done. I'll come back for you in an hour and see how you're doing.'

When the door closed behind him, I literally ran into the bathroom. An hour is not enough! Especially to style my hair. I took a quick shower and, wrapped only in a towel, started doing my make-up. Today I decided on a bold eye. I placed a delicate band of white pearls on my head and left my hair down. It fell down my back in gentle waves. I wore a long dress in a shade of bottle green. Sue insisted that I had to wear it at the party. Once again, she was right. My fair skin and red hair contrasted perfectly with the dress colour, which hugged my body at the top and ended with a slit down one leg. I was just fastening the straps of my black high stiletto sandals when Alex came back into the room.

'I'm ready.' I stood uncertainly on the carpet. I didn't usually wear such high heels. I picked up my clutch purse.

'Beautiful as always.' He gave me his arm and kissed my cheek. 'I wanted to ask you something. I don't know what time the party will end. Could you please not come to the room until after three in the morning?'

I looked at him suspiciously. I thought he was joking. He was pretty serious.

'You could go to the library. I'm sure you can think of something.'

'You're serious?' I know the customers had all sorts of bizarre demands, but sending girls away was hardly the norm. 'Okay, fine. Hold on. I'll leave a few things in the library.' I packed my cell phone and wallet in my clutch bag and my sneakers and sweater in another. I expected the party to end sooner. At least I'd have shoes to change into. We left my bag in the library and walked down the stairs where the party was held. Only now did I notice that bottle green was the theme colour of the decor for tonight's party.

We entered a room full of people. The people at the door took a closer look at me. There were so many elegant men and women that I suddenly felt uncomfortable. This was not my world, not my league. What if I said something silly, and Alex would be ashamed because of me?

'Hey, what's wrong?' he whispered in my ear.

I looked at him with confused eyes.

'You look beautiful, and you need to relax. You need a drink.' He directed us toward the bar. He poured champagne for me and something that looked like orange juice with vodka for himself. I accepted the drink gratefully.

'Sarah, you look stunning!' Elizabeth greeted me. She looked very refined in a simple, black, elegant outfit at George's side. 'Your dress is my favourite colour,' she laughed. 'George, will you get me a glass of champagne?' she sent her husband off in the direction of the liquor bar.

'Alex, do you think she will come?'

Elizabeth asked with hope in her voice.

'I'm sorry. I talked to her this morning. She won't be here.'

I didn't know who she was talking about, but I could see that the sparkle in Liza's eyes had dimmed slightly.

George handed his wife a glass, and she emptied half of it in one go.

'It's for courage,' she added, laughing. 'Come, let's invite the guests to the table. They are all here now.'

After dinner, Alex and Boris gave a congratulatory speech on the occasion of their parents' wedding anniversary, during which I felt like hiding under the table, because if someone hadn't noticed me before, now they were surely wondering who I was. My attention was drawn to a pretty blonde woman who was sitting on the right next to Boris. She was smiling and talking to him throughout dinner. It was obvious that they knew each other well.

'She is a childhood friend of ours. She lives nearby,' Alex explained to me, seeing that I was looking at the girl.

'Why are you telling me this?' I pretended to be indifferent.

'You seem to be interested in her.'

'That's not true,' I snorted indignantly.

'Maybe this horse has done more damage than you think?' he whispered directly into my ear.

I wanted to throw him another sharp retort, but the band started playing a waltz. The hosts were the first to get on the dance floor. They looked beautiful together, as if they were swimming rather than dancing. After a few moments, other couples joined the spinning wheel. Every now and then, more guests approached us. Alex introduced us politely and engaged me in the conversations. After some time, Boris came up to us with his friend. He made a short introduction. I saw the judging eyes of the girl. Something told me that we would not become friends. She touched Boris' arm to let others know that he was already taken. I felt a slight pang of jealousy. I admonished myself for my attitude. I was here with Alex, and I should be the one to look in love. I smiled at him as sweetly as I could, imitating the girl's gesture. Alex, slightly confused, asked me to dance.

'What's going on?' he asked.

'Nothing. I wanted to dance.' He accepted my lie without comment.

'Thank you again for coming with me. It was very important to me.'

I didn't understand any of it. But the important thing was that I had quite a good time and met many wonderful people. We danced to the next two songs. The straps in my shoes were starting to dig into my ankles.

'I'll sit outside in the garden. I'm really hot. Will you get me some champagne?'

'Yes. I'll be there in a minute.'

I walked past the string quartet and slipped outside. The night was cool and starry. I could still hear the sounds of music coming from inside the house. I squatted on a bench, enjoying the fresh air. I was already slightly tired with so many people and a smile glued to my face.

'Here, champagne for you.'

I twitched slightly when I heard a male voice. My body trembled. I justified my reaction was due to the coldness outside.

'Thank you,' I accepted the glass, avoiding his gaze.

Alex was swept up in a conversation about business. I'm supposed to keep you company.

'Oh, right. What about your friend?' it got out before I could think about it.

'She can handle herself,' he shrugged his shoulders.

'Look, I… I wanted to thank you for….' I lost my train of thought when he sat down next to me on the bench, '…for saving my life,' I finished.

He looked into my eyes, and I wanted to lose myself in their honey colour. My mind was turning to mush. His scent enveloped me and took away my ability to listen to reason.

'You're welcome,' he replied calmly. He always controlled his emotions. He didn't say anything else. He just looked at me with great intensity.

'There you are. I've been looking for you everywhere.' Boris' friend joined us in the garden with a smile plastered onto her face. She looked at me, then at him, not liking what she saw.

'I'll be going now.' I took the opportunity to go back inside to find Alex.

I had the impression that the party had no end. With great relief, we said goodbye to the last guests. All the household members went to their rooms. Only I had nowhere to go. I was about to go to the library to read something, as the collection was really impressive, when I saw Boris entering his room with a bottle of whisky in his hand. Apparently, he had decided to have another drink. I thought I might as well keep him company. I had a deal with Alex, and it would be a long time before I could go back to my room. I knocked softly. I didn't want to wake the other occupants. The door opened. A surprised Boris stared at me for a moment.

'Is something wrong with my brother?' I could hear the concern in his voice.

'No. He's fine. He's sleeping,' I lied smoothly. 'I can't sleep. I was about to go to the library, but I noticed you were carrying whisky. Perhaps you could use some company?' I was still wearing the same dress from the party. He probably thought I came to him because I had a fight with Alex. He stepped back slightly and invited me inside.

'I have glasses and whiskey. Unfortunately, I don't have any cola or ice.'

'That's okay. It'll do.' I sat down on the small sofa. Boris handed me a glass and sat down in the armchair opposite me. There was an awkward silence. I quickly regretted my decision to come here. I didn't know what to say, so I took a big sip of the amber drink, making my throat burn, and I coughed. 'Strong one,' I added as I regained my voice.

He looked at me with an amused expression. He was probably wondering what I was doing here.

'Are you and my brother serious?'

I didn't know how to respond. Any answer I gave would be the wrong one. Alex was really keen for us to be seen as a couple.

'I don't know if it's serious yet.' I tried not to lie, but I didn't give an obvious answer. I quickly drank the rest of my drink. I held the empty glass in my hands. I already knew I shouldn't have come here.

Boris turned on the radio, and ambient music came from the speakers. My head was buzzing slightly. Mixing champagne and whisky was not a good idea. I was suddenly highly relaxed and calm. I watched his slow movements as he walked toward me, but instead of sitting back in his chair, he faced me. He took the glass from my hands and set it down on the table. He grabbed my hands and pulled me to a standing position. He was taller than me. His honey-coloured eyes mirrored me intently. It was that moment when I should have left the room immediately. Instead, I stood and waited to see what he would do. I had to lift my head slightly to look into his eyes. What I saw in them made me a little uncomfortable. Lust and pure desire beat from them like an invisible power that kept me from moving or thinking soberly. The music only intensified my sensations. I didn't know what was affecting me so much: him, the alcohol or maybe this amazing mixture of both. I moved my gaze to his lips, wondering what they tasted like. Boris lifted his hand and ran his thumb over my bottom lip. As if he was wondering the same thing. He raised his hand and grabbed me firmly by my hair, not letting me move my head. I looked at him with panicked eyes.

'I had never desired a woman belonging to my brother. Never, until today.'

After those words, his lips landed on mine. He kissed me greedily and passionately. A wave of heat coursed through my body. I had never realised until then, that

I had never been kissed properly before. What was happening between us was pure chemistry. His lips were warm and soft, yet possessive and lustful. He grabbed me and pulled me even closer. My body was on fire. I wanted more. Suddenly he pulled away from my lips, panting slightly.

'Stop me,' he stared at me for several long seconds. He was waiting for my reaction. I respected him for that. He had given me a choice. I could still run away.

'I'm not going to.' I blushed heavily in embarrassment.

A quiet yelp escaped from my lips as I felt him pick me up and head towards the bed. I wrapped my legs around him. I could feel his erection as my dress wrapped around my waist.

I landed on the soft mattress. The man reached into the clasp of my dress and helped me remove it. I was left in my flesh-coloured lace underwear and stiletto heels. Boris took a step back and removed his clothes. He stood in front of me in just his boxers.

'You are perfect,' he said, looking at me.

I only had a moment to assess his muscular, tanned body once again. He took my foot and removed the stiletto, threw it behind him, and it fell with a slight thud to the floor. He did the exact same thing with the other. He slid his hand up my leg, making my entire body tremble. He knew exactly how it was affecting me because he smiled deviously.

'Take off your bra,' he whispered right next to my ear, marking his way from my neck to my breasts with passionate kisses. He took my nipple in his mouth and sucked. I began to writhe under him. His hand dipped into my panties, rubbing my throbbing spot. I moved my hips even more, seeking fulfilment. The feeling that was growing inside me was unbearable. He moved his mouth to the other breast and began the sweet torture all over again, sucking and biting the other nipple. Combined with his hand rubbing my bosom, the sensation was getting extreme. I pushed my hips upward, seeking satisfaction. This kind of feeling was incomparable to the erotic toys I had tried recently. I rubbed even harder against his hand and came. He watched me as I reached an orgasmic peak. After a while, he pulled my panties off of me. Still not fully aware of what was going on around me, I heard the sound of the film being torn. He came back up to my face, kissing me insistently. He positioned himself between my legs. He gently paved his way inside me, leaning over me on one arm.

'Are you alright?' he asked. I shook my head as I couldn't get a word out. He didn't take his eyes off me, pounding into me. I closed my eyes as I felt the pain.

'Look at me,' he commanded.

I concentrated on him, kissing him passionately. I had to get used to the new experience of being filled.

He moved slowly at first, increasing his pace. My eyes became cloudy by the end of this hot ride, and

I started feeling foggy. My body was squirming under him with pleasure and begging for more. He held my hands above my head. He continued the frantic pace for a while longer. He let go of my hands, and I stroked the sweat-soaked skin on his back. He dipped his face into the hollow of my neck and came. I could feel him breathing heavily. His intoxicating male scent filled the air around me.

'I'll take care of your orgasm in a moment,' he said, laying down next to me on my back, scooping me up and hugging me close. He covered us with a quilt. I could feel the warmth of his skin and his heartbeat. Our breaths calmed slowly. Not a single word was spoken between us anymore. I felt like asking him a hundred things, but I stopped myself. I hugged him tighter and enjoyed the moment.

I realised that it was just an illusion. I could feel his breathing calming down. I thought he had fallen asleep. I lay there for a few more minutes to be sure and then gently eased myself out of his embrace. I looked at his handsome face one more time. The harsh features had smoothed out, and he looked more relaxed. I got dressed, and as quietly as I could, I left the room. I remembered that I had left my bag in the library earlier. I went back to get it and called a cab. I felt like I needed to get away from here. I texted Alex, saying that I had to leave urgently and I would message him the next day. We were supposed to leave tomorrow morning, so it didn't make much difference. I asked the driver to take me to the train station and slumped into the cab's seat.

I took the train back home. My bag with the rest of my clothes was left at Alex's. All I had with me was a sweatshirt, sneakers, and a long elegant dress. The people on the train were undoubtedly having a good time looking at me. I knew I would have to ask Alex to bring my things. I couldn't stay there a minute longer, not after what I had done. I'd probably never see Boris again anyway. I wondered why I'd rather be with him than sit alone on the train. I didn't understand the conflicting feelings this man evoked in me. He was reserved and diffident but unearthly handsome, even when he slept. The way he looked at me when I was naked. I felt, for that one little moment, like the most beautiful woman in the world. I had to shake myself off. I had a feeling that I would never again be as comfortable in bed with anyone as I was with him. I was also aware that one night was all I could give him.

Boris

The next morning, I was awakened by a streak of light coming through the windows. The bedside lamp next to my bed was still on. I had slept for several hours. I was surprised. Sleep problems and recurring nightmares were part my daily routine. I refused to take those nasty drugs that made me feel like I was no longer myself. All I needed was a woman. This woman. My brother's woman. I groaned in distaste when I realised what I had done. I checked the spot next to me. Instead of a seductive body, I found emptiness. She was gone, just like that. I thought she felt it too. We were good together. I knew we were. What did I expect? It was cruel of me. To betray my own brother. I wondered if she went back to him. If she climbed right back into his bed, pressing her breasts against his back. I was crazy about that redhead. I knew from the very beginning that there would be trouble with her. Right then, at the club when I watched her from above as she danced on the dance floor.

I threw off the covers and made my way to the bathroom. I looked in the mirror. My brown hair, slightly overgrown, was sticking up clumsily, each strand in a different direction. I needed a haircut. As I began to pee into the toilet, I noticed blood on my penis. At first, I was horrified. I was in no pain. Therefore, the blood did not belong to me. If it wasn't mine, then it must have belonged to Sarah. I went back to bed and checked the sheet. There was even more blood. What had I done to her? I had a couple of drinks, but no more than usual. I would remember if she was in pain. Like a flash, I noticed the look on her face as I entered her. Fuck. She was a virgin!

There were hundreds of questions running through my mind. I sat on my bed to digest this revelation. What an asshole I was! I had to talk to her. Immediately. I dressed in a hurry. I almost raced to Alex's bedroom. I didn't knock. I rushed into the room, increasingly furious and confused. How could she keep this from me? I saw the bedding moving and two figures underneath it. I looked at it and couldn't believe it. She jumped out of my bed just to jump back into his.

'You bitch!' I didn't mince words. 'How could you? Was one guy not enough for you?' I grabbed the edge of the duvet and threw it off the bed onto the floor in one smooth motion. I stood for a moment, looking ahead. The sight left me speechless. I found my brother with another guy. Only after a moment did I put together all the facts. My brother was gay. How could I not know that? Another person who was hiding something from me. His partner was Sue's driver. Everything began to fall into place. Alex glanced at me cautiously with surprise.

'Where's Sarah?' I asked.

His partner clumsily reached for the quilt to cover their naked bodies. I could see his crimson cheeks. I felt the urge to throw something.

'Where is she?' he repeated the question more sharply.

'I don't know. She sent me a message to take her things tomorrow. She took the train home. What happened?'

'None of your business,' I growled and went outside to the front of the house. Maybe she hadn't left yet, and I could explain everything to her.

Outside I found only darkness. Somewhere in the distance, an owl was hooting. Even that was pissing me off. Alex stood right behind me.

'Cigarette?' He held out a half-empty pack toward me. I took one and lit it with my lighter. To my surprise, he lit one too.

'I didn't know you smoked,' I tried to keep the conversation going somehow.

Alex inhaled and slowly let the smoke flow out of his lungs. I looked at him and wondered when it all became so complicated. I remembered when we played tag or soccer together and how we fished for newts in the lake down at the end of the woods. All those mutual endeavours made us inseparable. Even so, I didn't realise he was gay. What kind of brother was I?

'Don't tell our parents, okay?' He looked at me with insecurity, 'I'll tell them myself. I'll tell Dad myself.'

'I understand, we don't talk about cigarettes.' I knew how scared he was. How afraid he was of this conversation. I hugged him, and he let himself be hugged. 'Okay. I won't say anything, but don't delay it.' I looked into his eyes and saw again the scared boy he once was. My little brother. 'They love you. They always will. Remember that.' I tossed the cigarette on the ground. I went back inside and poured myself another shot of whiskey. I knew I wouldn't fall asleep again anyway. I took a shower, and immediately after, pulled the sheets off the bed and threw them into the corner of the room. I would call her first thing in the morning. Only first, I had to get her number from Alex. I sat alone for the rest of the morning, drinking the whiskey until the bottom of the bottle was visible. Maybe the alcohol would help me forget about my problems for a while…

Sarah

I was preparing for the performance, despite my thoughts being completely elsewhere. I hadn't slept much. I spent the whole night on the train back home.

'Boris? What are you doing here? You're not allowed in here.' I looked at him angrily.

Out of the corner of my eye, I noticed the horror on Amy's face and the girls' shock. Why were they looking at me? There must have been men coming over here on multiple occasions before this. After all, it wasn't my fault that he barged into our dressing room without permission.

He looked at me for a few moments. Silence fell in the room. All the girls focused their attention on us. Boris interrupted our eye duel.

'Ladies, could you excuse us for a moment?' he said smoothly.

I could see how furious he was.

To my surprise, they all left, leaving the two of us alone.

'Why didn't you say you were a virgin?' he started.

'You wanted to fuck me, I agreed, it wasn't important,' I turned to the mirror and started instinctively powdering my nose.

He turned my swivel chair and leaned over so that we were very close. I could feel his breath on my lips.

'Not important? Are you crazy? I could have been more gentle. If only I had known. What game were you playing?'

'What did you come here for?' I didn't understand what he wanted from me.

'You ran away. And you're not my brother's girlfriend. You can't work here.'

'Oh really? You're not going to tell me what to do. Leave! Get out of here, now!'

A knock on the door interrupted our exchange. A man I didn't recognise said that they had to go.

'This conversation isn't over,' he hissed right into my mouth.

And he left. Amy ran in first and knelt in front of me.

'What did he want? What did the boss want from you? Did he fire you?' she threw out her questions like a bullet from a rifle.

I only registered the word *"boss"*.

'Did you say "boss"?' I looked at her in disbelief.

'Well, yes.' She looked at me curiously. 'You didn't know? He is the son of the owner. He took over the business not long ago.'

I groaned loudly, burying my face in my hands. What the hell have I done?

'Is our sweet little Sarah in trouble?' Olivia teased me.

'Shut up!' Amy stood up for me.

'Oh, come on,' I pulled her away. 'We don't have time for this. We need to get ready.'

'Today is your first performance. Are you nervous?' Amy focused all her attention on me.

'I'm nervous as hell!' I admitted.

'You're pretty bad,' Olivia said casually. 'I saw you practising.'

The rest of the girls were silent.

None of them wanted to start anything with this nasty viper. She had been number one here for a long time, and you could tell she was scared to lose her position. I tried to ignore her as much as possible. Unfortunately, my patience was running out. I was still flustered from my confrontation with Boris. I reached out to her. I pushed her, making her take a few steps backwards. The attack surprised her.

'What's going on here?' Sue stood in the doorway. As always, she had everything under control. 'Amy, you're dancing, and Sarah, you're helping behind the bar.'

'Behind the bar? Why would you do that? I want to dance!' I protested. I had been preparing for a long time. I felt I was ready.

'Change of plans. You help behind the bar,' she said again firmly.

'I don't want to be a waitress.'

'I didn't say you were going to be a waitress. You are to help the bartender today and stay out of the lobby. Put on your red wristband.'

'But why?'

'Because I said so,' Sue ended the conversation. 'You have another fifteen minutes, and I want to see all of you in the lobby.'

'I told you, you're bad,' Olivia commented.

I felt like punching at someone. I was angry and resentful. What was the point of all these rehearsals if I couldn't dance? Amy looked at me with compassion. She knew how much time and work I had put into preparing for tonight's performance. The next opportunity wasn't until next month.

An hour passed, and I was still angry. My job was to stand behind the bar and not go anywhere. I was tempted to show Sue what I thought about the prohibitions. Usually, I had no objection to her orders. Unfortunately, this time my wild nature was taking over. On top of that, I got a red armband. According to the system, it meant that I was unavailable to customers.

Niko had been glancing at me all evening.

'What's going on? Come on, get it out.' I stood facing him, polishing the glass. 'You did something wrong. Tell me, what's on your conscience?'

'Nothing! That's the thing, nothing. More or less nothing. I pushed Olivia, but she's dancing tonight, so it was something else.'

'You pushed Olivia? You're brave,' he was grinning at me.

I stuck my tongue out, making him smile even wider. I was so busy making fun of Niko that I didn't notice that Boris had sat down at the counter.

'Can I have a whisky on the rocks, Sarah?' he said my name with emphasis.

'Yes, right away.' I decided to treat him like any other customer. I poured him a double shot of whiskey. His gaze was focused on what I was doing. My hands trembled again in his presence. I slid the drink across the counter toward him. At the same moment, he grabbed my hand and trapped it between the glass and his warm palm for a few moments. I was getting more and more nervous. His cold, impenetrable eyes stared at me. Memories of our night together came flooding back. I remembered the moment he came inside me. The closeness was too electrifying. I was turned on just thinking about him. What was happening to me? I pulled my hand away.

'I'll clear the glasses,' I said in Niko's direction, causing one eyebrow to go up in a gesture of surprise. If I hadn't been so turned on by the mere touch of Boris' hand, I probably would have said something stupid. At that moment, all I wanted was to get away, if only for a moment. I reached for the tray and squeezed my way to the lobby.

'Where do you think you're going?' Boris' silhouette appeared right in front of me. He looked even better than the last time I saw him. What was I doing? He was standing too close to me. I was able to smell his cologne. I was dizzy from the onslaught of emotions.

'I made it clear. You are to stand behind the bar and not move from there.'

My eyes widened in surprise. I'd just realised the meaning of his words.

'It was you who wouldn't let me dance!'

'You want to dance? It's done,' he turned around and left.

I saw the curious looks of the girls. I took the tray and went to get those damn glasses.

When I came back, I saw Niko's contented smile.

'Don't say anything,' I tried to look threatening.

'I'm not saying anything,' he laughed at me, then turned towards the counter and served another guest.

After all the girls had performed, the customers would start heading home or to other, more secluded places.

'You have a private show,' said Sue, smiling at me.

I shouldn't be mad at her really. After all, it wasn't her fault I wasn't allowed to dance.

'You want me to dance?' I asked, surprised.

'Yes. Go, get ready, and be backstage at 2 am, sharp.'

I took a glance at my watch. I had half an hour left. I said goodbye to Niko and went to the dressing room. Most of the girls had shed their stage attire, swapping it for silk robes. It has always made me laugh. They looked like colourful birds flitting around in a locked cage. I walked over to the mirror and fixed my hair and makeup. I hadn't been given an outfit recommendation, so I chose a pair of fishnet stockings, black panties with a red lip print on the bottom, and a matching black top. I put red stiletto heels on my feet which were covered in sequins. They should shine beautifully in the spotlight. I added lipstick the same colour as the shoes. A few more deep breaths and I was ready.

I felt both fear and excitement. All these emotions were mixed together. I was curious as to see who I would be dancing for tonight.

'Good luck!' Amy wished me a successful performance. At that moment, I noticed that I wasn't alone. Some of the girls hid backstage to watch me dance. I heard the first notes of the melody. I took my last breath and walked out onto the stage. I couldn't see who was sitting in the audience. The lights were shining directly on me. I tried to look as professional as possible as I glided toward a chair on the stage. I didn't feel confident pole dancing, so today, the chair seemed like a better choice. I could express myself better. I didn't have to focus on all the complicated figures. My body had recently become more slender and bouncy, but I wasn't ready to dance like other girls yet.

I focused on the music and began to move. Calmly, slowly, I rotated my hips sensuously. After a while, I lost myself in what I was doing. I forgot where I was. I felt like I was floating, and that was all that mattered at that moment. By the end of the song, I knew I had given my absolute everything. I had danced the best I could. The song ended, and I was as turned on as ever. I could dance to a few more songs. The lights on the stage went out, and a silhouette of a man emerged from the twilight. He was sitting in a chair right next to the stage. I hadn't realised he was this close. He leant forward. His elbows were resting on his knees, and his hand was massaging the back of his neck. His honey-coloured eyes were focused on me.

'Come here. Everybody out!' he ordered loudly.

I almost forgot that we were not alone. I was standing as if glued to the stage. In the distance, I could hear hushed conversations. I saw Niko leave and close the door behind him. It was only us.

'Please come here,' he asked this time.

I walked toward him in my high heels. I stood at arm's length. Boris reached for me. He grabbed my hip and pulled me towards him. I didn't know what he wanted from me. What could I expect from him? He leaned over and kissed my naked belly. Shivers ran through me as I felt his breath and then his lips. I tilted my head back and lost myself in the sensation. His hand went up to pull down my top, leaving me in a black lace bra. He embraced my breast and caressed it through the thin material of the lace. I tangled my hand in his hair. He looked at me with those honey eyes of his.

'Boris,' I said first. Unexpectedly, he pulled me in so that I was sitting on top of him. I felt his pulsating manhood, but instead of moving away, I moved closer. He grabbed my bum and squeezed hard. He began to move as if we were having sex. He kissed me hard, aggressively. He stood up and sat me down on the stage. He put his hand inside my panties and touched gently. A gasp escaped my lips, which I could tell turned him on even more. He pushed me to lie down. I felt the cold floor under my back. He put one finger inside me, only to add another a moment later. His hand pushed against me and moved faster and faster. I was so close to finishing. I pushed my hips out toward his hand and came, an orgasm sweeping through me. After a while, I realised I felt uncomfortable. I sat up slowly.

Boris was standing at the bar. He poured himself a large portion of alcohol, drinking it all in one gulp. Everything happened so fast with unearthly intensity. I picked up my T-shirt from the floor and put it on.

'You can go now,' he said, topping up his glass with alcohol. He didn't even look at me.

I had so many extreme feelings flowing through me. I took off my heels and ran to my room. What did I want? What did I expect? After all, I was just a whore. Would it always be like this? I felt awful. I felt disgusted with myself. My legs were still trembling from my last orgasm. I could still smell his scent on me. I had to wash it off me. I undressed and jumped into the shower. I rubbed my entire body thoroughly with the lilac-scented soap. I loved it. It relaxed me. I had survived the evening. That was all that mattered. I came out of the bathroom wrapped in a robe, my hair still wet. Amy was sat on my bed.

'Are you okay? I was worried about you.'

I sat down next to her. I handed her the brush, and she combed my hair.

'Don't worry about it. I'll get used to it.' I wiped my nose trying to hold back my tears.

She hugged me, and we sat like that for a while.

'Don't get your hopes up. You are new. You must have caught his eye.'

'I know my place,' I answered sadly.

'That's good. Do you want to eat something? How about some ice cream? I know there's a box in the freezer downstairs.'

'Thanks. I think I'm just going to go to bed.'

She got off my bed, and looked at me for another moment with compassion. She hugged me again. 'Good night.' She closed the door behind her.

I changed into my pyjamas. I slipped under the duvet and curled up in a ball, with the hope of falling asleep quickly.

* * *

I see a man. He's far away. He is facing away from me. He is wearing an elegant suit. He doesn't turn around. I don't know who he is. I approached slowly at first, only to run a moment later. I want to stop, but I can't. I am getting closer. He turns around.

I woke up covered in sweat. It was a strange dream. I didn't know what it was about. I didn't even know who the man was. I felt so scared. I still feel uneasy when I think about it. It was a terrible feeling. Over-powering. I think I was afraid of losing control of my life.

I got up, wrapped myself in my robe, and went downstairs in search of the kitchen. I was very thirsty. I didn't even think to take water to my room. The whole house had been plunged into darkness. I stopped. A door a few steps away opened. I was in the girls' wing. The rules clearly stated that no males were allowed in here. I saw a storm of brown hair. It was Katrina. She gave the man a goodbye kiss. I stood in a place where no light fell on me; where I was invisible.

I watched the tender scene and wanted to believe that what I had just witnessed was something special. I so desperately needed to believe that there was still something good waiting for me in life. After all, we were not just objects in the hands of men.

I waited a little while longer. The man disappeared behind the front door, and I went to get water. I was surprised to see the light in the kitchen. It was Sue, who was sitting at the table sipping tea. Like me, she was dressed in a robe.

'Are you awake?' I asked a little stupidly. 'I just came to get some water.' I felt the need to explain myself.

'A few bottles are in the fridge if you want it cold, and the rest are on the floor.' She pointed to a pack of water lined up by the cabinet.

I tore open the package and pulled out one bottle. The kitchen was perfectly stocked. It held everything you could possibly want, from water, wine, and other spirits to snacks and delicious ready meals.

'Are you hungry? There's a casserole in the fridge. Katrina made it earlier. Help yourself.'

'I'm not hungry,' I said truthfully.

'I heard that you gave a great show.' She smiled with satisfaction.

'I did my best.' Honey eyes came to my mind again. I blushed as I thought about what happened after the show.

'Tomorrow, I'll pay you a week's salary,' she paused for a moment to continue her statement, 'He's been hurt, you know?'

I was shocked. Were we going to talk about this now? I sat down in front of her. I opened the bottle of water and took a large sip.

'I don't know if he can ever love again as much as he loved before. Please try not to get involved.'

'Okay,' I nodded automatically. That's exactly what Amy said.

'No one knows what goes on in his mind. He's a complicated man. I don't want him to destroy you. Men of that lineage are dangerous.'

'Destroy?'

'I can't talk about it. Take care of yourself. I should go to bed now. At my age, I need to get as much beauty sleep as I can get,' she added to lighten the mood.

She left me with a lot of questions. What was I getting myself into? Correction. What have I gotten myself into?

* * *

The next day they cancelled my classes at the university. The professor got sick. So I ate a light breakfast and went to the lobby, where I practised another dance routine. My muscles were still too weak for the fancy stunts on the pole. So I chose a chair as a prop. Ever since Olivia insulted me, I've been practising to get even better at what I did. I trained for a good hour, until my body was begging for a break. When the song ended, and there was silence between songs, I heard applause.

'That was truly smoking. I brought a bag with your stuff,' Alex pointed to a small package on the floor.

'Thanks.' I wiped my face and neck with a towel. Another song started playing in the background. 'I've had enough for today.'

'Is it your day off? Do you want to go to lunch?' he asked with a hint of uncertainty in his voice.

'Sure. What should I wear?'

'Whatever you want. We're going to that trendy restaurant I was talking about earlier.'

'For lasagna?' I was as happy as a kid with a piece of chocolate.

'For the best lasagna in town. I'll be waiting at Sue's. Come over when you're ready.'

I took a shower, and even tried to style my hair, but I couldn't tame it after a bath. I had to leave it loose. I put on a grey knee-length pencil dress and high heels. I looked at my reflection in the mirror and saw a sexy secretary.

We drove to the restaurant in Alex's black Audi R8. The machine had unearthly performance, and the engine growled like a kitten. The acceleration literally pinned me to my seat at take-off. I liked fast cars. I was intimidated by the luxury I was surrounded with. I was still a simple girl with a ton of debt. I realised that my contract here would eventually end, and I would be forced to return to my former life. To the apartment I shared with Alan and to the old, decrepit Volkswagen. For the time being though, I decided to enjoy every little thing, like speeding on the highway in a luxury car.

In the restaurant, we took our reserved seats. The room was impressive. Everything here was perfectly arranged and very expensive. Exquisite, decorated chairs and crystal chandeliers.

The waiter brought an appetiser and took our order. As soon as he had left, I stuffed a piece of baguette with olive oil into my mouth. I felt starving after my intensive training earlier.

'You left so suddenly that night. What happened?'

'Nothing, I had to leave.' I decided to keep some of the facts quiet.

'I understand you don't want to talk about it. I hope he didn't hurt you.'

I stopped halfway to my mouth with a baguette in my hand.

'Did you talk to him? What did he say to you?'

'He didn't tell me anything. Everything is just a guess. He pours so much whisky into himself that I'm honestly worried about him.'

The waiter brought our dishes. The lasagne smelled delicious. I put a piece in my mouth, and it was absolutely delightful. It was served with garlic bread and a salad.

'I have to be honest. I should have told you this at the beginning. I'm gay. You were supposed to be my cover.'

'I'm a lousy cover, don't you think? My profession disqualifies me from being the girl of the year.'

'You're new, innocent. Nobody knew you. You're perfect. My parents liked you very much.'

'Tell them hello from me. They're lovely people. I hope you explained my unexpected departure.'

'Don't worry. They didn't pry. Are you mad at me?'

'No, silly. Of course, I'm not,' I smiled at him.

There was a fuss at the entrance. Women were looking in that direction with interest. I was sitting in front of the entrance so I could see everything perfectly. Boris was standing at the threshold. The owner of the restaurant welcomed him personally. He walked slowly towards his table behind the waiter. At his side, there was a long-legged blonde. Like from a fashion magazine. Hair, body, face - everything looked like it came straight from a cover. But the worst part was that he was holding her hand. This gesture usually meant possessiveness towards another person.

'What happened?' Alex noticed my confusion. He turned discreetly in the direction in which I was looking.

'Do you want to leave?' He asked.

'We're not likely to leave unnoticed anyway. We might as well drink our wine and enjoy each other's company.'

'Are you sure?'

I glanced in Boris's direction again. He was just moving a chair for his partner. He must have sensed my gaze on him because he looked at me. He frowned slightly. He took a seat at the table. His companion grabbed his hand, and he let her do so. I had to leave on the spot right away.

'I've changed my mind. Please, let's go.' I looked pleadingly at Alex.

'Ice cream from the booth on the corner?' he joked.

'Yes, please.' We had to walk past Boris.

Alex, to my surprise, stopped at their table. He grabbed my hand. I appreciated the gesture of reassurance me. Boris pulled his hand out of the girl's grasp. It caused a grimace of displeasure on her face. She quickly masked it with a sweet smile. After the forced introduction, the men exchanged a few perfunctory remarks, and we left the restaurant.

Outside, I breathed a sigh of relief. I automatically pulled Alex to the ice cream stand. I ordered two chocolate scoops.

'Are you alright?' he asked, licking his ice cream. 'She's a model. Her name is Vivian.'

'Why are you telling me this?'

'So that you wouldn't think about it.'

'I wasn't thinking about it,' I lied.

'Has anyone ever told you that you're a terrible liar?'

'Yes, many times.'

My friends would always tell me I was an open book. All my emotions were written all over my face. 'All right, tell me what you know.'

'I was hoping you'd say that.' he said, overjoyed. 'They've been dating for six months.'

'They've been a couple? That long?' I was shocked by this news. Clearly, faithfulness was not his strong suit.

'They see each other occasionally, rather than being in a relationship. Anyway, they don't live together. He hasn't introduced her to our parents.'

'Unlike you,' I joked.

'Yeah, you're right.'

We laughed.

'I am pretty certain she wants to be with him, but I am not sure my brother is ready for another real relationship.'

Another one? Sue mentioned something too but didn't want to say anything specific.

'Yes, he had someone, but it's a sad story, and he should be the one to tell you, not me. Do you want me to drive you home?'

I nodded affirmatively.

* * *

In the evening I decided to visit my grandmother. I prepared her favourite apple cider for her. In residence, it's difficult to cook anything in small quantities. I'd spent around 2 hours making a cake. All the girls came into the kitchen. Each wanted a piece, of course. I ended up cutting off two pieces and leaving the rest for the girls. They made me promise to bake another one tomorrow.

I walked down the clinic hallway where my grandmother was staying, praying that this day would be a good one. When she remembered facts, people, and you could talk to her as usual. I really missed those conversations and the warmth she radiated.

Before, I used to call the nurses and ask them how she was that day before the visit. I was then mentally prepared for her reaction. However, I stopped calling since I started falling behind on my payments. I felt embarrassed enough. A more significant amount of money came into my account, but there wasn't much left after buying the outfits on Sue's list. I mean, there was a lot left, but still not enough to pay off all the debts.

Grandma sat in her chair and looked out the window. She hadn't wanted to leave the room lately. She glanced at me and smiled broadly. I involuntarily let out the breath I had been holding. I already knew she was having a good day.

'Hi Granny,' I hugged her tightly and kissed her cheek. I prolonged the moment to feel like a little girl again. Back then, she would often read me stories while I sat on her lap.

'Honey, it's good to see you.'

'The weather is still not that cold out there. Would you like to take a walk in the garden?'

'I just got back. I was gossiping with Evelina from room number five. Her granddaughter visited her yesterday with her one-month-old daughter. I saw the baby. It was as small as you were when you were born. Only you already had hair, and she's bald. I already knew you were going to be unique. There you go!' she pointed to the mess on my head.

As always, I felt a tightness in my chest when I thought about my childhood. I was only six years old when my parents were killed in the car accident. I moved in with my grandmother then. I know it was a horrible experience for her too. She was my only family from then on.

'I brought apple pie.' I reached into the kitchenette for plates and spoons. I boiled water for coffee for myself and tea for Grandma. In the corner of the room was a sofa and next to it a small table. I noticed a beautiful bouquet of tulips.

'Grandma, where do the tulips come from?'

'Your friend brought them. He was very elegant.'

'Alan was here? He didn't say he was coming to see you.'

'No, it wasn't him. Your new friend was—a really nice man. I told him about when you went to school and met that boy with the big glasses. Do you remember?'

'Yeah, I remember.'

'Good morning,' the clinic's manager cautiously looked into the room. 'Sorry to bother you, can I speak to you for a second?'

I hoped that I wouldn't meet her and I wouldn't have to explain that I didn't have money to pay for my grandmother's stay. As soon as we stepped out into the hallway, I began to explain:

'I know I'm behind on my payments. I'll pay when I'm…'

'I'm just on the subject. The debt was settled and the stay paid for another six months ahead.'

'But how so?'

'Mr. Smith paid for everything.'

'Boris?' I asked in surprise. I felt relieved. On the other hand, how dare he interfere in my private life!

'Give him my regards,' she smiled dreamily.

'Yes, I will,' I said. The mystery of the bouquet of tulips on the table was solved. I went back to my grandmother's room and spent the next two hours with her, laughing and watching a quiz show on TV. I drove back to my apartment shortly after leaving my grandmother's. Despite the late hour, I found Alan in the kitchen. He was cooking spaghetti sauce. He embraced me in greeting. I felt relief and, at the same time, regret that everything had changed. It felt good to be home again.

'What's that face? Don't you dare cry here! You know how much I hate tears. Do you want some wine?'

I just nodded. I was afraid that my voice would break and I would burst into tears. I didn't want to be sad. I took a big sip. Alan looked at me with the sauce spoon in his hand.

'Come on, tell me. I can't stand the tension. I've been waiting to ask you how the trip went, and you haven't written or called. Niko said you put on a good performance last night. I'm sure he'd have a hard-on if he had a taste for women. Come on! I can't stand it a minute longer. What happened after the dance? I know everyone had to leave. Did you do it?'

'Yes, I did. But not yesterday, on the weekend away.' I could feel my cheeks burning.

'With Alex?'

'No, with Boris.'

'Wait, wait, wait. I don't understand.'

I told him everything that had happened. He listened intently. When I finished, he looked at me with wide eyes. He was thrilled with the news. 'I knew he had the hots for you. Even then, at the club. He was watching you.'

'How do you know that?'

'Niko pointed him out to me. He's pretty hot. He was watching you dance. And he had this look on his face that gave me a hard-on. So, I dragged Niko to....'

'Wait, wait, wait. I don't want to know the details. Why didn't you tell me?' I was completely confused.

'It slipped my mind. I was busy.' He looked at me apologetically.

I hid my face in my hands. Everyone knew except me. It takes a lot of luck to sleep with a guy who turns out to be your boss. And for him to pays your debts for you.

'Oh, really? He paid off your debt?'

'Yeah, he did. He also went to my grandmother's place. He gave her tulips. Can you imagine? He paid off my debts and paid for another six months in advance.'

'You're screwed.'

'I know. Pour me some more wine.' I drank enough not to think or worry about tomorrow. There's probably already a lot of gossip about me at the residence. I had to last six months there. I had a contract for that long. After that time, I would pay him back all his money and be free.

* * *

During the following meeting at the residence, I could feel the gaze of the gathered girls on me. Amy brought me coffee. It had already become our little tradition since my first day in this place. Boris was present at this meeting. Everyone fell quiet when he entered the room behind Sue. He walked confidently. His eyes fixed on me. Every time I saw him, he seemed to look even better. He was wearing a dark suit. Embarrassed, I looked down at my coffee, and my red manicured nails. I tried my best not to look at him. I knew he sat down next to Sue, who, as always, had begun to lead the meeting.

Amy poked me and whispered, 'He's staring at you.'

I couldn't continue to pretend he wasn't there. As soon as I lifted my gaze, I felt it was a mistake. I lost myself in his eyes. I felt the unconscious need for him to touch me. I clenched my thighs tighter to quell the growing pulse sensation in my lower body. Sue handed out meeting schedule folders to everyone. This time none of the girls teased her or commented on what she had to tell them. They all looked at Boris and me. Finally, Sue made her formal presentation, assuring them that Boris would be taking over some of Alex's responsibilities.

How did I miss that detail? They are brothers, and the residence is their family business. A few days ago, Boris stated that he had no time for it. Seeing him sitting right in front of me made me think, what had changed? I thought I knew, and I didn't like the answer.

Sue turned the reins over to Boris.

'Sue overexaggerated my responsibilities. She and Alex are doing a great job together. I've been aware of the reports throughout this entire time. I'm not going to change anything. All of your matters will continue to be managed by Sue. I trust her one hundred per cent,' he smiled at her sincerely. 'Thank you, that's all for to-day,' he ended the meeting.

I picked up my folder and was the first one out the door.

'Sarah, can you stay a minute?' A male voice reached me.

Amy whispered, 'Good luck,' and she was gone.

The room was deserted. Boris stood in the same place as before.

'Come here,' he said. He indicated on a chair, 'Sit down.'

I approached him but made no move to sit down. I leaned with my hip against the table. I didn't want him to think he was in a position to give me orders!

He smiled slyly as if that was the reaction he expected.

'I'll give you all the money back. I didn't ask you to pay my debts.'

'You're welcome. You don't have to thank me.'

'You heard me. I don't want your money.'

'You don't? Then why are you here?'

'You're an asshole! You know that?' I turned to leave. He put his arms around me in an iron grip.

'Watch your mouth,' he threatened in an icy tone, and then, in contrast to what he had said, he kissed me on the neck.

I was furious with him. My body, on the other hand, was telling me something completely different. With one silly kiss, he aroused my senses. He kissed my neck softly without loosening his grip. I leaned my head back, giving him permission to caress me. He loosened his hands a bit, grabbed my hips and pulled my bum closer against his manhood. I could feel his erection despite the layer of clothing. I kept moving up, down. He hissed right next to my ear. He turned me around in one decisive motion. He was aroused. I could see the animalistic lust in his eyes. He plunged into my mouth without warning. He kissed me hard and possessively. We were alone in the room, but the door wasn't locked. Someone could enter at any time.

'No one would dare to come in here,' he said as if he had read my mind. 'Relax.'

He glided his warm hands under my top. He gently tickled my hips and the skin on my belly and then caressed my breasts through my lacy bra.

'Raise your hands.' I did as he asked.

He took off my top. I was now standing in front of him in just my jeans and a bra. He left one breast exposed. He took the nipple in his mouth, bit and licked, bringing me to the brink of pleasure. I wanted to sit down on the table, but the chairs blocked my way. Boris continued to suck on my breast as he swung two chairs into the middle of the room and sat me on the table. He exposed my other breast and began the sweet torture all over again. Each touch triggered a wave of pleasure in my crotch. I spread my legs slightly and pulled him closer to me. He unzipped my jeans and let his hand slide deep into my panties. As soon as he touched my vagina, I lifted my hips slightly.

'So wet,' he whispered. All this for me?' He whispered.

I glanced nervously at the door.

'Don't think about that. It's just you and me. Stand up. Take them off.' I stood up on soft legs, and I let my jeans slide to the floor.

He pressed a wet kiss to my lips. He took my hand and turned me towards the table. He pushed firmly but gently against the polished surface. The disparity between the warm touch of his hands and the cold tabletop was tremendous. I held my breath as he swiped his finger through my lace panties across my pussy.

'I really like this underwear. Let's leave it on you as I fuck you.'

He squished my butt, enjoying himself at the mere touch of my skin.

'Hold on to the table.'

I had to stretch my arms far out in front of me and grabbed the other end of it. My cheek rested on the cold tabletop; my feet still planted on the ground. I heard the characteristic sound of foil being torn. He moved my panties aside but didn't remove them. The condom was cold. I trembled when he touched my entrance. He caressed me with one hand as he entered me. Panicked, I looked at the door once more.

'Don't think, just focus on the feeling.' He thrust all the way in. I closed my eyes in ecstasy.

He began to move steadily. I was moving all over as I was pushed into the table.

'Grip it harder.' He lifted my legs, held them in the air just at his hips level. He turned up the pace. I felt the table slam into my body, my breasts moving rhythmically across the tabletop. I gripped its edge even harder. Boris picked up the pace even more. I was close to orgasm. Then he released my leg so that I was back on the ground. He pulled my hair without slowing down. I came powerfully with a groan. Shortly after, he peaked as well, falling on top of me. It wasn't until now that I felt pain wash over my body. I couldn't feel my hands. He kissed my shoulder blade and rolled off me. He left a cold breath of air on my skin.

'Get dressed,' he ordered.

I snorted, crawling off the table. He fucked me, but I was not his property. I would do whatever I wanted.

'Get dressed,' he said more softly. 'Unless you fancy another round.'

I looked at his still erect manhood. Instinctively I licked my lips.

'Jesus, get dressed,' he growled. 'I don't have any more time. I have a meeting in fifteen minutes at the other end of town. Next time though, we won't have to rush.'

He took off the used condom and threw it in the trash next to the coffee machine. I managed to get dressed in the meantime.

'See you tomorrow,' he said as if nothing had happened. As if we had just had a business meeting. I was so mad at him! At him and at my treacherous body. Because I liked it, I came to the conclusion that I liked sex. I just had to remember that this was my job and not my life. That way I could come out of this situation in one piece.

I threw my folder on the bed in my room, and took a long bath with lots of bubbles. All I needed for complete relaxation was a glass of wine. I wasn't sure about my plans for the evening yet though, so I held off on the wine. I put on my fluffy bathrobe and I reflexively combed my hair. A girl with blushed cheeks looked back at me from the mirror. I tried not to think about Boris. It wasn't easy. All my thoughts were focused on this complicated man. His gaze itself was enough to ignite my senses. Not to mention the touch. With a snap, I put the brush down on the dresser. I needed to calm down. He simply surprised me this time. Who was I trying to fool? I enjoyed it, and I certainly wanted more. I was excited by the vision of another rendezvous. I was curious if sex with every guy was this intense. I feared that, unfortunately, it wasn't.

I fell softly on the bed. I pulled a plastic folder out from under my butt. I sat down with my legs crossed and began to read the contents. Training, training charity ball on Wednesday, which is precisely in two days. Client's details: Boris Smith. Oh, fuck! I was in a heap of trouble. I wanted to be angry that he was dragging me into his games, but I couldn't. I read the instructions on how to look that day. I took the papers. I had to show it to Amy. The door to her room was open, and the room looked like a battered mess. My friend was standing in front of an empty closet and mumbling something unintelligible. All the clothes were sorted and stacked in different parts of the room.

'What are you doing? Laundry?' I sat down on the bed, after moving what was lying on it.

'I'm cleaning.'

'I can see that. But the closet was tidy. Why did you pull everything out?' I always envied her organisation.

'I have to get rid of half of my clothes. My sister's coming to visit me, and I'm making room in the closet.'

'She's coming to visit?' I was surprised. Not long ago, she said her sister wasn't going to see her.

'She's staying for a while. Not sure for how long. But she has had some problems, and she wouldn't tell me over the phone.' She looked at the folder in my lap. 'What do you have in there?'

'I'm going to a charity ball on Wednesday.'

'Shopping time!' She exclaimed happily. 'Come on; I'll show you my favourite boutique. You need a dress, shoes and a handbag. You already have underwear. We bought too much last time,' she laughed happily.

Soon we were on our way to go shopping. Amy was chattering excitedly, as she always did at such moments. I had already suspected that she was a shopaholic. Now, I was sure. The shop assistant greeted her like a good friend. A moment later, she was busying herself with the creations crammed on the hangers. This was not a typical boutique, where only a few things were displayed. Here, the hangers were overflowing with goods. After just a moment, Amy pulled out dresses of different lengths and colours. The saleswoman patiently took all the dresses and hung them in the fitting room. I was screwed. It could take forever to try them all on. At first, I put on the ones I liked the most - the ones that drew my attention with their colour or cut. I wanted something elegant, something I felt comfortable in. All the dresses were well cut; I was beginning to understand Amy's excitement. My heart was stolen by a simple black dress. It was ankle-length and tied at the neck. There was no neckline, but the back was covered by a lace insert that ended below the line of the panties. This meant that I would either have to find a pair of nude underwear, or just go without. I walked out of the fitting room to show my choice to Amy. My choice made her clap her hands in excitement. I glanced at the price and sighed with resignation. It was excruciatingly expensive.

'Don't worry about the price. You know, we'll put it on the bill for that rich guy you're going with. Actually, you didn't tell me who you were going with.'

I moved my gaze from the price to my friend.

'I'm going with Boris. Do you think he'll pay for this dress?'

'Wait a minute. You're going with Boris, slash by the creamy pie, slash the owner?' She made a strange face, 'Why are you only telling me this now?'

'You didn't ask,' I shrugged my shoulders.

'Girl, now you have to buy that dress.'

She asked the saleswoman to pack up the dress and shoes to complete the outfit. I also had my mind set on a green fur coat. The nights were getting colder, and I'd always wanted one.

After shopping, Amy dragged me to a chain store for a burger. She claimed we needed our daily dose of carbohydrates. She was really slim, considering the amount of food she consumed. I ate what I wanted, but in moderation, although lately, my body had slimmed down. It was due to all the regular hard workouts.

'Will you do my hair tomorrow?' I asked, biting into a burger.

'Of course. You need to put your hair up so your back is visible. We'll book a makeup artist, too. You'll look phenomenal. Besides, you attract the eyes of men even without it.'

'Me?' I was surprised. I never paid attention to it.

'Yes, you!' she rolled her eyes. 'Look. There are three guys sitting on the right.'

As soon as I glanced in their direction, they stopped talking. One of them even waved at me.

'See the one on the left. He keeps looking at you even though he's with a girl.'

When I looked at him, he turned his eyes away and focused his attention on his phone.

'They're looking at us, if anything, and not at me.'

'Yeah, right… I've already noticed this recently when we were shopping for lingerie. No wonder Boris lost his mind. Did you have sex with him?'

'Keep it down.' I looked around to see if anyone was listening in. She was staring at me with her big eyes.

'Yeah.' I was a little embarrassed by my own words.

'I knew it! Last time in the conference room?'

'Yes. I guess everyone knows now.'

'Everyone at the meeting. The way he was looking at you! It made me want to shag.'

'Shut up! People are watching.'

'So what? Everybody's having sex.'

'Let's go back.' I started to collect the leftovers from the table on a tray. 'I have class tomorrow morning. I still have to prepare a presentation.'

* * *

In class, I couldn't concentrate on what the teacher was saying. The day before, Amy had helped me prepare my presentation. It turned out that she had another talent that no one knew about. She could draw. Thanks to her, what I wanted to present gained shape and colour. Fortunately, the teacher didn't call my name. I would have performed poorly today. I was so excited about the evening and couldn't concentrate at all. I had never been to an event like this before.

After class, Amy didn't leave me for a second. She had a meeting that night. Instead of getting ready, she helped me. She pinned my hair high on top of my head so that the lace on my back could be seen. The make-up artist added extra emphasis to eye makeup, adding depth to my eyes. I had never looked as pretty as I did today. I packed some more condoms in my purse. After my last meeting with Boris, I had to be ready for anything. Just the thought of him made me feel a little stressed. I glanced in the mirror for the last time. I was ready to go one hundred per cent.

I threw my fur coat over my shoulders, grabbed my clutch bag from the dressing table, and went downstairs. I stopped halfway down the stairs to admire Boris, who was busy talking to Sue. His body was framed by a classic black tuxedo. The white-collar contrasted with his tanned face. He was explaining something frantically to Sue. He wasn't happy. He was pissed, confident, and unearthly handsome. He saw me and kept his eyes on my figure. He fell silent, causing Sue to follow his gaze. I could see her smile widening. She nodded slightly in a gesture of appreciation. She was very demanding, and it wasn't easy to win her approval. Boris apologised to her and approached the stairs with his eyes fixed only on me. I thought of my high heels, my long dress, and his magnetic gaze. That's exactly how he looked at me that day at the ranch when he covered my hand with his.

I released the breath I was holding once I managed to get down in one piece.

'Hello gorgeous,' he kissed the back of my hand. 'Ready to go?'

'Yes.' I took hold of the arm he stretched towards me.

The very innocent touch released a wave of heat through my body. I was really hoping he would be driving. Then, I could have some time to get used to the situation. Unfortunately, a shiny black limousine was waiting for us in front of the building. The chauffeur opened the door for us. I slid into the seat first. As soon as the door slammed behind us, I smelled his cologne. Despite the massive interior of the limousine, I felt out of breath. Boris took the seat next to me. I wanted to discreetly increase the distance between us. I moved a little. The material of the dress slid down my leg, exposing my thigh. I had completely forgotten that the dress had a long slit along my right leg. His gaze rested on my bare thigh. I tried to cover it, but I couldn't pull the material up. His face, still tense after the exchange with Sue, relaxed slightly as he watched me struggling desperately from the corner of his eye.

'Leave it,' he said and placed his hand over mine, locking it in a warm embrace. He didn't move his hand the whole journey. I was afraid to make any move. I kept my eyes fixed on the windscreen while Boris got more comfortable, still keeping his hand on my thigh. I was glad when the car arrived at the destination. As before, he lent me his arm, and we walked down the long hotel corridor. Before entering, he handed an invitation to a young girl. She led us into a room full of people.

'Would you like something to drink?' We headed toward the liquor bar.

'White wine, please.'

'You're all tense. Are you afraid of me?' he quipped.

'You are irritated, and I don't want to make you angrier,' I confessed honestly, taking the glass from his hands. He looked deeply into my eyes.

'I'm not irritated.' I made him laugh with that statement.

'You were arguing with Sue.' I remembered their sharp exchange of words.

'We had a different opinion on a particular subject. That's all.

Encouraged by the alcohol, I went on, 'Was it an important matter?'

'She thought you should return to the residence for the night, but I had a different opinion.'

I choked on my wine. My uncontrollable cough attracted the attention of everyone within close vicinity. Boris took the glass from my hand and lightly patted my back. When my breathing returned to normal, I picked up the glass and emptied its contents.

'Don't I have anything to say?'

'You don't agree with me?' he pierced me with his intense gaze.

I wanted to deny it, but I couldn't. Boris was definitely pleased with this turn of events. He smiled radiantly as if he had won the lottery.

'I need more wine,' I added. My request was fulfilled. After two glasses of alcohol, I felt a slight buzz in my head. It turned out that Boris knew many people at the ball, especially the men. Probably they were customers of the residence. The women also greeted him effusively, ignoring me very effectively. I should have felt offended. Unfortunately, I realised that I was merely his decoration. I sipped another glass, trying not to think about what would happen when we got out of here. Would we go to his place or somewhere else? Cheers and applause spread throughout the room. The event organiser thanked all of the donors. He especially wanted to thank the Smith family, and he also asked Boris to say a few words to the audience. Before he moved towards the stage, he leaned over and whispered:

'Wait here for me. I'll be right back.'

His breath tickled my ear pleasantly. Only now did I notice that he hadn't been drinking alcohol. Could it be that he wanted to drive in the evening?

'How does it feel to be at such a lavish party?' I heard a mocking voice.

'You tell me. You're here too,' I snapped.

Vivian came and stood next to me. She was smiling charmingly, and her words were dripping with sarcasm.

'You think you can get him?'

'I don't think anything.'

Boris just got to the stage and started giving a speech. Unfortunately, I couldn't focus on his words, being so close to his girlfriend. I wondered why he came here with me and not her.

'Just because you came with him doesn't mean you're with him.'

'Doesn't it?' I decided to play her game.

'No. He'll have his fun with you and come straight back to me. In all honesty, not even I can have him,' she swirled the alcohol in her glass, wobbling dangerously. 'His heart doesn't belong to either of us.'

Boris had finished his short speech and was already pushing his way through the crowd towards us. His face took on an angry expression again when he saw Vivian standing next to me.

'Boris, darling,' Vivian grabbed him tightly by the lapels of his tuxedo, spilling some of the liquor on his clothes. He received a kiss on the cheek as he turned his face in my direction. He looked at me menacingly as I took a step back. I didn't need to witness the scene this girl had set up for him.

'Sarah, please stay!'

I stopped.

'Honey, it's good to see you,' Vivian continued her performance.

'You're drunk,' he hissed in disgust.

'Maybe I drank one too many. Who's counting?'

'I'll order you a cab.' He took her hands off his jacket lapel and shrugged lightly.

'Come with me,' Vivian didn't give up.

She didn't even mind that I was standing right next to her.

'Come on. I'll take you to the car.' He walked away with her toward the exit, and I stayed where I was. First, he told me to stay, then he left. I walked over to the bar and asked for another glass of wine. Before I could even take a sip, warm hands wrapped around my waist. I smelled the familiar scent of cologne.

'Come on. I'm taking you away from here.'

'Taking me where?'

He just nodded, 'You'll find out in a moment.'

He kept me close to him the whole way. Maybe he was afraid I would change my mind and run away? He directed us to the elevator. I should have kept quiet, but my curious nature triumphed.

'Did you order Vivian a cab?' Her name barely came out of my throat.

He looked at me from under his squinted eyelids, 'Not exactly. I put her in our limo. I wanted to drive you back to the residence after the ball, but our transport just left.'

'You wanted to bring me back, and you still booked a room?'

'I was actually planning on dragging your sexy ass here during the party. But now...' he shrugged his shoulders, 'we might as well stay all night.'

'What does your girlfriend say about this?' I spat out without thinking.

'I don't have a girlfriend. I'm sure Alex mentioned that to you.'

'He did say you two were just having sex.'

'That's right. All I have in common with women is sex. Sex, and nothing else.'

The elevator stopped on our floor. I was nervous, even the considerable amount of alcohol I'd drank didn't help. Boris scanned his key-card and let me through. I went inside. The apartment was impressive. The room was bigger than my entire apartment. I ran my hand over the purple leather sofa, my stilettos sinking into the soft beige carpet. The lights went dim, and the skyline of the city emerged before my eyes. In the distance, coloured dots glowed and shimmered. The hotel was built on a hill so that I could admire the luminous spectacle down below.

'Beautiful, isn't it?' He kissed my neck. We stood like that for a few minutes, engulfed in complete silence. I leaned casually against his torso, soaking up every second of this fleeting moment. The right man and a scene that looked like it came from a movie. The thought terrified me. What was I suitable for? For sex, for spending time together. I couldn't get hooked on him. I still have four months left on my contract.

'What are you thinking about so intensely?' His lips began a slow journey down my neck to my ear and back again.

'Nothing.'

'Liar,' he whispered. 'Should I order something to eat?' he asked. He looked as if he wanted to eat me himself.

'I'm not hungry.'

He held me tightly, and we strolled towards the sofa. He turned on the music and sat down comfortably.

'Dance for me,' he asked.

I took a few steps back so he would have a better perspective. I moved my hips enticingly. I exposed the full length of my leg thanks to the slit in my dress. He kept his attentive gaze on me, following my every move. I grabbed the knot of the dress around my neck. After a moment, the top of it fell to my waist, revealing a black strapless bra. I caught his burning gaze. Seducing him with movements to the rhythm of the music, I slowly slid the dress off my hips. It fell to the floor. I was left in a black bra, flesh-coloured panties, and stiletto heels.

Boris took off his bow tie and put it next to him on the sofa. The temperature in the room automatically rose a few degrees. I grabbed the clasp of my bra. It quickly fell to the ground, as did my panties.

I walked up to him. His stare was on fire. I should have felt embarrassed. Boris was still dressed, and I was parading naked in front of him, but I didn't feel anything like that. The dim lights and alcohol had probably done their job. Seeing the approval in his eyes, I let go of my shame. I sat down on top of him, unbuttoning his shirt button by button, all the while looking into his eyes. His impatient hands caressed my breasts. The fire I liked so much was already burning in his eyes. I wanted him to reach me too. I kissed him confidently until I was breathless.

His hips were moving right under me. I wanted to feel him inside me as soon as possible. I struggled with the fastening of his pants. His movements became jerky. He helped me get rid of the rest of his clothes and sat me down again in the same position. This time I could feel his arousal between my thighs.

'Put it on,' he said and slipped a condom into my hand. I looked at it with consternation. He laughed, 'Let me help you unwrap the package. Grab the tip and unroll it over my penis.' My clumsy movements were clearly amusing him. 'Bravo. You've earned your reward.' He gripped my hips tighter and moved me into position. I fell on top of him slowly. He kept looking deep into my eyes.

When he was all the way inside me, I leaned my hand against his chest and lowered my gaze.

'Hey, are you okay?' He brushed away a few strands of hair from my face that had already managed to slip out of my bun. 'Look at me!' His honey eyes watched me closely.

'Are you okay?'

I moved.

'Fine, just…'

'Just what?'

'You're filling me up.'

'That's how it should be.' He laid his head casually on the back of the sofa. I could control the pace, so I sped up my movements, and after a while, we both came. I hid my face in his neck. All sweaty, I couldn't catch my breath. It took a long moment before our breathing calmed down.

'My legs felt numb. I had to get up.' I slid clumsily onto the carpet and went to the bathroom. I let my hair down. There wasn't much left of my elaborately combed bun. I walked out of the bathroom. I was still naked.

'Come over to me,' I heard a quiet voice. Boris was lying on the bed, leaning against the headboard. 'Come here.' He patted the spot next to him.

I was getting a sense of unease. What was I supposed to do? What was I meant to talk to him about? We hadn't talked much since the beginning of our acquaintance. I sat down carefully on the bed and lay down next to him. I didn't touch him. He looked at me, creased his eyebrows ridiculously, and pulled me closer to him. I felt a strange sensation. His chest moved steadily in rhythm with his breaths. I laid my head against it. I could feel his warmth and intoxicating scent. I liked it. He covered us with the sheets and turned off the lamp on his side of the bed. We were enveloped in darkness. He didn't speak to me. I wonder what he was thinking about? I knew he wasn't asleep.

'Sleep now,' he whispered to me.

'I won't fall asleep in this position.' I lay on my side, facing the wall. He put his warm hand around me, cuddling into my back.

'You still have four months left on your contract. I want you exclusively,' he spoke the words with hesitation. As if he feared rejection. But did I even have a choice?

'Okay,' I replied. 'Good night.' I didn't know what else to add.

'Good night,' he whispered. He placed one last kiss on the top of my head.

* * *

Rays of sunlight flooded the room. It took me a moment to remember where I was. The place next to me was empty. Only now have I had the opportunity to admire the decor of the bedroom. The room, like the whole apartment, was kept in light tones. In each room, only one thing stood out in colour. In the living room, it was a purple sofa and in the bedroom, there was a navy blue armchair.

'Are you getting up?' A freshly shaved Boris, dressed in jeans and a dark T-shirt, stood with a small sports bag in his hand. 'I had some of your belongings brought in. I doubt you wanted to wear yesterday's dress.'

I propped myself up on my elbows and wrapped the quilt tighter around me. Yesterday I was quite brave, but today, during the day, all my valour had disappeared. He put the bag on the bed. I moved nervously. The way he looked at me was unmistakable.

'I ordered breakfast to come to the room in twenty minutes. Is that enough time for you to get dressed?'

'Yes. I'm on my way to take a shower.' I had to hurry to make it in time. I was aware that I was completely naked, and he was stubbornly standing and waiting for my reaction.

'You were going to take a shower?' He was clearly making fun of me.

'Don't you have to do something important?'

'Important?' He leaned against the door frame in a very sexy pose.

'Call the company or the accountant or something…'

'No. Not a thing. I'm off today, but you've already missed some classes. We'll eat, and I'll drive you to college.'

'I'm not going in today.'

'You are. You have ten minutes until breakfast. Get up!'

I sighed wearily.

'Can you get out of here now? I'm naked.'

'I know, that's why I'm standing here.'

In a gesture of surrender, I got out of bed, grabbed my bag, and rushed naked to the bathroom.

'Child,' I muttered under my breath.

'I heard that! You have eight minutes.'

'I doubt it,' I snorted, closing the bathroom door. I don't know who packed the bag, but all the things I needed were there. I took a quick shower. I usually liked to stand under warm water for a long time, but I had to hurry this time. In the bag, I found a toothbrush, toothpaste, and makeup products. There was even a folder I needed for college. Someone had done an excellent job, but at the same time, they were rummaging through my personal belongings. I put on clean underwear, a t-shirt, jeans, and sneakers. I put on some more light makeup and gave up drying my hair. Well over eight minutes later, I was ready.

'Coffee, please!' I shouted from the threshold of the living room, where I smelled the aromatic fragrance.

At the table filled with food, Boris was reading a newspaper. He put it down and focused all his attention on me. I poured myself a cup of the fragrant black drink. I tried to behave as naturally as possible under his watchful gaze. I took a slice of toast and spread butter on it.

'Not hungry?' He kept looking at me intensely. He stood up and walked over to me. He wrapped a lock of my hair around his finger. 'You haven't changed your mind overnight? Can I have you exclusively until the end of the contract?'

'Nothing has changed,' I said confidently, although everything inside me was trembling with fear. He would destroy me. I could see it in his eyes. Nevertheless, I was ready to take the risk.

'I like the colour of your hair.' He kissed me on the lips and returned contentedly to his chair.

'I want to continue learning to dance and take part in shows.'

'Dancing is okay, shows – not so much. Your only job is to stand behind the bar.'

'You can't do that to me. What will the girls say? Besides, when the contract ends and I decide to stay, no one will be interested in me. I'll be labelled "the boss's whore."'

'Enough!' he banged his fist on the table until the cups jumped up, and so did I. 'I don't know what will happen next. At this point, I don't feel like sharing.'

'Typical man,' I muttered.

'I heard that,' he hissed menacingly, 'I didn't plan this. I don't know how it's going to work. I will arrange the details with Sue, and we will talk about this over dinner?'

'Are you asking or announcing?'

'Is there a difference? The effect is the same.'

Further conversation was pointless. He was going to get what he wanted anyway. In this instance, me. I took a bite of scrambled eggs and tried to eat at least a little. I guess I should be getting used to the situation. My gut told me that we would often eat breakfast together. On the other hand, it was better than immediately going home after sex. Actually, upon further reflection I decided it meant exactly the same thing.

'You ready? Let's go.' Boris waited until I finished eating.

I had already grabbed my things and stuffed them into a sports bag. Boris offered to drop it off at the residence. Despite my requests, he refused to drop me off a block earlier. Instead, he ostentatiously drove as close as he could. As a rule, students cannot afford expensive cars, so getting out of his Audi caused quite a bit of confusion. Fortunately, he did not get out of the vehicle. I said goodbye to him with a short "see you later" and ran towards the university building.

I kept thinking about last night during class, and as a result, I wasn't paying attention to the lecture. If I kept doing that, I'm wasn't going to pass the year. I constantly thought about something I shouldn't.

Right after class, I got on the bus and made my way to see my grandma. Since yesterday, my car had been parked outside the residence, so I was forced to use public transport.

It made me very happy to see my grandmother in a cheerful mood. I chatted with her about my friends from the residence. I also told her about the party, missing out some of the key details. There was no point in hiding that I would be spending a lot of time with Boris over the next few months. My cell phone once again buzzed in my purse. I had ten missed calls from an unknown number and three text messages. The first one, I guessed, was from Boris that there would be a car waiting for me outside the university. The following two were not so nice. *I'm at my grandma's.* I tapped out a short message. *Marco will pick you up in thirty minutes*, was the reply.

Grandma gave me a suspicious look as I texted but didn't say anything. She was just smiling brightly. I didn't want to spoil her mood by explaining that it was nothing important, not permanent. I said goodbye to her and I stepped in front of the building just as Marco was parking Boris' car. He got out and opened the back door for me. I felt stupid.

'You don't have to open the door for me. I can do it myself.'

'Mr. Boris told me to bring you back, so I have to be sure you're safe.'

I burst out laughing, not very elegantly.

'Marco, I'm Sarah, and that's what you can call me, okay?'

'Okay,' he smiled and asked, 'Shall we go now? Mr Boris is very upset.'

'Yes, he is. Let's go now.' Ten missed calls was really a lot. He was probably angry.

Today I had another dance workout scheduled, which I didn't feel like doing. I was tired and hungry. Pulling up outside the residence, I saw a bunch of people. Maybe someone had fainted? I couldn't see an ambulance. Marco didn't have time to turn off the engine. I jumped out of the car, running toward the gathering. Just before I entered, Alex and Boris were rolling on the ground. Both were covered in dust and badly battered. I pushed myself between the people as close as I could.

'What's going on here?' I asked Amy.

'They are fighting.' The crowd was cheering, heavily divided depending on who was getting the upper hand at any given moment.

'I can see that. What are they fighting about?'

'About you,' announced Amy and moved her eyebrows suggestively.

'Get Sue here. This has to stop.'

I entered their field of vision.

'Stop!' I yelled as loud as I could. Marco and Niko tried to separate them. Marco held Alex tightly, holding his hands behind him, but Alex still tried to break free. Niko, on the other hand, was too weak to stop Boris. The man, releasing himself, jumped back and punched Alex in the jaw once more. Blood was pouring from his cut lip. They glared at each other menacingly. Without thinking, I stepped between them.

'Stop it!' I shouted at Boris. I pushed him away, resting my hands on his chest. I forced him to take a few steps back. He shifted his enraged gaze to me but backed off.

'The show is over! Get back inside,' ordered Sue. 'You two, into my office! Now!' She turned on her heel and marched away furious.

The square was deserted. Alex shook off the rest of the dirt. Boris stood opposite with his fists clenched.

'Can you explain this to me?' I spoke first.

'I was just explaining to my brother what we agreed on last night.' he emphasised the last words.

I looked at Alex in surprise. Marco stood right behind him. He looked like he was about to have a heart attack. I shifted my gaze back to Alex.

'You can't do this,' he tried to convince me.

'Why not?'

'I can't tell you. Just don't do it.' He got closer. He touched my cheek. 'Please! Don't do this.' His eyes were pleading.

I was baffled. Marco shakily looked at me with a hostile expression on his face. Our temporary truce had just been broken.

Boris grabbed me around my waist, pulling me back a few steps. He leaned me against his body and kissed my neck. I knew what he was doing. It was a totally messed up game of possession. I watched as Alex's eyes grew sad. His whole body tensed up. I couldn't get a single word out. I couldn't. I didn't know what to say. At the same time, I didn't want to lose my friend. Alex shook his head one last time with resignation and walked away. Marco followed him, sending me another hostile look. We were left alone in the empty yard.

'He's your brother! How could you?'

'My adopted brother,' he hissed.

'What!?' I twisted around to face him.

'You heard. Come on, I need ice, and you should eat something.' He moved his jaw with great difficulty.

In the kitchen, I handed him a package of frozen peas. He sat down at the table. With a groan, he pressed the frozen peas to his face. I couldn't believe that these two intelligent men had beaten each other up in front of everyone. I put the pot on the hob a little harder than I intended. The sound of cast iron colliding with metal echoed through the kitchen.

'My parents adopted four-year-old Alex when I was seven. I remember our first meeting. He was skinny and seemed smaller than he really was. He was afraid even of his own shadow. It was a long time before he spoke to me for the first time. I was constantly chattering at him like crazy. Alex answered all my questions by just nodding his head. He followed me everywhere all the time. He annoyed me at first, but then we became best friends.'

'Who are his parents?'

'We don't know. We never raised the subject. George and Elizabeth are his parents.'

'And you're his brother, so what's the point of all this today?'

He just shrugged his shoulders, avoiding answering. I ate my soup, washed the bowl, and put it on the drying rack. I had so many questions in my head. I watched Boris' handsome face across the table.

'Did you make any arrangements with Sue? I assume yes, otherwise there wouldn't have been a fight.'

Olivia came into the kitchen. She looked at me with a look of disapproval. She spread out her food on the worktop.

'Boris, would you like a sandwich?' she asked so sweetly that I felt nauseous. She was actually very attractive. I was not surprised by her success among men. My face must have expressed surprise when Boris reached across the length of the table for my hand and started drawing little circles on it.

'No, thanks,' he politely replied and focused all his attention on me. Olivia had lived here for a long time, so they certainly knew each other well. I was surprised by what I had just felt: anxiety, jealousy? No, for sure, not jealousy. I was lying to myself.

Olivia cleaned up after herself sluggishly. Just before leaving, she stopped and turned towards us. She addressed Boris directly, 'Once you've had your fun with your new girlfriend, you know where to find me.' She winked at him and left.

I blinked in surprise.

'What was that?' I took my hand out of his hand.

He smiled at me in a boyish, slightly embarrassed way.

'Don't worry about her. It's in the old days.'

That was enough for me.

'You two were together?' I circled my finger in the air, pointing between them. 'Were you wit all of them?' A terrible realisation came to me. 'You've slept with all of us? That's sick and twisted.'

Instead of feeling guilty, he laughed at me, as I stood there getting mad. I didn't know what I really wanted. Everything was all messed up.

'Only with her,' he assured me. 'Twice, if that interests you.'

'No, I didn't want to know at all.'

'You did.'

'I didn't.'

'You did.' He grabbed my hands that were clenched into fists at the level of my breasts, and held me tight. Instead of arguing with me, he threw himself on top of me and started kissing me. He pushed his tongue into my mouth, one-touch, and I was already his. I tried to break the kiss. I didn't want to be at his every beck and call. I had to prove to myself that he wouldn't do whatever he wanted with me. Unfortunately, I lost myself in him, just as much as he did in me.

'Hmmm…' We heard.

Someone was standing in the doorway to the kitchen. I stepped back, feeling embarrassed. Sue and Amy walked into the kitchen.

'I called your father. He will be here in an hour,' Sue declared.

'I can't believe this,' complained Boris. He looked like a little boy who got a beating.

'I can't believe you are behaving so irresponsibly.'

Amy signalled to me discreetly that it was time to get out of the kitchen. We left them alone. I could still hear raised voices in the distance. I had never heard Sue yell at anyone. She was usually very self-controlled in every situation. It was difficult to surprise her, not to mention upset her.

Amy and I walked down the footpath next to the property. Trees lined both sides of the gravel road. I needed fresh air. A moment to think.

'What a mess,' Amy said.

'What actually happened before they started rolling around on the ground?' I was curious.

'Not that I was eavesdropping.'

'Of course, you weren't,' I laughed.

'Boris sat with Sue in the study for a long time. I know because I wanted to make sure my sister could live with us for a while. I waited for two hours. Then Alex joined them, but he quickly ran outside. Boris followed him out. You already know the rest.'

'Is it normal for a client to want to date one girl exclusively?'

Amy's eyes got as big as saucers from a teacup. She stopped and stared at me.

'Is that what this is about? Boris wants you exclusively?'

'Yeah. Is that so weird?'

'Very. I've never heard of anything like it before. The girls gossip a lot. They've been here longer than I have, so…' she hesitated, 'they say Boris dated someone at the residence. That was three years ago.'

I tried to take the news calmly.

'And what happened to her?'

'I don't know. Apparently, they were living together. Then it went quiet. No one saw her, and he stopped coming over. His father withdrew, and Sue and Alex took over running the business.'

'Did he love her?' it slipped out before I thought about what I was saying.

'Really?' Amy sighed heavily, 'What did I tell you at the very beginning? Not to get emotionally involved.'

'I know what you said. It's not like I love him…' Oh, fuck! I said that out loud.

'Don't make excuses. Just remember that I warned you.'

A sports car passed us on the path. George was just heading toward the mansion.

'Let's go back. It's getting dark, plus I'm curious to see what's going on out there.' Amy was almost jumping up and down out of excitement. I didn't share her enthusiasm. This was going to be my first meeting with George after I ran away from their house. On top of that, I was fooling them with a smile on my lips. How had I gotten myself into all this?

I had intended to walk into the room unnoticed. Unfortunately, it didn't work out.

'My dear, would you please join us?' George's voice came from Sue's office. Unluckily, I had to walk past him to get to my seat. I went inside. Sue was holding a glass of wine. Apparently, she had already drunk some because she was smiling involuntarily from ear to ear. Boris was watching me with his eyebrows pulled together. George greeted me too enthusiastically.

'Would you like something to drink, my dear?' he suggested. The others were silent.

'No, thank you. I still have a project to prepare for college.' I tried with all my might to get out of this.

'It'll only take two minutes.'

'Okay.' I sat down in the chair. George perched on the edge of his desk. 'Your contract is valid for four more months. You have the option to extend it, like all the girls here. You're bound by discretion.'

I wanted to say something, but he brushed me off with a wave of his hand.

'But you probably already know that. The salary for the whole period is here.' He handed me an envelope. 'And it will be divided into four months. You will receive weekly payments. You are still required to attend all events at the residence. You will not be given any preferential treatment. In one week, you will be expected to perform on stage.' I was happy to hear that.

'Dad…' Boris tried to interject.

'Quiet!' He looked menacingly at his son.

'The fact that your client is my son does not distinguish you in any way. Do you understand?'

'Yes.' I lowered my head. I felt like a little girl being reprimanded by her father.

'You've caused a lot of confusion here. Officially, Boris isn't your boss. I am. Any questions?'

'It's all clear. May I go now?' That was the only thought that came into my head. I wanted to get out of here as soon as possible.

'Of course.'

I was a coward. I'd run up two stairs at a time up to Amy's room.

'Vodka, I need vodka!'

Amy gave me a strange look.

'You need wine.' She decided.

'I need booze and lots of it.'

She agreed. She pressed a full glass of vodka into my hand.

'As far as I know, you don't pour wine all the way to the edge of the glass.' I remarked with a sneer.

'I won't be running downstairs for wine the chole night.' She turned on the music and started dancing.

She was right. I emptied half the glass in one go. I put the rest down and joined her in the middle of the room. I wanted to forget about the whole messed-up day and Boris waiting downstairs somewhere.

* * *

I was walking with some college friends to the parking area of the university. One of them was talking about a new boy she had met. Suddenly she fell silent.

'Who is he?' I followed her gaze. Boris was waiting near my car. With his back turned to us, he was talking on his cell phone. He slammed his fist on the roof of my car. I hoped he didn't make a dent. He turned around and quickly ended the call. He tucked his phone into the pocket of his jacket. His eyes rested on me and his gaze softened.

'He's a friend,' I said a quick goodbye to the girls.

'You have to introduce us!' I heard a shout behind me.

'Next time.' I sped up my step.

He was sinfully handsome. Sexy beyond belief.

'Hi,' I timidly probed, testing his mood.

'Hi.' He pulled me in and kissed me quickly. 'I'm taking you out to dinner. You were busy last night, so dinner was a goner.'

'I was busy?' I pushed him back an arm's length away. It was hard for me to think in his arms.

'I saw you dancing in Amy's room. That looked a lot better than putting up with my cranky mood.'

I placed my hand on his jacket again, looking into his eyes. He pulled me toward his Audi, effectively ending the subject. He opened the passenger side door. I remembered what my grandmother used to say. She claimed that men only open car doors for their lovers. On the other hand, the wife just opens it herself and gets in. I was willing to agree with her. I had never been married, so I had no comparison.

Boris sat behind the wheel and looked at my smiling face, so I told him what I was thinking. He started laughing too.

Alex wasn't answering my calls. It turned out that he wasn't answering Boris's calls either. He obviously didn't want to talk to us. He had also taken a week off work. I couldn't believe this was all because of me. His behaviour was a big mystery to me. After all, he claimed to be gay. He was even in a relationship with Marco. I felt sorry for him.

I sat down with Boris in a cosy pub. He talked about his parents and his childhood. It was good to listen to his memories of his youth. He talked a lot about Alex. It was evident that they were grew very close as they grew up. I thanked him for the cake while I happily sipped on my coffee. I tried to bring up the subject of paying for my grandmother's clinic, but Boris dismissed me by changing the subject. I had to accept the fact that I had an unpaid debt. On the way back, I didn't ask where we were going. I was completely unprepared for a night together. I was panicking in my mind about what I should do. I was surprised when we stopped at my car at the university car park. Tonight, I was free. The goodbye kiss was tender and sensual, though it increased in intensity at a dangerous pace. Lately, we kissed like a couple of teenagers. One more moment and he would be dragging me to the nearest hotel.

He tore himself away from my mouth.

'I'm working tomorrow night. Will you come to the club? Then I'll take you somewhere.'

'Okay,' I agreed cautiously.

He pulled a VIP badge with my name on it out of his pocket. It assured me free entrance without any unnecessary explanations to security or anyone else. I said goodbye to him, knowing that we would be spending tomorrow night together. I liked that plan.

I returned to the residence in high spirits. Somewhere in the distance, I saw Marco washing his car. He turned his back on me when he noticed me. I'd expected that reaction. I wasn't even mad at him. I understood him completely.

I walked straight into Sue's office. Amy sat behind a large mahogany desk.

'Don't even ask! Everyone here has gone crazy. I've been answering phones all morning. I can't get through to Alex, and Sue's lying there drunk.'

'She's drunk?' I've only seen her drink alcohol once. 'That doesn't sound like her.'

'She must have started right after Boris left.'

'That was twenty-four hours ago.'

'Apparently, she woke up and got drunk again. Don't look at me like that.

And before you ask, no, this is not normal.'

The phone rang again, and Amy, sighing, put the phone to her ear. With a flick of her wrist, she showed me that she was going to come over in half an hour with some wine. During that time, I had time to shower and change into a comfortable tracksuit. I also wondered what I would wear to the club tomorrow. I checked my phone, no answer from Alex. I texted him to contact me when he was ready.

I went downstairs to the kitchen. There was a guy sitting at the table. I had never seen him before in my life. He greeted me, clearly amused by my surprise. Right next to him sat Sue. She presented herself like one big disaster. Dressed in a robe, without make-up, she looked older and tired.

Nevertheless, the man was staring at her with total adoration. He was very handsome. Even I had to admit that. I took some crisps out of the cupboard and quickly left the two of them alone. I shared my news with Amy. She explained to me that the man in the kitchen was Severin. He had been friends with Sue for years, apparently hoping for something more. She, however, stubbornly rejected his advances.

* * *

On Saturday morning, I visited my grandmother. Then at the residence, I had my first pole dance workout. It didn't go as well as my trainer had hoped. I also got reprimanded for missing training a few days ago. It was almost as rigorous as school. After, I packed everything I may have needed for my trip with Boris.

I drove my Volkswagen to the club. I didn't want to waste money on cabs. I didn't know what Boris meant when he said he would take me somewhere. In front of the club, as always, the line stretched around the building. I showed my VIP badge and went in without any questions. The club hall was even more crowded than last time. It was the first time I was here alone. Boris should have been around somewhere, but he hadn't specified exactly where. I ordered a drink; the waiter glanced at my badge and didn't ask me to pay. I liked being a VIP. I leaned against the bar, looking for the spot on the first floor from where Boris had last watched me. He was there. He was standing exactly in the same place as last time. He was dressed all in black. Was he waiting for me? I had a perfect view to follow his every move. A blonde girl put her hand on his chest. She laughed lustily. Boris said something to her and left her. Apparently, her proposal was not very tempting. I smiled discreetly. I was the one he had chosen, and I was the one he was going for.

'Hey!' I tried to shout over the music.

'Come with me.' He grabbed my hand and pulled me toward a familiar door with an "*Admission for staff only*" sign. I hurried after him with my drink in my hand, trying not to spill it on the dress I had chosen for the evening. The short silver dress clung to me like a second skin. When the office door closed behind us, the noise subdued. I could still hear the music, but it was possible to talk freely. He took the glass from my hand and put it on the desk.

'You look bootylicious,' he embraced me, spinning me around. I had trouble accepting compliments, so I dismissed him with silence.

'I was wondering how I would find you. It wasn't that hard.'

'We have cameras everywhere. I knew exactly when you entered the club. Plus, security was supposed to be watching you.'

'Watching me?' I was surprised.

'You came alone. You never know who's hanging around. Especially when you're wearing that tiny piece of material.'

He ran his hand along my bare shoulder. I trembled. His pupils dilated, and I already knew what was coming. He stroked my lips with his thumb. He wanted to repeat the motion, but I caught his finger with my teeth and began to suck. His other hand slid down the dress directly to my crotch. He moved my panties to the side and rubbed my sensitive spot. I pushed against his palm, moving my hips. I stared at him with my thumb in his mouth. I imagined what it would be like to take his penis into my mouth, and suddenly I wanted to do it. I unzipped his pants and knelt in front of him.

'Are you sure you want this?'

As an answer, I licked the tip of his hard cock. It trembled under my tongue. I licked its entire length.

'More,' he hissed.

Encouraged, I took him into my mouth, licking and sucking. Boris grabbed me by the hair, quickening the pace. He wasn't being brutal, but rather showing me exactly what he wanted.

'There's a condom inside the desk. Top drawer.' I moved away from his penis, lifting my gaze to him. How many women has he invited here that he had condoms on hand?

I stood up, feeling pain in my knees. I walked around the desk and pulled out a package. I hurriedly put the condom on with a bit of help from Boris. He clearly didn't want to wait any longer. He threw the documents off the desk and onto the floor in one move.

'Come here,' he said softly. He sat me down on the cold desk. My panties quickly disappeared, and his impatient fingers filled me up. I had already been wet for a long time. I didn't need any additional encouragement. After a while, his hard penis took the place of his fingers. I wrapped my legs around his waist, and he led us to climax. All this time, he looked deep into my eyes. I felt that this was not just ordinary sex for us. Afterwards, he kissed me sweetly and lazily. I stood up on my soft legs and put on my panties.

I was picking up papers from the floor when someone knocked. Without waiting for an answer, he came inside. I looked at Boris in panic. The corners of his mouth lifted slightly. He knew very well what I was thinking about. The door wasn't locked, and we had just had sex.

'Boris! The DJ says he's only staying until midnight because that's what you paid him. Oh, hi Sarah!'

I quickly got up, which proved to be a challenge, considering the length of my dress and said, 'Hi. Good to see you.'

'You more so,' Mick smiled flirtatiously.

Boris squinted slightly, following our conversation.

'I'm going to talk to the DJ. And you…' he pointed the finger at his friend, 'Keep your hands off her. Pick up the papers from the floor. Have something to drink at the bar. I'll be back when I can.' He gave us a warning look and left.

Mick gathered up the papers, and he put them on the desk.

'What caused such a paper Armageddon?' I must have blushed because he looked at me with all-knowing eyes.

'I see,' he smiled even wider. 'Come on, let's have a drink.'

I ordered a vodka with orange juice. I told him a simplified version of how I met Boris, skipping the sex and the residence. Mick was a sincere and funny guy. He was the manager of the club. He made all the decisions in Boris's absence. I felt someone's presence behind me. Mick nodded slightly in greeting.

'Sarah.' I twitched at the sound right next to my ear.

'Alex?' I was pleased.

'Let's go and talk somewhere quieter,' he suggested.

'Could you get me another drink? I'll be right back,' I said to Mick, walking away. I felt like I might need it any minute.

We walked outside into the backyard, where crates and empty beer kegs were piled up. The girl I had seen behind the bar earlier put out her cigarette and ducked inside. We were left alone. It was only in the light of the lanterns that I saw Alex's battered face. Instinctively, I touched his cheek. He closed my hand in his. It was cold outside, so it was hard to ignore the warmth of his touch. Warmth and nothing else. No butterflies in my stomach or fireworks. I pulled my hand away.

'Don't look at me with pity. I don't want that,' he threw in my direction.

'What do you want? You look like a battered apple. I don't understand any of this. You don't like the arrangement between Boris and me. I understand. But you can't mess with my head. Do you hear me?' With every sentence I said, I raised my voice an octave higher.

By the end, I was furious. The emotions of the last few weeks had kicked in. 'You said you were gay.' I finished in a quieter voice. 'So why all this?'

'I know what I said. I'm still sticking to it. But you. You!' He shook his head in a gesture of resignation, 'I can't stop thinking about you. I can't sleep. Something strange is happening to me. Can I kiss you?' he asked with hope in his eyes.

'No!' I protested sharply. 'What am I, some kind of guinea pig? What the hell do you think you're doing?'

'I want to see if this is all just my imagination.'

He took a step towards me. Despite my firm denial, I didn't move. Nor did I do anything to stop him. I thought he was going to throw himself at me, with passion and desire, as Boris usually did. Instead, I felt him take my face in his hands. He looked into my eyes and begged for permission. I stared, mesmerised, into his irises. He placed a kiss on my lips, like a gentle caress. Encouraged by my decreasing resistance, he deepened the kiss. I couldn't say it was uncomfortable. His lips were warm and soft. He smelled of mint. He ended the kiss and watched me with a hopeful look in his eyes. He hoped that I felt it too.

'I'm sorry… I…' I wanted to explain myself.

'I understand,' he was utterly devastated. 'I'll deal with it somehow,' and he just walked away.

'Wait!' I called out again because I couldn't let it end like this. 'I like you, but as a friend.' My confession probably made him even more depressed.

'Don't worry. I'll be here if you need me. Now, and when Boris is done with you.' The last bitter words echoed in my head. Again and again, and on and on.

I got back inside. I was cold. I sipped my drink like it was lemonade. Seconds later, Boris announced that he was done for the day and we could go. He still didn't say where. I grabbed my bag from the back of my car and got into his Audi. Without a word, he turned up the heat. I felt the warmth, and my body relaxed. I was slowly getting dreamy. We drove for another twenty minutes in complete silence. We got out in the underground garage of the apartment building. Boris was carrying my bag. I knew something was wrong. The atmosphere was a little tense. On the top floor, he opened the door for me and finally spoke:

'I didn't plan this, so there may be a bit of a mess.' He let me pass in front of him. The light illuminated the room, and I realised then that we were in his apartment. I looked at him with a silent question.

'As I said. I hadn't planned this. Are you hungry? I have lasagne in the fridge. I made it this morning.'

'You cook?'

'I don't want to starve to death, so I cook sometimes.' We walked into a bright, modern kitchen.

'Wine, a cocktail?'

'Tea, please.'

He put a kettle on. He took the lasagne out of the fridge and reheated it in the oven. I watched his fluid movements in the kitchen. He obviously liked to cook. He placed the tea and a large piece of lasagne in front of me. He sat down next to me with his portion by the kitchen island.

'We were going to go to a hotel,' he admitted honestly, 'but I'm tired.'

I watched him devour his meal and couldn't understand why he had brought me here in the first place. He noticed that I was watching him.

'You don't like it?'

I tasted the first bite.

'It's delicious.' After a while, my plate was empty.

Boris took the empty dishes and put them in the dishwasher. It was obvious he lived alone. He didn't like mess. Despite his words about tidiness, the apartment was clean to the extreme. He showed me the living room, bathroom, bedroom, and study. As I walked past one door, he mentioned that it was always locked. He kept unnecessary things there. We went back to the living room. The apartment had a modern décor and was very cosy. The only thing missing was pictures - not a single frame on the dresser, wall, or fireplace. It was a bit impersonal, but maybe it was just a typically masculine decor, without any unnecessary ornaments and trinkets?

'What now?' I felt strange and out of place here. It was the middle of the night, and I was already feeling tired.

There were two bathrooms in the suite. We went to get ready for bed, each in a separate room. When I came out dressed in sexy little PJs, he kept his eyes on me but immediately climbed into bed.

'Come to bed.' He had a tired and sleepy voice.

I laid down next to him. I couldn't fall asleep. I kept staring at the ceiling. He did exactly the same. Finally, he turned off the light. The room fell silent and dark. After a while, I turned on my side, and he hugged me, wrapping his arms tightly around my waist. I could feel his erection. I tense up, waiting for the caressing to continue. It didn't come. Instead, my breathing calmed. I could get used to this. I felt warm and almost asleep.

'We have cameras at the club.' A quiet whisper reached me. 'They monitor every nook and cranny of the club.'

I was waiting for him to say something else, to continue his thought, but he was obviously not going to do that.

'Good night,' he whispered again.

After a while, I heard his steady breathing. Did he just tell me that he saw me with Alex?

* * *

In the morning, the place next to me was empty and cold. After a shower and a quick retouch of my makeup, I got dressed. My body was screaming for its daily dose of caffeine. I found the kitchen. It was already after ten. I had no plans for today yet. I also didn't know if I would spend it with Boris. Our arrangement was clear, but I had no idea where the boundaries were. I was afraid there were none. I found him with the phone to his ear and documents spread out on the kitchen island. The same place where we'd eaten lasagne last night. He hadn't heard me get up. I watched his broad, tanned back; he stood shirtless, in sweatpants. He was arguing about drink prices for the new club. I'd managed to deduce that much. I walked over, hugged him around the waist, and kissed his shoulder blade.

I pressed my cheek against his back. His warm skin smelled of soap. We stayed like that for a while. I inhaled his scent. My body was stirring to life. Another moment and I would have started licking him. I came to my senses enough to walk away and pour myself a cup of coffee. I opened the fridge and added milk. I could feel him watching me. He was following my every move. He ended the conversation. He came up to me and kissed me, long and wild. I nuzzled into his hair, pulling him closer to me. He gripped my chin tightly. He held my face still.

'Breakfast?' he asked, his eyes burning with desire.

'Can I have you?' Abashed and excited at the same time, I tried to look confident.

He smiled like a cat that had just caught a mouse. He threw me over his shoulder and carried me back into the bedroom. He literally threw me onto the bed and tugged at my pants. I propped myself up on my elbows and watched him desperately trying to pull them down.

'Help me,' he hissed.

I helped. We were both naked and horny. The fast pace he set meant that in no time, we were both lying wet and satisfied. It was wild sex. My stomach was rumbling. Boris heard it too.

'Come on. Let's get you fed.'

We had breakfast in the kitchen. Boris prepared scrambled eggs with bacon for us. I didn't like cold coffee, so I made myself a new one. We were both relaxed and in a good mood. I was going to visit my grandmother. Boris also had some plans. He didn't say what sort, so I didn't push it. I didn't know him well enough to ask. I just remembered that my car was still outside the club. I had two options: he could drive me to my car, or be my chauffeur for the day. I objected to option number two. I had my own car and didn't need a babysitter. I insisted that he drop me off at my Volkswagen. He went into the club to see how they cleaned everything up after last night's party.

I went straight to my grandmother. She said I was glowing. The comment should have worried me. It meant I was getting attached to Boris. It was true, that I felt comfortable in his company. I also knew the rules. It would all be over in less than four months. I knew I should leave there as soon as possible and return to everyday life. The emotional rollercoaster I had put myself through was not good in the long run. After my contract ended, I had to be thinking about myself and college. I have always wanted to be a pharmacist, which is why I started college in the first place. That should be my ultimate goal.

That afternoon, Grandma felt tired. She forced me to go home with the excuse of taking an afternoon nap. I could see her getting tired faster and faster. She didn't complain because she didn't want to worry me. She was always stubborn. I kissed her and said goodbye, 'I love you, Grandma,' and left. I passed the manager of the clinic in the hallway. She told me to say hello to Mr Smith with a dreamy smile. Clearly, his personal charm had caught up with her as well.

I popped into my apartment and grabbed a couple of things I needed. I wrote a note and left it on the tabletop for Alan. He should know that I still lived with him. Then I drove to the residence. Tonight, was a gentlemen's evening, and I wanted to help the girls.

I walked into the dressing room. All eyes were on me. I saw the reserve with which they treated me. This was what I was worried about. Amy was frantic, telling me what had happened in my absence. The implication was that Sue's temporary crisis was over, and she was back at work. The mysterious Severin hadn't shown up again. Alex was scheduled to return to work after the weekend. She tried to pry some details from me about Boris, but I brushed her off. I could see the curiosity around me, so I was even more reluctant to divulge details.

'You have ten minutes until the bar opens,' Sue rushed us. She spotted me. 'What are you doing here?' She was slightly surprised and concerned.

'I want to help. Let me help you.'

'All right. But only behind the bar. You can tell him that yourself.'

Does she care what Boris says? I pulled out my cell phone and sent a text message saying that I was in residence and would work behind the bar. The reply came immediately: "Forget it. I'm on my way to pick you up." What was that supposed to mean? Some kind of power struggle for control? I showed the message to Amy. Together we couldn't stop laughing.

I had been serving drinks behind the bar all evening. I had to get rid of two intrusive customers. With the second one, Niko's intervention came in handy. I was beginning to understand why he was the bartender. There was something about him that made him difficult to oppose. Maybe it was because of his tall physique or maybe just his menacing look?

I saw Boris. He was walking quickly towards me. He was angry. I had a feeling that he would take me away by force. He sat down opposite me.

'Have you been drinking?' he asked.

'No.' I was surprised, trying to figure out what he meant.

'Great, you'll drive. Pour me a whiskey. I'll wait for you to finish your work.' By the time I left, he was persistently stuck to the chair at the bar. The next day in the morning, I had classes at the university. I repacked my bag again. He was waiting for me in the hall. He was explaining something furiously to Sue.

'He had kissed her! Can you imagine?'

Sue didn't say anything. She hugged him like a little boy.

She noticed me and moved away quickly. Boris straightened up and handed me the keys of his Audi Q8. 'This is my little baby. Don't hurt her.'

'Is she a woman?' I was teasing him.

'My favourite.'

'Don't worry. She is in good hands'

I adjusted the seats and the mirrors. I'd never driven an Audi before. I felt like trying to find out what all the buttons on the dashboard were for. Boris watched me with amusement.

'Shall we go? Because I assume you have a driving license.'

I ignored him. I turned the key in the ignition, and the engine woke to life. I looked at it in panic.

'Where's the gear shift?'

He laughed out loud. My gaze must have been hurling lightning bolts because he quickly fell silent. He pointed to a button that told me nothing. It turned out that all I had to do was press the gas, and the car would start automatically. My car was old and didn't have such modern features. I had a right not to know. I liked this car immediately for its heated steering wheel and seats. I backed out slowly. I was afraid of driving fast in a car that wasn't mine. By the end of the journey though, I felt confident enough to speed up. We went to his place. We didn't want to sleep. I made popcorn while Boris switched with the remote control through the channels. He found a movie that caught his attention. He stretched out comfortably on the sofa. He pulled me to his side. My body automatically relaxed. He had a good effect on me.

'I would like you to sleep at my place on weekends and Wednesdays.' A quiet voice reached me.

'And the rest of the week?' I asked cautiously.

'You have studies and your own life. That's enough for me. On weekends I come home in the morning. I want you to be here. I'll give you the keys. I never know what time I'll be back.'

'Okay. Why Wednesdays?'

'No reason. It could be Tuesday or Thursday.'

'Oh, that's great. Wednesday works for me. I'll drive myself. Then there won't be too much hassle with driving me to college.'

He agreed to this solution.

A piece of popcorn got stuck between my teeth. I asked for dental floss. I took absolutely everything except the floss with me. In the bathroom, where Boris pointed, I found it. I also found something else. A pill called Zolpidem. A very powerful sedative. I knew the name from college classes. If I had any doubts, on the package was a description and dosage. Besides that, I found two more identical packets. I cleaned my teeth and went back to the couch.

'Are you a drug addict?' I asked straight out.

'What, no, where did that come from?' I think he started to guess. 'I haven't been able to sleep for a while.'

'Really? You get up earlier than I do. You don't sleep at night? Then how do you function?'

I could see by the expression on his face that he was thinking about the answer. Maybe he didn't want to admit it, or maybe he didn't want to scare me. I didn't see him taking those when we were together.

'They help me sleep. They also have side effects. I feel sleepy and confused throughout the whole of the next day, but I can't sleep without them. If I'm exhausted, the pills put me to sleep only for a couple of hours. It is more of a nap than deep sleep. My doctor prescribed me these pills. I don't like taking them, though. I hate any kind of pills.' He hesitated. 'After our first night together, I fell asleep. Deep and hard. No sleeping pills. When you're with me, I manage to get five hours of sleep. That's enough to function normally. It's a nice change.'

'Wow!' That's all I managed to say. I also noticed that he cleverly dodged my question. He didn't answer how long he'd been taking them. I kissed him on the lips and grabbed his hand.

'Let's go to bed then. I won't be here again until Wednesday.'

Making our way to the bedroom, we passed a locked room. I promised myself that I would find a way to look in there, and something was telling me that this handsome man was hiding more secrets than he let on.

* * *

Fields with giant windmills stretched along either side of the motorway. Driven by the energy of the wind, they turned slowly. There was something magical about them. I got more comfortable in the seat of the car.

'Are you going to sleep? Should I turn down the radio?' Boris turned down the music.

'I don't know yet. Why won't you tell me where we're going?'

'It's a surprise.' He glanced at me before shifting his gaze to the road again. He was very mysterious this morning. He was taking me on a trip but wouldn't say where to.

Sometime later, I opened my eyes. I sept through part of the journey. We passed a beautiful house with two turrets, just like in a fairy tale which was behind a decorated metal gate. I had already seen this building. I imagined that an enchanted princess lived in it.

'Stop the car,' I demanded calmly but firmly.

'Are you feeling unwell?'

'Stop the car. Now! Now!' I shouted at him.

Confused by my outburst, he braked sharply and stopped at the side of the road. I got out and pulled my suitcase out of the boot.

'What are you doing?' I saw the confusion in his eyes.

'I know where we're going. I'm going home. I'm not going to your parents.'

He wanted to say something but changed his mind.

'What were you thinking? Last time, I was there as your brother's girlfriend, and now…' I was throwing out words with the speed of a machine gun. 'This is not a surprise. This is a trick! A nasty trick. Have you thought about how I feel about this? I bet your parents don't want anything to do with me.'

He silenced me by deeply forcing his tongue down my throat. It couldn't be called a kiss. I wiggled my legs to free myself from his grasp.

'It was my mother's idea. She wants to talk to you.'

'About what?' I was in shock.

'I don't know. She said it was important. She specifi-cally demanded that I bring you.'

'That's something she would do.' I agreed. 'However, that doesn't change the fact that it's a mean trick. I'm going to have a fuss until we get there.' I pushed him away and got into the car. I saw him shaking his head in disbelief. He packed my suitcase back into the boot and returned to the driver's seat.

'There's a gas station around the corner. I need to fill up the tank. Would you like me to buy you anything?'

'Don't try to bribe me.' I turned towards the window. 'Dar chocolate Bounty and a can of Coke. Please.'

'I didn't hear that.'

'You heard right. I'm still mad at you.'

I ate the bar and sipped the sugary drink. Only then, did I feel a little better. When I got there, I didn't wait for him to open the car door for me. I wanted to let him know that I was still angry. Childish behaviour on my part, but I didn't care.

The last time I left this house, was at night. In the daylight, it had something magical about it. I felt nervous about my meeting with Elizabeth. She must have been waiting for us because she was already standing on the porch. I wrapped myself tighter in my autumn jacket. Near the sea, the wind was always more vigorous, but the air was fresh and crisp.

'There you are!' She came up to me. She hugged me tightly in greeting. Surprised, I stood straight as a stick. When she finally let me go, she told Boris to take the luggage upstairs to the room. We headed for the kitchen.

'Are you hungry? I made a pasta casserole and a plum cake.'

'I'd love to have some cake. I'd also like some coffee.' I sat down at the kitchen island. Liza was bustling around the kitchen, taking out coffee mugs.

'I'm sorry I left last time without saying goodbye. It was rude of me.'

Liza put a piece of cake in front of me.

'It's good that you're here. You brought Boris back to life. I haven't seen that spark in his eyes in a long time. Thank you.'

'Because of me, Alex and Boris got into a tussle.'

Liza sat down next to me on the bar chair.

'Alex will be fine. He's just finding his own way. I feel his pain, like any mother, to know her son is going through a difficult time. He needs to find the answers to his questions on his own. He was here last week. We had a long talk. He needs time because that is the one thing that heals all wounds.' Her face grew a little sadder. She stood up and handed me a sugar pot. 'Boris has had a difficult time too. He'll tell you when he's ready. Enjoy each other's company.' She shook my hands. 'Thank you for making him happy.'

'I'm afraid you don't know everything.'

She laughed.

'I know everything. Even more, than I should. I found the sheet in the dustbin.'

She moved her eyebrows suggestively, and I blushed.

'This needs to be celebrated.'

She pulled chilled champagne from the fridge and two glasses. Boris took the bottle from Liza's hands and asked, 'What are we celebrating? It's only noon.'

At that moment, my face became the colour of a tomato. Blue ran into the kitchen. He greeted us, jumping and licking Boris, before he got to me. After a while, George joined us. The last time I saw him was at the residence, and it was not a pleasant memory. He nodded to us in greeting. He handed a rose to Elizabeth and kissed her. A long and indecent one.

'Dad!' Boris protested.

'You should know that your folks are in good shape.'

Now, Liza was clearly feeling embarrassed.

'Who wants coffee?' She tried to get out of her husband's embrace.

* * *

Liza and I were sitting on a comfortable couch, and Blue was delightfully pressing his nose against my side.

'Check this out.' Liza pointed to a photo in a hefty album. 'I love this picture.'

It showed Alex and a teenage Boris proudly displaying a gold medal around his neck.

'First place in the swimming competition. I remember that day like it was yesterday. I was so proud. I still am.'

'That explains his love for swimming.' I recalled the day I first saw him in swimming trunks.

'Look at this.' She pointed to another photo. Both brothers were eating a huge portion of ice cream. Alex, without a tooth, was smiling for the camera. 'They always supported each other. There was never any rivalry between them. Other mothers complained about how their sons would quarrel and fight. Boris always supported Alex and vice versa. Boris took care of him. The children are growing fast. Now I am waiting for grandchildren, you know?' She suspended her voice significantly.

'But we…' I hesitated. What was I going to say? That we are not in a relationship and we just sleep with each other?

'Darling, you have to believe in the power of love.'

'But we don't…' I tried to make her understand that there were no feelings between us, only lust. Did I have the right to do that? To destroy her idealised image of her son? But I decided to keep quiet about our relationship. Boris himself should explain it to her.

'I was working at the residence when I met George.'

I looked at her, shocked. I'd realised we had a lot in common.

'It wasn't a simple relationship. A happy ending requires sacrifices. And you know what, it's worth it. Believe me.' She turned to another page of the album.

I looked surprised at the photography, then at her, and then at the photo again. Two familiar faces were smiling at me from the photograph. Much younger, more carefree, but still the same: Liza and Sue. They were enjoying themselves. A magical photograph. Sue rarely smiled. She was usually focused on the task at hand and was very serious.

'Sue is my sister.' Liza moved her hand over the photograph. As if she wanted to touch her and comfort her.

'I didn't know.'

'Yes, it's understandable. We don't see each other often. It's one of those things you regret but can't change. Life is so complicated... Promise me something.'

'Yes?'

'Don't put anything off. It's not worth it.'

'I can promise you that.' I laughed. We continued looking at the pictures. I couldn't stop thinking about Sue. It was such a surprise.

George came back from the stables with Boris. They went off on their own, which gave me time to look through the family album and learn some interesting facts about little Boris.

'Are you alright?' George asked when he saw the album on Liza's lap. His concerned look said more than words.

'I was just showing off our boys when they were little.'

'Really?' Boris interjected. 'You could have spared her that.'

'Now I know how many pimples you had as a teenager. And who you went to prom with.'

'Old times. I'm going swimming. Are you coming with me, Sarah?' It wasn't a question, even though it sounded like one. 'We'll be back for dinner,' he excused himself quickly.

***

I loved watching Boris swim. It gave me as much plea-sure as it did him watching my bum. Even the first time at the pool, I wanted to impress him. I had to admit it. I liked him from the very beginning, and I've suddenly realised how crazy I was about him. Apparently, it's easier to come to life's conclusions in cold chlorinated water.

'Are you swimming or sleeping?'

I was lying on my back. The water was lifting and rocking me.

'I was thinking about our first meeting here.'

'I'll never forget the sight of your butt.'

'Hey!' I splashed water in his direction.

'Did you just splash me? You better run! I'll give you a head start. I'm counting to five. One, two…'

I swam as quickly as I could to the other end of the pool. I heard five. He was fast. Then something pulled me under the water. I didn't even have time to swim to get halfway through. I choked; his strong arms wrapped around me. He pushed me to the surface. Panicked, I felt the bottom of the pool under my feet. Fortunately, it was not deep. I could swim, but I preferred to feel the ground beneath my feet.

'Hey, relax.' He brushed a wet strand of hair away from my cheek. 'Are you okay?'

'I panicked. It's okay.' I wrapped my legs around his waist.

'Are you teasing me?' A smile wandered on his lips.

'As if I would dare!' I moved my hips suggestively in denial.

His pupils dilated. He kissed me, simultaneously advancing towards the end of the pool. I guessed what his intentions were.

'We can't. This is your parents' pool.'

He wasn't listening to me. He pressed my back against the tiles. I stayed still. He dipped one hand in the water. With the other, he supported me. He stroked me through the thin material of the outfit. He shifted the fabric of my panties and touched me. Kissing furiously, he dipped one finger into me.

'I wanted to do this the first time we were here.'

It turned out that he was more than ready. He entered me quickly and brutally. We could only hear our gasps and the regular movement of the water around us. I entwined my hands in his hair. I returned his kisses with full intensity. A condom - a thought crossed my mind. We didn't use a condom. But it was quickly replaced by pleasure and an orgasm raging through my body. He held me for a while longer. Our breathing calmed down. He pressed his forehead against mine.

'I love you.' He said nothing more. My heart fluttered. I hugged him tighter, sliding my tongue down his neck to his ear.

'I adore you too.'

I was horrified at how it sounded all by itself. Not exactly the way I wanted it to be. I think he felt it too. He slipped out of my grasp.

'I'm going to swim a little more. Dinner will be ready in a minute.'

'Okay, I'll go and dry my hair.' I thought of something on the fly. I left him alone. On the way out, I turned around. He was swimming fast and was shaking his hands furiously. What had I done? I could have bitten my tongue instead of coming up with some stupid text about feelings.

Boris

Someone was calling my name with manic persistence. It repeated over and over again. I opened my eyes. There was darkness in the room. It took me a moment for my mind to break free from the nightmare.

'Boris! How are you feeling?' I heard a woman's voice. She turned on the lamp by the bed. I could see her big worried eyes. She was staring at me as if she wanted to know the answers to all her questions. As if she wanted to touch my soul. To know the secret I kept from her.

'Sarah?' I asked stupidly. She croaked slightly. She must have felt touched because I thought there might be someone else with me.

'I'll be right back.' I sneaked off to the bathroom. The watch indicated three o'clock in the morning. I rinsed my sweaty face with water. I brushed my teeth. I put off going back to bed. I owed her an explanation. She asked nothing, though she was very curious. She respected my silence.

In the beginning, she was supposed to be my foundation. My good-luck charm. Today I had my first nightmare since she slept next to me. Maybe it was the look in her eyes? She looked at me differently than she had at first, in that specific way. I was aware of what it meant. I had already seen it in someone else.

She knocked quietly and entered the bathroom. I stood still, bent over the sink. I felt sick. It made me sick to think what an asshole I was. I felt her warm hands. She pressed her cheek against my cold back.

'Do you want to talk about it?' she asked shyly.

'You know I don't want to.'

'Talking sometimes helps,' she insisted.

'No, thanks.' It sounded rough and unpleasant.

I turned to her. Her big eyes were almost begging to talk. I didn't want to hurt her. I should tell her to go away. End these games. I couldn't, not yet. I kissed her, putting all my feelings, longing, and promise into that kiss. I didn't want her to leave. Not yet. She kept my nightmares away from me. So why did they come back to me again? Fear. I was scared of what she told me. I was scared of her feelings.

Later, when she fell asleep in my arms again, I could only be furious with myself and my stupidity.

Sarah

In the morning, Boris wasn't in bed. His mother said he was at the pool. He made no further mention of the previous night. I understood that he didn't want to bring up the subject. After breakfast, we took Blue for a walk along the seashore. It wasn't raining, but it was windy. Boris held my hand the whole walk. I walked in an oversized windbreaker that he had dug out of his wardrobe. We talked about his new club and the trip it would involve. The new club already had a manager. But he wanted to supervise the opening personally. He wanted to go away for a week, maybe longer. He offered to bring me along with him. But I preferred to be here, closer to my grandmother. I had never been away for such a long time. Lately, Grandma looked more tired than she did just a few months ago. More and more often, she lost the thread of the conversation, or became aggressive towards me. The feeling of helplessness was overwhelming. I could not help her other than to be there for her and pay for specialist care.

Boris squeezed my hand tighter.

'You weren't listening.'

'I was lost in my thoughts. I'm sorry.'

He took my face in his hands and kissed it.

'Let's go back. It's going to rain.'

I looked up. Nothing seemed to herald a storm. However, with every step, the sky was getting darker and darker. He was right. Close to home, the first drops of rain fell on us. Alex was just getting out of the car. When I saw him, I was about to let go of Boris' hand. I didn't want him to suffer more. Boris, as if reading my mind, squeezed my hand even tighter. The males marking their territory was unbearable. They behaved as if I had no say, and they had to decide everything for me, each claiming me as theirs. I jerked my hand away, which didn't escape Alex's attention. Blissfully unaware, Blue was as happy and wagging his tail as ever. He was the only one who seemed to be enjoying himself.

Liza drew us out of the awkward silence. She was muttering something about the family being complete and the meal being ready. In the overall confusion, I still managed to find out that Alex had arrived for dinner, unaware of our presence.

At the table, I was awkwardly seated between Alex and Boris. Considering the number of empty seats at the table, this was odd. George tried to make up for it by talking business, which Liza hated. In this situation, however, she did not protest. After soup and the second course, we received an unannounced guest.

A childhood friend of Boris', as they first introduced her, named Nina, decided to drop by for a visit. I met her at Liza and George's wedding anniversary party. She would not leave Boris' side then.

'Good evening. The door was open, so I came in.'

Blue lifted his head from his warm hideout to lay comfortably on the cushions again. This could mean two things: Nina was here so often that it was a waste of time for him to say hello, or - which seemed more likely to me - Blue didn't like her, so he ignored her.

Liza greeted her and invited her to the table. In no time, she had a plate and a set of cutlery placed in front of her. It must be said that her housekeeping was perfect. I thought of my wardrobe and the pile of dirty clothes and the constant mess in the bathroom. I was not perfect in any aspect of my life. Just the fact that I was sitting wedged between Alex and Boris was evidence of that.

Nina placed a large portion of salad onto her plate, as if she were a rabbit and not a woman. She hinted something about the stables, where she'd found out that Boris had come to visit. I listened with stoic manner as she flirted with Boris throughout dinner. I kept repeating in my mind that it wouldn't be long before I was back to a normal life without the Smith family.

'Boris, I wanted to show you my new mare. A beautiful specimen of Arabian blood.'

'Maybe next time.' He looked at her apologetically.

She was sitting opposite me so that I could see the disappointment in her eyes. Obviously, she was not used to being refused. She smiled charmingly, masking her disappointment.

Boris, aware of her games, was having a great time.

'Sarah and I are going home. We want to go to bed early.' he stressed the last word. He grabbed my hand, resting on the counter halfway to the water glass. He laced his fingers with mine. There was silence at the table. I didn't know if it was my imagination, but I heard Alex's jaw clench loudly. Another moment and I would be witnessing a fratricide.

The lady across from me stared at me with a puzzled look.

'I thought it was Sarah and Alex….' She searched for support from Alex.

'You thought incorrectly,' he hissed. 'Mum,' Boris turned directly to his parent, 'we're going to go. Thank you for a lovely weekend.'

'Yes, thank you very much,' I interjected, reminding them that I was here too.

Nina gave me an unpleasant look, and Alex made a face as if his favourite pet had died.

We packed our suitcases and were in the car just a moment later.

'I'm glad we managed to escape' I got more comfortable in the seat. We had a drive that would take two hours ahead of us.

'I had to get out of there. It was suffocating.'

The sound of the phone resounded in the car. Boris answered with a button on the steering wheel. 'Mick, you're on speakerphone,' he pointed out by way of introduction. 'I'm not travelling alone.'

'Are you with the mega sexy Sarah?'

I laughed.

'Hi, Mick.'

'Don't push your luck,' Boris threatened him. 'What's the matter?'

'We had a little problem last night.'

'And…' Boris urged him on.

'Three thugs demolished one of the bars in the club, and they smashed everything up with baseball bats.'

'What do you mean, with bats? Who let them in?'

'I don't know. The police are working on it, and we're checking surveillance. Have you done anything to anyone lately?'

'No more than usual. Why are you only calling now?'

'Because… you know… you haven't been away for a while. You deserve a rest. You don't need another thing to worry about. Anyway, they caught them. They're in custody. Tomorrow you have an investigation at the police station. Maybe you know them.'

'I'm on my way. I'll be there in two hours. I'll drive Sarah home and come back. Have you counted your losses yet?'

'Yeah, I got a preliminary estimate. I'll see you soon. Bye, Sarah.'

'Bye,' I said goodbye, and Boris ended the call.

'I'll drive you to your flat unless you want to go to the residence?'

'What?' He surprised me. 'No, I'm going to your place. I'll wait.'

'I don't know what time I'll be back.'

'That's all right. I want to be near you. Today is Sunday.'

He smiled at me. He stroked my leg tenderly.

'Good. We'll go to my place.'

Just as he said, he came back in the morning. I didn't even know what time it was. He snuggled into my warm, sleepy body. By morning, the bed was empty. He probably hadn't slept at all. When I asked him about it, he dismissed me with a kiss.

Nevertheless, I had some coffee and breakfast was ready. He had made pancakes. A man in the kitchen is so sexy. A man taking care of his woman is even sexier. I watched him as he sipped his coffee and searched for documents in a pile of folders. He mentioned something about a contract with an insurance company. I could watch him as he wrinkled his forehead in thought and nervously fixed his hair, which had recently become too long. He caught my gaze a few times, held it longer, and I felt him take possession of my heart as well. I was endlessly in love with him. I couldn't deceive myself any longer. The question was, did he feel the same? Did he even like me? The thought terrified me. Suddenly I found myself wishing I could stay here, instead of going to university. I wished I could stop time. To lock us in our little world. It wasn't feasible. We both had a ton of things to do that day. He had to show up at the police station while I wanted to visit my grandmother. There were also such mundane matters as grocery shopping and laundry left to do. This week it was my turn to clean the apartment. After all, I lived with Alan and only temporarily at Boris' or the residence.

Alex's vacation was over, which means he should be back at work. I didn't feel like seeing him. The atmosphere at yesterday's dinner was extremely awkward. He kept looking at me like a hurt puppy. Was I supposed to feel guilty? Boris was no better either. He did everything he could to piss off his brother. And then there was Nina. I definitely had to tell Alan everything. I typed out a short text message to him saying that I would make dinner tonight because we needed to gossip. In response, I got a message with a few lines of kisses. It had been a long time since we had spent a friendly evening together.

For dinner, I roasted a chicken following my grandmother's secret recipe. I also bought some wine. I had plenty of time until Alan returned, so I cleaned the apartment. I was just finishing vacuuming the living room when my roommate returned.

'That's what we're talking about! That's the kind of view I like to come home to.' He was referring to me on all fours with my butt sticking up. I had just finished vacuuming a hard-to-reach spot under the dresser, and I still wanted to take a quick shower before dinner.

'Do I smell food?'

'I made a roast chicken.' Seeing his delight, I added quickly, 'No baked potatoes, just vegetables.'

'Did I do something to hurt you? Have I been mean to you? Why no potatoes?' He made a sad face.

'I decided to limit the carbs.' I turned off the vacuum cleaner and rolled up the cable.

'I didn't agree to anything like this.' He pretended to be offended and went into the kitchen. 'There's wine! I forgive you.'

I smiled subtly. I knew it would turn out like this. I jumped quickly into the shower. After dinner, we moved to the couch. Dressed in leggings and a sweat-shirt, I stretched out comfortably. I told Alan what had happened recently. I could see his excitement. Every-thing was clear to him. I loved Boris, so I should fight for him. Make him fall in love too and not want to leave me. The truth was that I didn't know what Boris had going on in his head. He was secretive about his feelings. I didn't know much about him, only exactly what he wanted to reveal to me. At first, I didn't want to know more than what was necessary. I explained to myself that then, there would be no emotional bond between us. I was wrong. My fascination with this man increased with every moment we spent together. By the second bottle, my head was buzzing. I was very relaxed. The doorbell interrupted our fierce discussion about which actor Boris resembled.

We were not expecting anyone at such a late hour. The sight of a glum Boris took me slightly by surprise. It wasn't the fact that he showed up even though we didn't have any plans. I was more the disturbed look on his face. He looked sad, depressed. He didn't want to talk about his problems. Very typical of him. He stood on the doorstep as if wondering if he had done the right thing by coming to see me. I kissed him softly. In response, he drew me close and deepened the kiss. Alarmed by my prolonged absence, Alan came to see who had come. However, he quickly returned to the room.

I served Boris the rest of our dinner. Alan finally had a chance to get to know Boris. They took an instant liking to each other. My friend had a knack for getting along with everyone. He also sighed surreptitiously, thinking I couldn't see. I couldn't hold it against him. I was impressed by Boris as well. If he noticed Alan's strange behaviour, he ignored it. He was very friendly and even started smiling in his peculiar seductive way. It was getting late, Alan went to bed, and we sat at the kitchen table. He told me the details of the police reconnaissance. He didn't recognise these men. The police were still determining how they had brought the baseball bats inside. Despite the charges against them, they had not disclosed who had ordered the robbery.

'It's time for me to go. I just wanted to see you.'

'Stay for the night,' I uttered it just a little louder than a whisper. Despite my quiet voice, my gaze was fixed on Boris' eyes.

'Alright,' he just said, making me the happiest woman on the Earth. And that's exactly how I felt, falling asleep in his arms. I woke up during the night. He continued to sleep next to me. I snuggled tighter into his warm body and fell asleep again.

* * *

I felt a series of kisses on my exposed shoulder before I even opened my eyes.

'Good morning,' he whispered. He didn't stop kissing my body with his lips. 'I have to go.' He got up. I felt a sudden emptiness next to me. I watched him put on his pants and shirt. He was the first man to spend the night with me in my room. The first time, I had spent the night at his. His handsome face was covered with two-day old stubble. I liked him even better like this.

'Are you leaving without breakfast?' I tried to convince him to stay a little longer.

'You tempt me.' He smiled charmingly, climbed back onto the bed, and stole a quick kiss. 'I'll call you tonight. Sue mentioned something about needing you at the residence. Ask her what she wants.'

'I have a dance lesson today. Maybe she wanted to remind me.'

'Maybe,' he agreed with me. He looked at his watch once again. 'I have to go,' he repeated for the umpteenth time in a row. However, he did not move from his seat. 'I'll call you later.'

'Okay.' His behaviour amused me. 'Go, or you'll be late wherever you have to go.'

'Yes, that's right.' He went back to bed once more and kissed me. 'I'll call you. Am I repeating myself?'

I looked at him seriously and burst out laughing uncontrollably. 'Go now, go.'

I skipped college that day. The prospect of spending the morning within closed walls was not appealing at all. Instead, I went straight to the residence. I didn't have dance lessons until the afternoon, so there was a chance that I could gossip with Amy.

The cold wind blew my hair away, and I felt the cold air in my bones. It would soon be Christmas, which I planned to spend as I did every year with my grandmother.

In the driveway on the other side of the yard, I spotted Marco. He was looking at me defiantly. So here we were, the same old story. Even if I wanted to fix it, I didn't know what to do. What was I supposed to say to him? I'm sorry your boyfriend prefers me over you? It was a hopeless situation.

I left some things in my room and went down to Sue. At that moment, I got to the assembly in the conference room. Traditionally, Amy brought me coffee. I was annoyed by the curious glances tossed in my direction. Apparently, I was still the number one subject of gossip. Every girl got a folder with the meeting schedule for the week—all of them, except for me. The room slowly emptied, and I didn't move from my seat.

'Do you want to talk to me?' I directed the question to Sue.

She waited until the door closed.

'You didn't get the folder because I didn't know if you'd be here today.'

'Boris mentioned that you wanted to see me.'

'Yes, I mean,' she began confused, 'Elizabeth is my sister, but you already know that. Our relationship is, how shall I put it, good but tense. I didn't talk about it because these issues don't concern you. I see, however, that you have almost made your way into the family. You should know what is going on around you.'

'What do you mean, I almost made it into the family?'

'Let's face it. You and Boris….'

'It's just an arrangement,' I quickly explained. 'I'm with him because he pays me.' Even if I didn't believe it, I couldn't proclaim to everyone that I was in love with him.

'Is that so?' she asked, staring at me with all-knowing eyes. 'What goes on between you is your business. I just wouldn't want, and I'm saying this as your boss, for things you find out to come out. We don't need family dirt being dragged out.'

'What are you afraid of?'

'Nothing.' She looked away. She walked over to a table in the corner and poured herself a cup of coffee. I could clearly see her hands trembling. She returned to her seat a moment later, already more in control.

'I also talked to Alex. Nothing is reaching him. Please don't think that any of this is your fault. Nothing whatsoever. The problem is that for the past few days, he's been walking around either sad or angry. He's not acting like himself. Maybe if you talk to him, explain everything.'

'There's nothing to explain. I'm with Boris whether he likes it or not. He can't make me feel sorry for him.'

'All right,' she muttered, satisfied with what I had said. 'Are you going with Boris to Liza and George's for Christmas?'

'No.' I was surprised. 'He never asked me about it. I spend every Christmas with my grandmother, and this one isn't going to be an exception. I'm supposed to go with him to the opening of the new club.'

'And then what?'

I knew exactly what she was asking. I hadn't yet thought about what I would do when my contract ended.

'Are you asking if I'll stay? I don't know. I still have two months to decide.'

'We'll come back to this conversation. Don't forget about the dance tonight. You're helping the bartender in the evening.'

She had once again adopted her formal tone, meaning that our chit-chat was over.

* * *

I returned to my room, all sweaty after my workout. Amy was lying on my bed.

'Finally! Life here without you is getting unbearable,' she started to complain. She lay on her back, lifting her hips up and down.

'What are you doing?' I looked at her sceptically.

'I'm exercising. I've put on some weight lately.'

'Move over.' I lay down next to her on the bed. My cell phone was vibrating. I looked at the screen. There was a message from Boris. He wrote that he was very busy but thinking about me.

'Hey,' Amy poked me with her elbow. 'What's with the face? Is that Boris?'

'Yep.'

'I see hearts and butterflies on your face.'

'Are you starting again?' I sent her a warning look.

'I'm worried. Stories like this don't have a happy ending.'

'Give me a break.' I got out of bed. I was beginning to make up a happy ending to the story in my head, although I could see that Amy was right. For some reason, Boris kept women out of his life for a long time or abandoned them quickly. I wanted to believe that things would be different with me. I wanted to be someone important to him. But what if Amy was right?

'Do you have any wine?'

Amy was happy.

'I thought you would never ask.'

Throughout the evening, Boris kept sending me messages. Instead of focusing on serving drinks, I nervously glanced at my phone. When the object of my affection finally sat down at the bar, my brain turned to mush. All I wanted was to be able to leave this place with him.

'I'm taking you to my place,' he whispered directly into my ear. The tray with the empty glasses almost fell out of my hands.

'Today is Monday.'

'I want you. Right now!' He took the tray from my hands and set it down on the counter. 'She's done for the day,' he shouted to the bartender and led me out of the residence. To be precise, he pulled me towards his car. Instead of opening the door, he leaned me against the hood.

'I've been thinking about you all day.' He kissed my neck, moving towards my mouth. 'Do you need anything from the residence?'

'My purse. Give me a minute.'

He stepped back, making way for me.

'Sixty, fifty-nine, fifty-eight… time flies.'

'You are crazy, man!' I laughed. I ran up the steps two at a time. I wanted to get back down as quickly as possible. I think I broke my packing speed record. I literally threw a few of my things in my bag, and moments later, we were driving towards Boris' apartment.

We rushed through the dark streets at a dizzying pace. In the middle of the night, the roads were almost empty. The lights of the stores turned into one colourful blur of colours. Boris was looking straight ahead, his hands clenched on the steering wheel.

'What did they say at the police station?' Until now, I hadn't had an update on how it went.

'Not now,' he only hissed.

Confused by his tone of voice, I moved restlessly in my seat.

'I'm trying to make it home, so I don't have to fuck you on the side of the road in the car, so be nice and don't distract me.' He only looked at me for a split second before shifting his gaze to the road again.

My body's reaction was immediate. Fortunately, it was dark outside because my face turned crimson. I liked the way he spoke to me. I moved once more in my seat. I clenched my thighs tighter, anxious and excited. All it took was one sentence, and my brain thought of only one thing. It didn't matter to me, where. We might as well have done it in the car. I changed position once more.

'Stop wriggling. I can't concentrate on driving. All I can think about is wanting to be inside you already.'

'Stop! Stop!'

'Why?' He looked at me confused.

'Let's do it here,' I suggested, confident in my decision.

We drove along a road where a forest stretched on both sides. He pulled over to the side of the road, abruptly changing direction. I squealed in surprise. He stopped in a small parking lot. During the day, people came here to take their dogs into the woods for a walk. Currently, it was dark and empty.

'Are you sure?'

'Yes.' I liked that he asked. He never forced me to do anything. He always made sure I got as much pleasure out of our sex as he did.

'Come to the back.' He got out, but first, he moved the front seat as far forward as possible to make more room for us. I kicked my sneakers off my feet and took off my jeans. I regretted not wearing a skirt. It would have made this much easier. I got out of the car in just a sweater and panties and made my way to the back. I no longer cared about whether anyone would see us. The only thing that mattered in this small space was us. I wanted to feel him inside me as soon as possible.

Instantly after I closed the door of the Audi, I threw myself on him, craving his touch and smell. Boris had barely managed to take off his jacket, and I was already sitting on top of him. I kissed quickly and greedily. He raised one eyebrow and looked at my ass in just my panties. He embraced my bum and pulled me closer to him. I could feel his swollen cock. It was ready, just like me. I moved my hips suggestively. I grabbed his hair, making him look at me. I kept rubbing against him.

'I'm going to fuck you now,' I said as seriously as I could.

The corners of his mouth went up slightly. He struggled not to laugh. Without a word, he nodded in agreement. I opened the zipper of his pants, gripping his penis tightly. My hands were cold. He hissed softly. He lifted his hips, and I slid his pants off him. Without further ado, I slipped out of my panties. After just a moment, thirsty and connected, we moved rhythmically. I felt his hands clamped on my waist. He held me tight. He pulled up and down, speeding up his movements. My orgasm was close. I moved even closer, rubbing my clit hard against him. With a deep kiss, he quieted all the sounds I made. Sweaty and hot, I rested my head against his shoulder a moment later.

'Are you okay?'

'Yes.' I smiled in the darkness. 'Can we sit like this for a while?'

'Sure. I'm not in a hurry anymore.'

I got the feeling that he was smiling too. I hugged him even tighter. Steam dripped on the windows, creating patterns and streaks. We stayed like that until I felt cold.

We returned to Boris's apartment feeling much more relaxed. On the way, he told me about the prosecution of the perpetrators of the robbery at the club. He didn't know them. Instead, he suspected that they had done it on commission. They had no prior criminal record, so they faced only a fine and a probation sentence, and a restraining order against the club. The perpetrators justified themselves by saying that they had consumed too much alcohol that night, and it just happened. They did not admit where they got the baseball bats or how they brought them into the club. The insurance company took photos. He has to wait for the claim to be paid, and in the meantime, order a carpenter to fix the bar. I was glad he shared this information with me. We have come a long way in our short friendship. We had a great time together in the beginning, but our conversations were based on what was going on at the time. Discussions were about trivial things, such as a movie we watched together. This had changed over time. The taboo topic between us was still the feelings we had for each other. He hadn't yet specified how he felt about me, other than "I love you" in the pool. Nor did he talk about us in the future tense. Everything pointed to the fact that everything we had in common was only here and now. He gave me no hope or illusions of a future together. He made no promises. Still, I found it hard to remain unmoved by his charms. I liked everything about him. The way he spoke, the way he moved, the way he smelled, the respect he had for his parents. Every thought of him increased my pulse rate, made my heart beat intensely.

I woke up in the middle of the night. I was alone in bed. It was obviously one of those nights when Boris couldn't sleep. Usually, he would sit in the living room and read a book. He loved crime fiction. He also had quite a vast library. Sometimes I would get up to make sure he was somewhere close by and go back to bed.

I had a fear then that he would leave me and never come back. It was nonsense. After all, I was in his apartment. My need to see him was strange and inexplicable.

It was four in the morning. I was thirsty. In the corridor, Boris locked the secret room with the key and put it in his pants pocket. I didn't know what was behind that door. It had been locked from the beginning. I asked about it only once. He brushed me off, saying something about dust and unnecessary things. When he couldn't see, I secretly pressed the handle, hoping to find out what was behind it that day. What normal person locks a room in their house with a key?

'Have you been standing here long?' he asked sharply. I didn't like that tone of his voice.

'I was thirsty.' He accepted my explanation and relaxed slightly. He assumed that I hadn't seen anything. At that moment, I decided I needed to find out what secret he was hiding behind the closed doors, as soon as possible.

'Are you keeping a sex slave in there?'

'The only sex slave here is you.' He laughed.

In the kitchen, he sat me down on a chair like a wayward child. 'What would you like to drink?' he asked suspiciously as if he suspected me of lying or spying.

'Water, please.' I drank a full glass under his watchful eye. 'You can't sleep?'

'A lot is going on right now. The bar. You.'

'Me?'

'Yes, you. All my thoughts during the day are about you.'

I was speechless. Maybe I misheard. He stepped toward me. He lifted my face to look at him. I nuzzled my cheek into his warm hand. I loved the moments when it was just us. Nothing else mattered.

'I'm grateful to my brother for bringing you to my parents' house that day. Our meeting was something unexpected, but at the same time, one of the few good things in my life.'

'Tell me.'

He stared at me for a long time in total silence. My eyes were pleading. He didn't say anything. I could only hear the ticking of the clock. I couldn't get him to confess the truth, yet something was clearly bothering him. At least I tried. It was impossible to heal a soul around which a wall has grown too high. I stood up and hugged him. I took in his scent.

'Are you sniffing me?'

'I'm getting hooked on you. I'm like a drug addict. Every day I want you more.'

His chest was rising in irregular breathing. He was laughing at me.

* * *

I was with my grandmother. She had slept through most of my visit today. The nurse checked in several times during this time. It was obvious that she was just as worried as I was. Grandma's strength was decreasing with each day. Until a month ago, I would walk with her in the garden, but she had neither the health nor the desire for that kind of activity anymore. I did not allow myself to think that one day I would be left alone, without a family. I wiped away the few tears that ran down my cheek.

'Hey, little girl.' I heard her sleepy, worried voice. 'Tears should flow only from happiness. Don't be sad because of me. I'm already old. My time will come sooner or later.'

'Don't say that, Grandma.' I grabbed her hand.

'It's true. I'm glad you have found someone. You won't be alone.'

'Grandma. He… it's complicated.'

'Every relationship is complicated. Do you think it was different with Grandpa? We had our bad days, but they didn't matter as long as we were together. In the end, we only remember the good moments. The happy moments. And that's how you're supposed to think: only about the good moments.'

'I'll try.' I wiped away a few more tears.

'You can go now. I'll sleep for a while.'

I kissed her and hugged her as hard as I could.

'I will come visit tomorrow.' She didn't hear me anymore. She was asleep.

On the way home, I stopped for a coffee. I was shattered. I had no plans for the afternoon. I sat by the window with a hot drink in my hand. I watched people on the street. Everyone was running somewhere in a hurry. The wind started to blow, and rain began falling from the sky. Raindrops were trickling down the window.

My phone beeped with an incoming message. Boris wrote that we wouldn't see each other today, but he was thinking of me. I shifted my gaze back to the street. My thoughts revolved around last night, the locked room and the kisses. I stopped my gaze on a couple across the street. They were both standing with their backs to me. I could have sworn I knew the silhouette. The man next to the woman was holding a large umbrella, shielding them from the rain. The woman kissed him on the cheek and walked away.

The man turned and caught my gaze as if he sensed I was watching him. It was Alex. He walked briskly to the other side of the street, dodging the moving cars by inches. One of them honked at him, the driver shouted and waved his hands. Alex didn't even look at him. A moment later, he was standing next to me. He smelled of the cold and the rain.

'Do you want another one?' He looked into my cup.

'No thanks, I've reached my caffeine limit.'

He went to get the coffee and sat down next to me.

'You look good without the bruises,' I said.

'Yeah. I prefer that version of myself.' He smiled crookedly.

'I definitely do too.' I lowered my gaze to my hands. 'I don't want things to be like this between us.'

'Like what?'

'I don't want to struggle to think of what to say.'

'Look at me. Nothing has changed between us. You said what you thought. I'm your friend. You don't have to feel embarrassed. I can handle my own feelings. I'm a big boy. Just no bedroom details.'

I smiled, encouraged by his words.

'Thank you. Who was that woman?'

'Vivian. She wanted to talk.'

'That's who I thought she was. You didn't mention you were seeing each other.'

'Because we're not. She was looking for someone to complain to. Boris wouldn't take her calls or return her messages. She wanted me to have some kind of influence on him.' He laughed at his joke. 'As if it were that simple….'

'How was your day?'

'So, this is how he acts when he's done with a woman?'

'Are you asking me if he will treat you the same way? What makes you think he'll end things with you?'

'The contract expires in two months.'

'Does it? Do you think that's what this is about? If it was about the contract, he wouldn't have slapped me in the face.'

'Don't make me get my hopes up.'

'I'm not. Just remember, I'm here for you. Always.'

I began to wonder if we would have had the chance to build something lasting if it weren't for this whole situation with Boris. I think we would. I touched his hand. 'Thank you for everything.'

'So, how was your day?' He looked at my hand, sighed heavily, and changed the subject.

* * *

I sat on a chair in the kitchen and contemplated whether to tell Boris about my meeting with Alex. Honesty won.

'I saw your brother today,' I fired out with one exhale before I could get second thoughts.

He focused his gaze on me. His hand hovered with the knife in the air over the uncut peppers. He put the knife down and wiped his hands on a washcloth. Now I had all his attention.

'And what had you two agreed on?' He clenched his hands on the countertop.

'I was having coffee in town, and he was across the street talking to Vivian. He noticed me and sat down. I didn't know Vivian was calling you, and you weren't answering.'

'You don't have to worry about that. It's not important.'

'Is that what you think of her? Is she irrelevant?'

His expression changed. He was pissed.

'Since when are women so unified?'

I didn't like that tone. When we break up, will he call me irrelevant too?

'You've been dating her, and can't even be bothered to have a normal conversation with her? Is this how you always end relationships?' My question hovered between us.

'That's your point! You're comparing yourself to her.' He moved closer to me, his anger boiling over. He looked really pissed off. Maybe I shouldn't have asked him about this.

'Let's get something straight. I didn't make any promises to her. I've been clear from the beginning of our relationship. The fact that she started thinking of us as a couple was her mistake. Then at the restaurant, I went to meet her to explain everything. I couldn't take it any longer. Clearly, she didn't understand what - *it's over* meant. I never introduced her to my parents. She didn't even have half the attention that I give you.'

If he thought he made anything clearer, he was wrong.

'You're an asshole! You know that?'

His eyes darkened dangerously. I shouldn't have tantalised him.

'I'm being honest. You're important to me, but I can't give you more than what you have.'

'Why not?'

'Don't push it.' He went back to cutting vegetables.

If I had any delusions that we could be a couple, I just got a straight answer. It hurt, and it hurt hard. But I hoped that time would make a difference. I could have waited, after all. I glanced down at his body and the broad back under the tight T-shirt. I liked the freedom I felt with him. No inhibitions. The memory of sex in the car immediately came back to me. I could definitely wait.

'What are you thinking about? You're blushing.'

'For some reason, it just got a little hot in here.'

'That's not true.'

He finished cutting the vegetables, and I didn't even notice. I was absorbed in processing my feelings.

'I hope this blush is because of me,' he began jokingly, lightening the heavy atmosphere that had fallen between us.

'Yes, definitely because of you.'

He sat me down on the kitchen counter.

'And what am I supposed to do with you?'

'Whatever you want.'

The boyish grin on his face suggested that I didn't need to repeat myself a second time. His impatient mouth took complete possession of me. In no time, we were naked, and I was squirting with pleasure. From now on, cooking in this place would no longer be the same.

A long while later, after showering together, we went back to cooking the meal.

'Do you have plans for Christmas?'

'Like every year, I will spend it with my grandmother.'

I could see the disappointment on his face, but he accepted it with calmness.

'Did you have anything planned for us?' It was too late for me to understand the meaning of my own words. I avoided talking about us in the plural. He didn't seem to notice and continued:

'I wanted to take you to visit my parents for Christmas.'

'More awkward situations? Thank you, but I think I'll pass.'

'They like you.'

'But Alex will be there too.'

His face got a little cross.

'There will be a Christmas party after the intimate dinner. I don't want to go to it by myself.'

An image of his friend, Nina, immediately appeared in my mind. She would be happy to see that I didn't come. The sting of jealousy was not pleasant. However, I valued my time with my grandmother too much to change my plans. I intended to take her to my apartment for Christmas unless the doctor objected. Alan wasn't going to his parents this year. We planned to spend the time together, just the three of us. We would watch old movies while eating yummy treats prepared especially for the occasion.

* * *

The intrusive ringing of my phone awakened me. It was only after a few beeps through my sleepy mind that I realised it was my phone. It was the middle of the night. Who was calling me at this hour?

'Is it yours?' asked Boris sleepily.

'Sleep. It's probably Alan, drunk and wanting to talk.' He used to have parties like this where he didn't remember much the next day. He didn't remember the night's conversations either. I also thought of a second possibility. I tried not to panic and to chase away the intrusive thought. Let it not be anything related to grandma - I repeated in my mind like a mantra.

Boris turned on the night lamp on his side of the bed. I answered the call. The first words of my caller made my hands start to shake. I couldn't control them. Boris watched me anxiously as I answered with single words. I was no longer able to form a complete sentence. By the time I finished talking, he was already wearing pants and pulling a sweater over his head. Tears were streaming down my cheeks uncontrollably. The phone fell out of my hand. Boris was already by my side. He held me in his arms until the sobbing stopped and my breathing calmed down enough for me to speak.

'Grandma. They took her to the hospital. She was struggling to breathe.'

'Which hospital? Do you know?'

'Yes, I know.'

'Get dressed, let's go.'

'I'll go alone.' I insisted.

He interrupted me in mid-sentence.

'You're shaking all over. I won't let you drive like that.'

I just nodded in response. I started looking for my clothes. The next thing I remember, was the hospital. Boris dropped me off in front of the entrance to the building and went to park the car.

The sound of my footsteps carried across the stone floor. The receptionist informed me that I couldn't see my grandmother. Visiting hours were over. I could return in the morning, and the doctor treating her would be there then, too. But I had to see her, at least for a moment. Boris stood behind me and put his hand on my shoulder, offering encouragement. The woman at the reception desk beamed at the sight of him. Instinctively she started to fix her hair.

'Mr Smith,' she said sweetly, entirely unlike the way she spoke to me.

'Is there any way you could override the procedures? All we need is a moment.' He sent her one of his best smiles.

She sighed theatrically.

'All right. You have five minutes. Room number three.'

'I'll wait here for you. Go.'

I hated hospitals. I moved quickly towards the room before the woman could change her mind. In the distance, I could hear her voice telling Boris about the change from clinic to the hospital and the better hours.

I knocked softly and pushed the door. My grand-mother was laying in the single bed at the centre of the room. I approached as quietly as I could. I took her hand. She was asleep. She had an oxygen mask over her face and was plugged into a heart-monitoring machine. She looked smaller and more fragile. Tears streamed down my cheeks. I had promised myself to be strong, but seeing her like this was heart-breaking. She had always taken care of me, but now I didn't know how to help her. My visitation time limit had passed. I kissed her hand gently. She moved but didn't wake up. In the doorway, I looked at her once more.

'I love you, Granny,' I whispered.

Boris interrupted the conversation and quickly said goodbye. He put his jacket over my shoulders. I didn't even notice that I wasn't wearing it. The cold air hit my face.

I got into the car and cried again. I wiped my nose again and again. I didn't want comfort or a conversation like: "everything will be fine". Boris obviously sensed this because he said very little. When I stopped responding, he stopped talking too. He didn't make me talk.

It was already dawn when we returned to his apart-ment. I looked around and realised that I was just a guest here. This was not my home. This was not my life. A puffy face with reddened eyes looked back at me in the bathroom mirror. I didn't even have any face cream. I packed the things I needed into a small sports shoulder bag. I kept unpacking and repacking. On the other hand, my apartment had a pile of clothes to wash. I had had enough. At this point, I had had enough of everything. Boris was sitting in the kitchen, his favourite radio station playing in the background.

'Would you like coffee, tea, anything stronger?' He smiled shyly.

'I'm tired. I will lay down for an hour, provided I fall asleep. I have a hard day ahead of me.'

'Did you talk to her? Did she wake up? You were so quiet.'

'She was sleeping heavily, but all those tubes and ….' My voice broke down again. 'She was so fragile. I can't lose her.'

Boris was already at my side in two quick steps. He didn't comfort me with unnecessary words. Nor did he promise that everything would work out. He had no right to raise my hopes. Neither of us knew what a new day would bring. He hugged me tightly. He let me cry, then took me to bed. He laid down next to me, hugged me tighter, and covered us with the quilt.

'Get some rest,' he told me, noticing my eyes were still open after a long moment.

'Can I leave some of my stuff with you? I keep having to pack everything in my bag and plan what I'll need.'

He didn't speak for a while. I even suspected that he had fallen asleep.

'I'll make room for you in the closet tomorrow. You're right. I hadn't thought of that. Will you sleep now?'

'If I'm demanding too much, say so. I don't want to force you.' I hated the fact that it was dark, and I couldn't see his reaction. Sometimes facial expressions say more than words, but there were only words left in this case.

'You can bring as many things as you want.' Even though the words came from his mouth, I wasn't entirely convinced.

'I will.' I snuggled into his warm body and, exhausted, fell asleep.

As usual, when I opened my eyes, Boris was already up. The smell of freshly brewed coffee and toast came to me from the kitchen. My thoughts immediately returned to my grandmother, and I felt nauseous just thinking about it. I rushed to the bathroom and emptied the contents of my stomach into the toilet. I looked even worse than the day before. My hair was tangled, bags under my eyes. I brushed my teeth and jumped quickly into the shower. Boris was in the bedroom, getting changed out of his sweatpants into some jeans. One look in my direction, and his eyes grew sad.

'How do you feel?'

'Exactly how I look.'

'I've made some space for you.' He walked over to the three-door closet and slid the left-wing open. Inside there were only a few empty hangers and nothing else. We had talked about it just the night before, and he had already moved his stuff. 'This part of the closet has been empty for a long time. You can fill it up.'

And the mystery was solved. I didn't even realise it was empty. I never checked. I thought he would say something more, but he didn't.

Despite my protests, he stuffed half a slice toast and half a cup of tea into me for breakfast. He also insisted on being my chauffeur. I thought we had already agreed on this matter. Apparently, I was wrong. I had neither the will nor the energy to argue about unimportant things. During the drive, I watched the people outside the window as they rushed to do their business. However, my life seemed to slow down when I saw my grandmother connected to the hospital machine.

'Hello?' Boris answered the call. 'Who's calling? You're on speakerphone.'

'It's Mick.'

'Did you change the number? What number are you calling from? Your number didn't show up on my screen.'

'I'm calling from my cell phone. Something must have gone wrong with your super-high-end car.'

'Could be.' Boris pressed some buttons, but the display still said 'unknown number'.

'I'll check with the service department. I'm busy right now.'

'Is Sarah there?'

'I'm here,' I said.

'Hi, gorgeous. How are you?'

'I've been better.'

'Why are you calling?' Boris got impatient.

'You were supposed to be here half an hour ago. They're coming to install the new bar. You said you wanted to supervise it yourself.'

'I'll be there in an hour. They probably won't be finished by then. Keep them there. I want to assess the work myself. We don't have time for corrections and complaints. During the holiday season, it's hard to get a professional.'

'Sure. I'll see you later. Sarah?' He changed his tone of voice to an appealing whisper. – 'Have a good day.'

I laughed.

'You too,' I replied, still laughing.

'Idiot!' Boris commented, but he also smiled.

I needed to lighten the mood. Mick was effortlessly great at that.

Boris stayed with me for another hour. He supported me while I talked to the doctor. He asked specific questions that I wouldn't have come up with. I couldn't keep my head straight. The prognosis was poor. For the time being, breathing assistance was needed. Grandma had frequent suspension of breathing, which could have ended tragically. On top of that, she had caught a virus, which had complicated name. Her body was exhausted. How could I not notice anything? I automatically blamed myself for not giving her enough attention.

Boris brought me some more coffee from the cafeteria and went to the bar. I sat by my grandmother for a long time. I didn't touch the coffee, which had cooled down in time. All I could hear in the room was the quiet beeping of all those menacingly-looking medical devices. She awoke twice but was unable to speak. I tried to be strong, but seeing her in such a state was not easy to accept. Every now and then, the nurses would come in to check on her condition, and we would be left alone again. I didn't know how long I had been here. Not until Boris's presence made me realise that it was already dark.

'Have you eaten anything?'

'I'm not hungry.'

'You have to eat. You have to be strong for her.'

I cried, swallowing my tears. Boris hugged me to his chest. His scent calmed me slightly.

'I have to pee.' I whimpered into his shirt.

'What?'

'I haven't moved since you left. Let's find a bathroom.' I said goodbye to my grandmother, kissing her hand like last time.

On the way back, we stopped at a small, quaint Italian place. The smells of the food finally made me hungry. By the time I saw the size of pasta portion, I had smiled.

'I knew you'd like it.'

'Am I that predictable?' I asked, surprised.

'No. Not at all.' He raised an eyebrow suggestively. 'I like to eat here, and you haven't eaten anything since this morning.'

He was right. The pasta was delicious. We ordered two more portions to take away. Tomorrow's day promised to be exactly the same. It was good to have something in the fridge. We made another stop at my apartment. It looked like I would spend the next night at Boris' place. Alan was watching the game and drinking beer. Boris sat down with him. He wasn't in a hurry, which gave me time to pack in peace. When I looked over, they were still watching the game. I wanted to sit on the couch, but Boris pulled me into his lap. I was aware that I would have hundreds of texts from Alan tomorrow morning. He was watching my every move. I kept telling him it was just a deal. This time I wouldn't get away so easily from an honest conversation.

As I predicted, there were several texts from Alan the following day. In the last one, he even begged me to call him back. He was the most curious person I knew. He cared for me like a brother. If there was a crisis, he was the first person I called. I could be sure he would drop everything and rush to my aid. That's just the way he was—my true friend.

I touched the coffee pot with my hand. It was still warm. I poured my morning dose of caffeine into the mug. I couldn't find Boris in the apartment, and I had no idea where he might have gone. He hadn't mentioned anything about a meeting. I quickly checked to see if the secret room was still locked. I had to find out what was in there. Unfortunately, the door handle didn't budge. For the next fifteen minutes, I talked to Alan on the phone. I felt like I had ran a marathon rather than a phone conversation. He flooded me with questions. The most important was - when are you moving out? - I repeated to him countless times that my packed suitcase was a temporary solution and I wasn't going anywhere long-term. Boris, meanwhile, had come home and placed the groceries on the tabletop. As soon as I finished talking, I got a welcoming kiss, after which I wondered if I should drag him to bed. He smelled of wind and cold air.

'I thought I'd do some shopping. I couldn't bear to wake you. Have you eaten yet?'

'No, not yet.'

'I bought fresh rolls for breakfast and your favourite cold cuts.'

It made me especially happy that he thought of me and bought my favourite products. I also found yoghurt, which I liked. It was evident that he was observing me more than I thought.

'Too bad you didn't wake me up after all. I have to go to the pharmacy to get some medicine.'

'Are you in pain?'

'No, silly. I have birth control pills to pick up.' I was embarrassed to talk to him about it. I've actually had sex with him plenty of times, and it made me ashamed to discuss the issue of contraception.

'We'll pick it up on the way to the hospital. Let me know when you're ready.'

'Thank you.' I didn't know exactly what I was thanking him for. Was it for taking me to the pharmacy, for his support, or maybe for the rolls for breakfast? My nerves were in tatters. One more meaningful moment, and I would have cried again.

'Hey! Don't cry,' he said, wiping away the tear that ran down my cheek. 'It will be fine, you will see.'

'You don't know that,' I said reproachfully.

'You are right, but you must have hope. Sometimes hope is the only thing that keeps us alive.'

Those words sent an uncontrollable shiver down my spine. Spoken aloud, with a distinct hint of bitterness, they sounded more like they were addressed to him than me.

'Sit down while I make breakfast.' Once again, I watched as he unpacked the groceries and arranged them in the cupboards and fridge. I enjoyed watching the skill with which he moved around the kitchen. He had been living alone for a long time, and I longed to stay here for longer.

It was Christmas break at the university. There were only four days left until Christmas. Boris still had plans to go to his parents. He understood my situation and did not ask again if I would come with him. Instead, he promised to be back as soon as he could.

We stopped at the mall where the pharmacy was located. I picked up my pills and, with a quick step, joined Boris. He stopped in front of a jeweller. My heart sped up.

'What are you looking at?' I asked in surprise.

'I don't have a present for my mother yet. Maybe you can help me choose something.' I was happy that he valued my opinion. At the same time, I hoped that he wanted to get a present for me. Unfortunately, everything indicated that we came for a gift for his mother. After lengthy negotiations, together, we chose gold earrings adorned with tiny diamonds. They were expensive. For him, however, the price was not important. He had them wrapped in Christmas paper. Then he took me to the hospital and went to the office.

The next day, everything was the same. It was my shift behind the bar at the residence in the evening, which I had completely forgotten about. Boris arranged a day off for me. Sue understood my situation perfectly. She told me to come back whenever I was ready.

I slept in my apartment. That evening I had dinner with Boris, and after that, when it was time to say goodbye, I got a very wet and obscene kiss. Boris planned to go to his parents' first thing in the morning. When I got back to the kitchen, Alan measured me with his eyes.

'Has a hurricane passed through the hallway?' Satisfied, he stirred the dish in the pot.

In the bathroom, I became aware that due to that brief moment with Boris, my hair was a mess and on top of that, I had smeared my lipstick. Tired but satisfied, I fixed my hair and went back to the kitchen to help him cook.

My friend took care of all the Christmas shopping, for which I was incredibly grateful. He also decorated the Christmas tree. We did it together every year, but I didn't have the time this year. He took practically all the work out of my hands, even though I knew how much he hated cleaning. I appreciated what he did for me. We managed to cook everything we had planned for the day. Traditionally, I made cheesecake using my grandmother's recipe. I regretted that she would not be here with us. Despite being terribly tired, I couldn't fall asleep. For the past few days, I had slept with Boris, snuggled into his warm side when bedtime had come. Now the bed seemed cold and uncomfortable. How had he managed to take over my life in such a short space of time? Every day I would wake up thinking about him, fall asleep with his name on my lips. It was some kind of madness.

The next day, Grandma was breathing more freely. The difference was clearly visible. When I looked into her room, she was sitting up in her bed. The doctors had removed her oxygen mask. She still looked miserable, but she was up, resting her back against the pillows. That was really something. I hugged her tightly.

'Honey, it's good to see you. You don't look so good. Didn't you sleep last night?' She was looking at me worriedly.

'Who said that?'

'Where's your handsome friend? I saw he was here with you a few times.'

I must have blushed because Grandma laughed and immediately started coughing. I quickly applied an oxygen mask to her that was lying at arm's length. When the attack was over, she was breathing freely again.

'No laughing,' I ordered. I held her hand tightly. 'Don't scare me anymore.'

'Honey,' she shook her head, exhausted, 'we've already talked about this. My health is getting worse and worse. You must learn to take care of yourself. Don't worry about me. You'd better take care of that handsome boy.'

'Don't say that!' I didn't give up.

'What did you buy him for Christmas?'

'Nothing. I didn't have time. Anyway, he went to his parents.'

'You have to get him a present. Not a tie, that's too cliché. Think about what it might be. The stores are still open.'

'I'll think about it,' I promised.

On the way back, I drove up to the same jeweller where we had bought Boris' mom's earrings. I saw that he was looking at watches before I approached him. The saleswoman was happy to see me. She carefully showed me which watch Boris was looking at. It was a very, very expensive one. I already had a lot of savings, anyway, all the money came from him, so I decided to splurge, and bought it for him.

That afternoon I felt more at ease. Grandma was recovering, and that was the most important thing. I went to do some more grocery shopping, did some laundry and changed the bedding. I had said goodbye to Boris just yesterday, and it felt silly to admit it to myself, but I already missed him. I missed his closeness. I liked it when he would embrace me and give me a kiss on the lips and then go back to his activities with a look of innocence. I had free time all to myself. I was in my apartment. I should have been relieved to have some freedom back. But all I felt was emptiness. Even Alan noticed my unusual behaviour. I dismissed it to the stress of my grandmother's condition. We both knew I was lying. For the hundredth time that day, I checked for messages from Boris. I didn't want to be pushy and flood him with texts. My cell phone was silent. I even checked the signal. Everything was working perfectly.

* * *

In the morning, Alan's cries woke me up.

'Gifts! Sarah, Get up! It's Christmas!'

I covered my head with a pillow, hoping to get at least a little more sleep. The night before, I couldn't get to sleep for a long time. It was raining, pounding on my bedroom window. I didn't fall asleep until morning, filling my time with a book. I rolled out of bed, begging Alan for a cup of coffee before we descended into the madness of opening presents. Under the Christmas tree, like every year, most of the gifts were addressed to him. His entire large family sent him gifts. I didn't understand why he didn't spend Christmas with them. All I knew was that his father did not accept his sexual orientation, and his mother was afraid to oppose his father. His brothers and sister sent him gifts through the post.

There was only one gift waiting for me under the Christmas tree. I opened the box. I got wireless headphones. I had looked at them hundreds of times in the store, but they were too expensive.

'Just what I wanted. Thank you.' I was happy with the gift.

'Anything for you, you know that.' He reached for the gift from me. I wasn't sure if he would like it. He unwrapped it and took a confused look at the package of pralines. Not just any kind, because they were handmade. He opened the envelope attached to the sweets. His eyes grew big with surprise. The envelope contained a voucher for a baking and cake decorating course. At first, I thought he disliked the idea. He loved to cook and bake, but maybe it was a wrong choice?

'This is awesome! Do you know who this guy is?' He showed me the name of the instructor on the course brochure.

'I have no idea,' I admitted, wrinkling my forehead.

'He opened a chain of some of the best candy stores in the country. He's a confectionery guru. How did you find this?' He was looking through the contents of the envelope with pious reverence.

'Boris helped me arrange it.'

'I have to give him a big hug for that.'

'I don't know if that's a good idea.'

'Jealous?' He was teasing me.

'Maybe a little. Open the rest of the presents and let's have some breakfast. I'm starving.'

After breakfast, we visited my grandmother in the hospital. I brought her some delicious food. She ate because she didn't want to worry me, but I could see she had no appetite. I bought her a warm grey robe with embroidered white stars. It was supposed to be waiting for her at our house under the Christmas tree. This was not how I imagined my Christmas. Grandma, on the other hand, was worried that she couldn't give me anything. For me, the greatest gift was her recovery.

In the afternoon, she ushered us home. In a much better mood, Alan and I ate a late dinner. Then we sat comfortably on the sofa in front of the TV with a glass of wine. I enjoyed the Christmas movies. Our argument about what we were going to watch was interrupted by the sound of the doorbell. We weren't expecting visitors, which made me even more surprised.

'Check who it is, and I'll open another bottle,' Alan declared. I smoothed my dress and moved towards the front door.

'Boris!' I squealed excitedly and even dashed towards him, shoving my tongue into his mouth. He looked at me suspiciously as soon as I stepped away from him.

'How much have you had to drink?'

'Not enough. I missed you.' I snuggled into him, rubbing my whole body.

I guess he didn't expect it because he wobbled perilously, holding me in his arms.

'Why won't you let him in?' Alan's voice reached us. 'Would you like wine or whisky?' He turned to his guest.

'Coffee, please.' He looked at me with amusement. 'I have a feeling that we could use someone sober here.'

Alan went to make the coffee, and I moved to let Boris into the apartment. I locked the door, and he grabbed me, pressing my ass against his crotch.

'I like this dress,' he whispered directly into my ear, and he kissed my neck, exactly the way I loved it.

'Okay, lovebirds, coffee is ready.' A call came from the room.

'Just what I needed. I usually stop for coffee on the way, but I wanted to get here as soon as I could.' He looked at me with such intensity that it made me hot.

'What about your mom's party?' He should be with his family right now.

'Nothing.' He shrugged his shoulders. 'I said I couldn't stay. She understood, and she liked the earrings very much. It was a good choice. Oh, that's right. I almost forgot.'

He put his coffee cup down on the table and went to the hallway where he had left his coat. I admired how great he looked in his classic black suit with fascination. He sat beside me and handed me a rectangular, dark green suede box. 'Merry Christmas.' He kissed me fleetingly.

I looked at it.

'Open it!' Alan urged me. His excitement was equal to mine.

I slowly lifted the lid. I gasped for air. Only after a while did I realise that I had been holding my breath. I held a bracelet in my hand. Not just any bracelet. The braid of tiny flowers was decorated with rubies. It glittered in the light of the chandelier. It was beautiful. I stroked it carefully with my hand.

'Put it on!' Alan was impatient.

'The bracelet is beautiful! It must have been expensive.'

'Worth every smile you give me.' Boris took the box from me and fastened the ornament on my wrist. I moved my hand a few times, enchanted by the effect.

'I love it,' I said. 'Oh, I have something for you too.' I reached under the tree and handed him the last Christmas paper-wrapped package. 'Merry Christmas.' I smiled unsurely.

Boris ripped the paper apart. He looked like a little boy who was finally allowed to unwrap his present.

'It's the same one I had been looking at the other day at the store.' He took off his watch and put on the new one. He carefully packed the old one in the box. 'I wondered if I should buy it.' He took my hand and kissed it. Apparently, he remembered that we weren't alone.

'Do you like the gift from Sarah?' He turned to Alan. He continued to hold my hand in his.

'I'm already looking forward to my first baking class. Have you seen who's going to be teaching the course? Of course, you have. You helped arrange that.'

'No problem. How's your Grandma?' He focused his worried eyes on me.

'Better. I talked to her. She's been disconnected. No word yet on when she'll be released from the hospital.'

'I'm glad she's better. I was worried about you. You were so sad. Why didn't you call? You could have at least sent a message that she was better.'

'I didn't want to disturb you.'

He pulled me close to him, and I snuggled against his side with my glass in my hand. What more could you want? I had a great guy by my side, two of them even, and a supply of wine to last through the holidays. I reached out my hand once more and looked at the jewellery on my wrist. I caught Boris' gaze. He was watching me with fascination in his eyes. This was definitely a good Christmas.

Slightly tipsy, I dragged Boris to my bedroom. In bed, I got a little silly. I was laughing so hard that the bed was shaking. Boris tried, with little success to quieten me down. It had the opposite effect. Finally, he gave up. Then, we made love long and slow.

* * *

Boris opened the car door and grabbed my hand. He didn't let go even after entering the building. I felt that I hadn't been at residence in a long time. Sue was busy talking to Marco, gesticulating heavily. On the other hand, Marco adopted his usual annoyed expression that he had whenever he saw me. He relaxed slightly only when he saw Boris and our entwined hands.

'There you are!' Sue extended her open arms towards me. She locked me in a strong, motherly hug. I really liked her. Boris moved back but still stood close to me.

'How is your grandma feeling?'

'Better, thank you.'

'That's great news. I was worried.'

'I can come back to work behind the bar tonight,' I suggested.

'If you're ready. I won't push you, though I have to admit you're helpful.'

'Sarah!' Amy was already running down the stairs. She was the next in line to lock me in a bear hug.

'There you are! I've missed you. I need to tell you something important. I feel like I haven't seen you in ages. Do you want coffee?'

She looked hesitantly in Boris' direction. I had noticed that she felt insecure around him. After all, he was our boss, at least in a sense. But I suspected that it was an excuse for him to come to the residence more often.

'Sure, go ahead.' He gave me permission, at which I rolled my eyes. He really could be an asshole sometimes.

'Sue, why don't you show me those documents and invoices you had mentioned over the phone. We're going away for two weeks. I want to supervise the opening of the new club personally.'

I was about to leave when the meaning of his words hit me.

'Did you say we were leaving?' I turned to him. 'I'm not going anywhere. I'm not leaving my grandmother alone.'

'We'll talk about it later, okay?' Clearly impatient, he didn't want to bring up the subject at this moment.

'I'm not going.' I said. 'Come on, Amy, let's go get some coffee.' I marched off without looking back. I heard his loud laughter. It was strange that it amused him because I was very serious.

In the kitchen, I reached for the cups while Amy poured water into the kettle.

'Okay, tell me. What's the news?'

'I've signed up for school.' She looked ashamed and ran her eyes to the side.

'That's great!' I hugged her tightly and asked, 'What course did you choose?'

'Hairdressing, just like you advised me. I put aside some money. I want to move on with my life. I can't live here forever.'

'That's great news. When do you start classes?'

'After the new year. I'm so excited. I already bought black pants and a blouse. We'll also have a traineeship. The uniform is mandatory. I also looked around for scissors. Ideally, I would buy everything I need right now. And then, who knows? I might be able to leave the residence. What about you? What are you planning?'

'Nothing.' I shrugged my shoulders. 'It's too early to plan anything.'

'I've seen the way he looks at you. He won't let you go.'

I was glad that she noticed it too. Maybe there was hope for us after all? I took a sip of coffee and reached for the cookie on the table.

'Damn! Where did you get that bracelet?' She looked at my hand in awe.

'A Christmas present from Boris. It's beautiful, isn't it?'

Just then, Olivia came into the kitchen. She glanced at the ornament on my hand. I was sure she would comment on it with some stupid text. Instead, she just said, 'I'm glad that you're here. I hope your grandma is doing better.'

I looked at her, shocked.

'I may be a bitch, but that doesn't mean I don't have a heart.' With those words, she walked out of the kitchen. I looked at Amy's surprised face, and she laughed.

'Well said,' I commented, regaining my voice. I hadn't suspected her of human reflexes. Life can hold many surprises.

After our last exchange of words, I thought Boris would insist that we travel together. Instead, he stated that he understood and would not force me to choose between him and my grandmother. He surprised me with that because he could be a relentless asshole at times, but on the other hand, he could also be a decent guy. Lately, he has been showing the other side of him more and more often.

'Darling...' Grandmother's voice pulled me out of my reverie, '...You have been visiting me for four days straight, but your thoughts are somewhere else. Tell me, what is going on?'

She was right. Ever since Boris left, which was exactly four days ago, I've been walking around as if absent. I couldn't find my place. I did everything I could to keep my hands and mind occupied and not glance at the phone display. I would get messages from him, and I was happy that he was thinking about me, even though he was really busy. My face was beaming at the thought of him.

'Grandma, I think I'm in love.'

'Hallelujah!'

'Grandma?' I was shocked by her reaction.

'Why are you looking at me like that? It's about time. Is this the new friend who brought me flowers?'

'Yes, that's Boris.'

'You were here with him. Bring him next time.'

'He's away for two weeks. Besides,' I hesitated, 'He still doesn't know about my affection for him.'

'You haven't told him?' Grandmother grasped my hand. 'My child, I am sure he knows.'

'Do you think so? What if he doesn't feel what I feel?' I feared that my stated fears might come true.

'You won't know unless you confess your feelings to him. Tell me more about him,' she asked with dreamy eyes.

I was afraid of her reaction. That was unnecessary though, as she was as excited as I was. I told her about Boris, what he does, about his family. I neatly skipped the part about the contract and the residency.

'You must go to him,' she announced with her eyes sparkling with emotion.

'I will not leave you here alone.'

'You must go! I can see how you are withering with longing. I have excellent care. Besides,' she smoothed the folds on the quilt, 'I'm not going anywhere. Go to him.' She insisted.

'I can't.'

'I don't want to hear it. How much I would give to be in your place. You're young and in love. Make sure to pack something sexy.'

'Grandma!'

'What, just because I'm old, I can't say things like that? Come on. Give me a kiss and go.'

I hesitated but obediently kissed her on the cheek. I practically ran back to the apartment. Alan looked at me with a suspicious look in his eyes. My cheeks were flushed, and the wind tousled my hair. I indicated to him that I was going to see Boris. He was happy and helped me pack my suitcase. He claimed that I had been walking around like a zombie for the past few days. I was worried that my car might not make it through the several hour trip, so I took the train. In the meantime, I got the name of the hotel where Boris was staying from Mick. I also stipulated not to tell him anything about my arrival.

I arrived at the place before midnight. At the reception desk, I was informed that Mr Smith had not yet returned to his room. I lied that I was his wife and finally got a spare key to the suite. It was my first time at the Marriott Hotel. It was impressive. I finished exploring the rooms. I stopped, when I heard Boris talking to another man, and then the sound of the door closing. I walked out of the bedroom. He noticed my movement out of the corner of his eye and stopped, alarmed by someone's presence.

'Sarah?' He asked, confused.

I felt that coming here wasn't such a good idea after all.

'Surprise?' I forced myself to smile. I stepped nervously from foot to foot.

Then everything happened at an accelerated pace. Boris covered the distance separating us in a few steps. He reached for the clip in my hair, undid it, and threw the ornament on a nearby sofa.

'I missed you,' he whispered. His eyes scanned all over my face. Then he looked appreciatively at my elegant pants and blouse. 'You look beautiful.' He returned his gaze to my eyes and finally kissed me. Hard, possessive, passionate. Exactly the way I loved it. I wrapped my legs around his waist.

'Bed, sofa?'

'Kitchen?' I suggested cheekily.

He raised one eyebrow and, without delay, moved me to the kitchenette. He sat me on the table. His swollen manhood pressed against my crotch, asking to be released. I unzipped his pants and touched him. He sucked in air as my hand moved steadily. I loved looking into his amber eyes. He closed his eyelids and tilted his head back, simultaneously extending his hips toward me.

'That's enough,' he hissed. He took off my blouse and bra. He kissed first one breast, then the other. Each stroke of his skin caused another wave of pleasure that I felt between my legs.

'Take off your pants and lay with your belly down on the tabletop.'

I couldn't explain it, but his words turned me on even more. I preferred to have my say in everyday life, but in bed, I liked him to take control. He touched my wet pussy and purred appreciatively. He pushed me gently though firmly onto the tabletop. Memories came alive when we had done the same thing at the residence.

'Hold on tight,' he ordered once again.

I held the tabletop with all my strength, and for that, I got the best sex of my life. Exhausted, the two of us took a shower together in the impressively sized bathroom. Pleased and satisfied, I fell asleep with the intention of telling him about my feelings tomorrow.

In the morning, I woke up with a warm hand on my bum. It was a nice change because usually, Boris got up much earlier than me. Today was the opening day of the club. In all the rush, it turned out that I hadn't brought an elegant dress with me. The opening was to be held as a lavish party. I was completely unprepared. We spent the morning looking for a suitable outfit. I bought a lace dress with a flared bottom in a beige colour. It was beautiful and fit perfectly. I wasn't quite sure what to choose. It was more suitable for a wedding than for an evening party. Boris decided for me.

'Do you like it or not?' he asked, at last, seeing me indecisive.

'Well, I like it, but the colour...'

'We'll take it,' he turned to the boutique saleswoman. 'Please wrap it up.'

He paid before I could take out my credit card. Then we had lunch at a nearby restaurant. The smile never left my face. I was with my beloved man who fed me well. The dress of my dreams was waiting in the car. The evening promised to be fantastic.

After arriving at the hotel, Boris headed off to ensure everything was in working order before the grand opening. I had time to take a long bath and get ready for the evening event. I wished Amy had been with me. There was no way I could have managed my hair on my own. Everyone said it was beautiful. The truth was that my red locks were very problematic. I wondered what to do about them when someone knocked on the door.

'Did you order a hair and makeup artist?' asked a young girl in a uniform.

'No, there's been a mistake,' I began to explain.

'Mr Smith warned me that you would say that. Can I come in?'

'Yes, of course.' I moved to let the girl with the big suitcase on wheels pass. Before I could recover from the shock, she was already laying everything out on a table in the middle of the living room. It was a surreal feeling. What did I do to deserve such a man? I sat down, slightly tense, on the stool. It turned out to be completely unnecessary. I quickly found Kate and I had a lot in common. To the point that she offered to meet me for coffee if I were to stay longer in the city. I was glad. Boris would probably be very busy. I could use someone familiar in the new place. I put away her business card, assuring her that I would call her.

I didn't even notice when my hair and makeup was ready. I stood in a robe in front of a large mirror. I was speechless. The girl was good at her job. She assured me that everything was paid for. I didn't even know when Boris had managed to order this lovely girl for me. I stood there, my hair pinned up and decorated with a thin band with rhinestones. Even in this light, it sparkled with every movement of my head. The hairstyle and the makeup would go perfectly with the dress.

Boris returned, took a quick shower and changed into his suit. He stopped at the sight of me. He silently mouthed the word, "gorgeous," before I even had the chance to put on my dress. I knew that he wouldn't be able to keep his hands to himself. He tried to untie my robe, but I chased him into the bathroom. I was well aware that there would be nothing left of my beautiful look if we ended up in bed. He walked away with slight disappointment, but he had made it clear that we were going straight back to the bedroom after the party.

A limousine was waiting for us in front of the hotel. I had a feeling that Boris wasn't telling me something. However, I forgot to ask when I saw the limousine's interior—a luxury in every sense of the word. A glass of champagne quickly found its way into my hand, one of many that night. I looked sensational, and that's exactly how I felt. The confirmation was the gaze of my man staring at me. Because more and more often, that's what I thought of him.

'What's going on?' The car slowed down. We were following other vehicles in traffic. This was not what I had expected. There were people everywhere, separated from us by barriers and security. Lots of security. Boris smiled from ear to ear and reached out his hand towards me.

'Ready?'

'Ready for what?'

'For a good time.' He smiled again, immensely excited.

I slowly stepped out of the vehicle so as not to damage my dress. I trotted across the soft carpet to the main door of the building. Someone on the side shouted Boris' name, and flashbulbs flashed. We walked into the building under the fire of photojournalists.

'What was that?'

'I invited some friends, and it became a sensation.' He gave me his arm, and we entered the vast hall. Boris greeted people I was seeing for the first time in my life. For the next hour, all the faces and names blended together for me. I also had time to drink some champagne. The bubbles relaxed me. I felt less tense, and I even started to joke around.

Boris held me close to his side. I saw pride and possessiveness when compliments were given to me.

I imagined the opening of a discotheque with colourful lights and loud, thumping music, not an elegant banquet. Waiters were handing out champagne and other drinks, and a string quartet played in the background.

The buffet was overflowing with the amount of food. There was also an auction that evening, with the proceeds going to a worthy cause. Now I knew why Boris had been so busy lately.

'Would you like to dance?' I heard right next to my ear. He took my glass and put it on the passing waiter's tray.

'Of course.' I was very serious. We could finally be alone for a while.

He led us to the dance floor. I was not a fan of ballroom dancing, but it seemed to be easy with Boris.

'Mom insisted that we learned to dance. Alex and I went to summer dance school when we were young. I hated it, but as you can see, it paid off.' He stared at my lips for a moment, with the intent on tasting them. He shook himself off when the song came to an end.

We continued dancing for two more songs. I felt like I was floating in his arms. Boris went to get us drinks, and I watched the dancing couples. Elegant men and even more dressed up women created a colourful mosaic on the dance floor.

'What is such a beautiful lady doing alone at a party?' I heard a voice right behind me. I turned abruptly, measuring the man with the sexy voice with my eyes.

'I'm Lucas.' He took my hand and kissed it lightly. He kept his gaze on me. A tailored suit framed his broad shoulders. I doubted that he could buy it in an ordinary store with such a body shape. Besides, the entrance price to today's banquet was staggering, which made me think that the suit was also exorbitantly expensive. He was most likely hiding a great body under all the layer of clothes. The man smiled wryly as if he had read my mind.

'You've met Sarah?' Boris handed me a glass, and Lucas reluctantly let go of my hand.

'We've just met, haven't we?' the smile on his face widened.

I took a sip of champagne to mask my confusion.

'He's a friend of mine. We went to the same school.'

'How are your parents?'

'They're great. They spend all their free time at the stables, which is just like old times.'

They both laughed.

'I heard that you were named sportsman of the year,' Boris asked.

'I scored some points for the team.' He flashed a smile again. 'It was a good season.'

'Lucas plays field hockey,' Boris explained quickly.

Now I understood why he had such an extraordinary figure. For the rest of the conversation, I listened to them both reminiscing about their childhood. Out of the corner of my eye, I watched the dancing couples. Lucas obviously noticed it.

'Can I ask Sarah to dance?' The question snapped me out of my reverie. It was directed at Boris, not at me.

'If she wants to. Just return her in one piece,' he joked.

'May I?' Lucas' eyes looked at me with great intensity. He stretched his hand towards me.

I was already feeling a little drunk. I had definitely drunk too much champagne. The man was taller than Boris, but he danced just as well.

'Have you been together long?' he asked, turning me around in the dance. I caught a glimpse of Boris standing at the end of the room. He was observing us.

'Not very long.' I gave an evasive answer. I didn't know how much I could reveal.

'He looks just like in the old days. He is smiling again. That's good.'

'I think so too.' I was about to ask him for some details, but I mistimed my step and wobbled. He grabbed me tighter and did a few faster spins, holding me tighter in his arms. As the song ended, he bowed in a gentlemanly manner. 'It was an honour,' he said, dragging the words out.

I liked him. He was funny and danced better than I did. I apologised to him and went to the bathroom. I could have used some help with my dress. It was beautiful but very impractical. I washed my hands and checked how my makeup looked. It was all intact. I would have to give my makeup artist a big hug. When I returned to the hall, my cheerful mood suddenly disappeared. Vivian was standing next to Boris. She looked like a star in her glittering dress. She had prepared well for this party. The worst part, however, was that she had her bony hand on my guy's chest. She was a bitch. How did she get in here? Maybe Boris had invited her? I didn't like the idea of having to talk to her again. As I got closer, I could tell that Boris was surprised by her presence too. He had said some nasty things to her earlier. I wouldn't want to be in her shoes. Too bad she was stubborn and didn't understand the first time, that it was over between them.

'Darling.' My voice was dripping with sweetness. I had never dared to address Boris like that before. This time I couldn't help myself, and I really wanted to show that he belonged to me and she had no right to him.

She took her hand off his chest, and she transferred all her rage to me.

'You bitch!' she began, "Do you think you can just take a guy from me and call him "darling"? She jabbed me in the arm with her finger.

I wanted to discuss the subject with her, but Boris shook his head. The people near us were watching the scene that had just taken place with open interest. The bitch was smiling mockingly, glaring at me angrily. It was only then that I noticed that she was wobbling slightly. She was drunk.

'Where are you staying? I'll order you a cab.' Boris was losing his patience.

'You're not getting me out of here!' She wobbled again and leaned back. 'You're not going to get rid of me like trash this time!'

'Don't be so dramatic. I can see you've had enough. Everyone's staring.'

'I don't care!'

Boris took a cell phone out of his pocket and put it to his ear. With his other hand, he grabbed me and pulled me so that I was standing right behind him. He effectively separated me from Vivian. He mumbled a few words into the phone, and after only a short while, two security guards appeared beside us.

'Make sure this lady gets to the hotel safely.' He turned to me as they led Vivian out of the room.

'You will regret this!' she shouted in our direction and disappeared from our sight.

'I didn't know she would be here,' he explained quickly. 'Sometimes, I think that she is mentally unstable. Did you see the way she looked at you?'

'Were you afraid for me?' I joked.

'Just for a moment. Darling, huh?' He grabbed the back of my neck and kissed me passionately.

We were interrupted by the auctioneer. It was time to start the next part of this evening. I must admit that there was no shortage of attractions. I noticed only at that moment that my hands were trembling. However, by the end of the auction, I calmed down enough to enjoy the evening all over again. We danced throughout the rest of the night. I fell asleep in the limousine. I didn't remember the journey back to the hotel. Boris helped me take off my dress and unpinned all the pins from my hair. His every touch was a foreshadowing of the pleasure he was about to give me that night.

* * *

We lounged in bed until noon. Unfortunately, Boris' duties called, so he went to look after his business, while I stayed at the hotel. I took a long bath. I got out of the tub only when my fingertips were all wrinkled. When I was a kid, my grandmother had warned me that I would dissolve like a sugar cube in coffee if I soaked for too long. And I believed it for a while until I learned the truth. The ingenuity of adults toward children is downright impressive.

I ordered lunch and called the hospital to ensure Grandma was doing okay. She didn't have a cell phone. She was an old-school woman. She claimed that a phone without a cord was unnecessary for her. I had a different opinion about that, but I couldn't convince her. The nurse assured me that my grandmother's condition was stable, and I didn't need to worry. I was happy to hear this news. I felt a little guilty for leaving her alone. I wanted to go into town for coffee and explore the area, but Boris returned faster than he predicted. He took me to a restaurant where they served delicious pork loin. We drank a whole bottle of wine to go with it and took another bottle back to the hotel. I felt happy and relaxed. We decided to walk back to the hotel. The crisp, cold air did us good. In a few days, we would return home. I was a little behind in my studies, which I wanted to catch up on when we got back.

Fireworks lit up the sky. Midnight struck, and with it came the New Year. I stood in the cold in the embrace of the man I loved. It was raining from the sky. I wouldn't give up this moment for anything in the world. Was this what happiness looked like? I gazed at his handsome face, and touched his warm cheek. He looked at me as if he knew what I wanted to say to him. My heart cried out, "I love you." But something was holding me back from saying it out loud. He kissed me in the pouring rain.

'Let's go back to the hotel.' He embraced me tighter, and I automatically felt warmer. I knew I would often think back to that evening. It was perfect.

The time together passed so quickly. Before I knew it, we were going back. In my mind, I made making a list of tasks I needed to do: laundry, shopping, don't forget the shampoo for my hair, call Sue, check on Grandma. - I pulled out my phone, writing down everything that came to mind in my notes. I felt Boris' warm gaze on me.

'Look at the road.' I reprimanded him.

He took one hand off the steering wheel and, looking ahead, put it between my legs. I slapped his hand. He laughed out loud. It was amazing how much energy this guy had. We practically didn't leave the bedroom for a week, and he still hadn't had enough.

'Hello, who's calling?' Boris said after pressing a button on the control panel.

'Haven't you fixed the speakerphone yet?' Mick sighed in disbelief.

'Lack of time. I've had my hands full.'

'I can imagine. Hi, Sarah. How did the surprise go?'

'Good, thanks. I've got to buy you a drink for that.'

'You know where to find me. I'm calling about something. Actually, I don't know how to say this, so I'll just say it straight out. Vivian trashed our office.'

'What do you mean she trashed it?' Boris was surprised.

'She came to me under the pretext that she wanted to talk, and suddenly she threw a chair. After a while, she threw everything that came her way. She was a real madwoman. She threatened to make you remember her. She said something about revenge. Dude, what did you do to her?'

'Honestly? I left her, but that's no reason to trash my office. She was at the opening. I kicked her out of the party. I could've guessed there'd be trouble with her. Show all the employees her picture and ban her from the club.'

'I already did that. I'll see you there. Sarah?'

'Yeah?'

'You owe me a drink.'

Boris disconnected the call.

'What are you going to do with her?' I wondered out loud.

'I don't know. She's crazy.'

We were almost to his apartment when the phone rang again.

'Hello?' Boris called.

I was convinced it was Mick who had forgotten to tell us something else.

'Can I speak to Mr. Smith, please?' A woman with a sonorous voice asked. 'On the phone.' He glanced at me nervously.

'Your wife had another seizure. She tried to kill herself. Please come as soon as possible. She's in critical condition.'

I didn't hear the rest of the conversation. I couldn't process anything except the word "wife". My whole world became a huge blur. I could see the panic in his eyes when the woman said that phrase. There was silence in the car. I was afraid to even breathe. He was married. That was all I could think about. He had a wife. He lied to me all this time. Tears rushed to my eyes. How could he, how could he do that to me? I crumpled my purse in my lap. I wanted to know and know nothing at the same time.

'You have a wife?' I asked in a broken voice, trying hard not to cry.

He clenched his hands on the steering wheel until his knuckles turned white. He stopped at the bus stop.

'Get out,' he demanded firmly. 'You can take a cab home.'

We were already close to my apartment. He took out some banknotes and pressed them into my hand. I looked at the money. Was that all I was to him? A paid whore? A thing? Someone he could pay for and send away when he got bored?

'Get out,' he said again.

'Is that all you have to say to me?' I was still able to manage a whisper. My whole world collapsed. Everything I had ever dreamed of was in ruins.

'I said, fuck off!' He lowered his head resignedly.

It was the first time someone had said that to me: the first and the last. I sat still for a moment, unable to move. Nevertheless, my hand went to the handle, and I opened the door. I got out without saying anything. I threw the money I was clutching in my hand to the passenger seat and slammed the door. He took off with a screech of tires, and I stayed at the stoplight. He drove off with my luggage and my heart.

Tears streamed down my cheeks. The salty drops smeared my makeup. No one at the bus stop approached me. Only one solution came to my mind. I took out my phone and called my best friend. The conversation was short and precise. A fundamental question was raised about where I was. Then I heard a noise, probably him putting on his shoes.

'Take the crowbar,' I cried into the receiver.

'A crowbar?' He was surprised. 'I don't have a crowbar.'

'We have to break down the door,' I decided seriously. There were no unnecessary questions—just specifics.

'We will break the lock. Stay where you are. I'll be there in a minute. Take care of yourself.'

He arrived very quickly. He opened the door, and I got into the car. I curled up on the seat. He was looking for external injuries on me. He breathed a sigh of relief when he found nothing like that.

'Where are we going?'

'To Boris's apartment.' I gave him the address, and he pasted it into the GPS navigation. I pulled out a pack of tissues, wiping away my smeared mascara. Curiosity was eating him up, but he didn't ask. He waited patiently. I was grateful because I didn't want to talk about it. We drove in silence. I was afraid that I would break down entirely as soon as I mentioned Boris's name. For now, shock and disbelief, and consequently adrenaline, pushed me to action. My hands were shaking from the overwhelming emotions.

Alan took the bag with the drill from the trunk and followed me to Boris's apartment. He kept saying under his breath that this was not a good idea. I opened the door with the keys Boris had given me earlier. I was happy and madly in love then.

'Here.' I pointed to the door. 'It's always locked. I need to know what's on the other side. You go ahead, and I'll pack my things.'

'I'll help you,' offered my friend. Perhaps he thought I would change my mind. Perhaps he wanted to keep an eye on me. Perhaps he was afraid I would get hysterical. So far, I had only mentioned Boris's wife to him. That much information was enough for him to grasp the situation. I didn't bother arranging my clothes. I threw everything inside my suitcase and closed it. I undid my bracelet and put it on the bedside table along with my keys. I would not allow myself to be treated this way. I took one more look at the glittering stones and left the room.

I fetched the extension cord. I remembered it lying in the cabinet with the vacuum cleaner. We plugged in the drill.

'Are you sure?'

'Absolutely. Drill.'

Before Alan could get close to the lock, the drill stopped working. I looked at him in disbelief. Was it broken? I wanted to check that everything was okay with the cable. I looked towards the contact and jumped up with surprise.

'What are you guys doing?' Alex was standing with the cable in his hand.

'None of your business,' I snapped back. 'What are you doing here?' I snatched the cable from him and plugged it back in.

Alex passed me and opened the door with a key. He had the key! He knew everything and had the key.

'Traitor.' My rage increased even more.

'There you go. Now you can go in without breaking down the door.' He stepped back. He gave me a choice. I could opt out.

I quickly opened the door. Cartons and boxes took up most of the room, and each one was signed. Shoes, purses, clothes, cosmetics, others. I went deeper into the room. In the corner stood a dusty guitar case. Dust floated everywhere, and cobwebs hung on the wall. Apparently, the room hadn't been cleaned in a long time. It was hard to believe since the rest of the house was perfectly clean.

I walked over to the first box labelled "clothes." I found summer dresses for a slim woman. In the next one, women's purses. In the "other" box were packed documents and photos. I opened the album. A smiling blonde girl with a guitar in her hand was looking at me. In the next picture was the same girl in a baggy sweater. A few pages later, a picture of Boris. He was smiling. He looked so carefree and happy. Another photo of him embracing a blonde girl and whispering something in her ear. It broke my heart once again. I slammed the album shut. I couldn't look at it. I also found frames in the same box. They fit perfectly on the fireplace. In each picture, he was embracing his wife. My hands began to shake even more. I dropped the frame. The glass cracked and scattered on the floor. I wanted to pick it up, but someone's arms lifted me to a standing position.

I was shaking all over. Alex wanted to hug me. I pushed him away.

'You knew and said nothing!' Anger was better than despair. I jumped at him. I pounded him with my fists, and he didn't defend himself. Alan grabbed me and pulled me away from him.

'I wanted to, but he's my brother. What was I supposed to tell you? Don't get involved, he's got a wife?'

'That's right! You should have warned me!'

'I tried, but you wouldn't listen.'

'Who is she?'

'Her name is Natalie. Right now, she's lying unconscious in the hospital. She tried to kill herself again, and Boris sent me to get her health records.'

At the mere sound of the name of the man I love, my tears flowed again. I realised that everything I had, everything I thought I had, was an illusion. I screwed myself into thinking there was a future for us. I was looking for an opportunity for us, when I was doomed to fail from the start. I didn't miss the fact that he said: "once again". This wasn't the first suicide attempt?

'Does...' I hesitated, '...Does he love her?'

'I don't know.' Desperately, Alex ran his hand through his hair. 'It seemed to me that she was everything to him.'

I turned to Alan and hid my face in his chest.

'Then he met you. I think you're important to him. The way he acts around you. He looks happy again. I'm jealous. He's managed to meet another wonderful woman. Sarah, I care about you. Even now. After all this time. Don't cut me out. Even if I can only be a friend.'

'Come on. Let's go. I want to go home. The keys are on the bedside table. I took my things.'

Alan took my suitcase. I wanted to show how strong I was, even if I was falling apart inside. Even though I felt defeated, I straightened up and quickly left the apartment.

* * *

As time passed, the adrenaline high subsided, and anger gave way to disbelief. Then, came the despair. Amy had brought my suitcase. The fucking coward had left it at the residence. He didn't have the courage to face me. He preferred to use Amy. I didn't like her sympathetic gaze. Maybe my hair was greasy, and I didn't smell very nice, but that was no reason to treat me like a child.

'When are your exams?' She dragged my suitcase into the bedroom.

'Soon.' I watched as she unpacked my things.

'Get a grip of yourself. He's just a guy. There's going to be another one. College is your future. He's your past.'

'Don't say that!' I fell apart again for good.

Amy put her arms around me and hugged me.

'You'll be fine. You'll see.' She pushed me back an arm's length. 'Girl, you need to take a bath. Now! You stink.'

'I don't want to!' I tried to protest.

Amy filled the tub and forcefully put me in it. Then I heard her fierce discussion in the kitchen. She was explaining something to Alan. I couldn't hear her words, just muffled sounds.

I closed my eyes. I tried to focus on the sensations caused by the warm water on my skin, on the smell of the bath foam. I tried to clear my mind. Unfortunately, it was impossible. The whole time, I had Boris' face in front of my eyes.

Finally dressed, I looked almost like myself again. On the outside, everything matched. Only my eyes were sad and dim.

Amy took me out to dinner. The fresh air did me some good. I was getting hungry, which was a good sign because I found it difficult to eat lately. Every day I felt a little better. In the beginning, I cried for days. Over my naivety, over my lost heart, over my failure. I was almost functioning normally during the day. The nights were the worst, where I would think of our moments together. His smile. The touch of his lips. The jokes. Then I remembered how he treated me in the car, and tears ran down my cheeks.

A week later, Boris called. I really wasn't ready to talk. I was sitting on the bed. Books were lying open everywhere. I didn't move. I didn't answer the call. I just stared at the display until the phone stopped ringing. I really wanted to hear his voice. Unfortunately, he couldn't tell me anything new. I couldn't forgive him.

Instead, I had a long, cleansing conversation with Sue. Once again, I was amazed by her life wisdom. She gave me time to decide what I wanted to do next. We agreed that the contract had expired, and she offered me another job. I could still help Niko behind the bar. I could also dance. Lately, I had been putting on more and more music and dancing until I was out of breath. It was a kind of therapy. All that mattered was the music and nothing else.

I spent a lot of time with my grandmother in the hospital. Her condition had worsened again; she was breathing with difficulty, barely catching air. She no longer took off her oxygen mask. I usually told her about the events of the previous day. I laughed a lot. Only in private did I allow myself to despair. I also went back to the residence to help at the bar. I thought I saw Boris out of the corner of my eye at the entrance several times. When I turned around, he was gone. After one of those evenings, I received a beautiful bouquet of red roses through the flower mail. The note only had one word written on it: "Sorry." I hugged the flowers, the thorns hurting my arms. I fell to my knees and cried. Alan found me in this position. He made me some tea, laid me down on the sofa, and took the flowers out of my sight. I fell asleep. In the meantime, he called for Amy. She was sitting right in front of me when I woke up. One thing I could say for sure - I had great friends.

I was surprised when Sue offered me a performance. At the same time, I was excited. She knew I was working on a new dance routine. I agreed right away. I could rub Olivia's nose in it, prove that I wasn't bad. Lately, she'd been successfully avoiding me, and she'd stopped being mean to me. She was too busy harassing the new girl. I was beginning to understand that this was a sort of test. Sometimes I would catch her worried look. That scared me more than her aversion. I knew how to deal with aversion, but pity; not so much.

I put on my stage outfit: black shorts and a one--shoulder shirt of the same colour. The last time I danced on this stage was for Boris. I shook off the unwanted memories. I glanced at myself in the mirror. On my feet, I had black stiletto heels and cabarets. I was ready. I went out onto the stage, and focused on the task to be performed. I heard the first notes of the song *Earned It*. Subconsciously I was looking for Boris with my eyes. I admonished myself for my stupidity. As the lights illuminated my silhouette, I was unable to see who was sitting in the audience. I put all my emotions, all my longing into that performance. I was rewarded with loud applause. In the dressing room, I was hugged by Amy.

'That was amazing! And that spin.' She demonstrated one of my steps, 'Perfect! It's obvious that you've been practising a lot.'

'Dancing makes me forget about my problems.'

'Ladies, can I ask you to step out for five minutes?'

I heard Boris' voice. He was here, standing in front of me. So many times, I imagined our meeting. Now, my mind was blank. The door behind him closed. I knew that I should avoid him and leave. Part of me, the masochistic part, wanted to stay. He was standing with his hands stuck in his pants pockets. It was as if he was afraid that he would unintentionally touch me. He looked around hesitantly, also wondering what to say. His face had lost its healthy colour. He looked tired and sad. Even his hair was in disarray.

'Did you get the flowers?'

'Why did you send them to me?'

'I wanted to apologise.'

'So do it.' I crossed my arms over my chest. I wasn't going to make things easy for him.

'Listen to me.' He walked up to me. He raised one hand with the intention of touching my cheek, but frowned. He shoved his hand deep into his pocket again.

'I didn't mean to hurt you. I'm sorry. I didn't mean to give you hope for something more.'

'Get out of here!' I demanded. That wasn't an apology. He wanted to mess with my head again.

'Understand…' He took my face in both hands. 'I don't want to hurt you. You're important to me.'

He pressed his forehead to my forehead, and I foolishly let him. I also let him kiss away the tears that ran down my cheek. I wanted one last time to feel the way I used to. One last time to feel wanted before I closed this part of my life forever. Very slowly, gently, he kissed me. It was just a touch as if he was asking for permission. I kissed him more intensely, despite the voice in the back of my head that told me I would regret it.

'Go away…' I whispered into his mouth. '…Go away and never come back. I'm done with you. Let me live a normal life and stay away from me. You lied to me, and I can't forgive you for that. Go away.'

'Is that what you want?' he asked with uncertainty.

'Is that what I want? Are you serious? What more have you got to offer me?'

'Not much…' He looked defeated.

'So come back when you can give me everything! As long as it's something you want to come back to. For now, I don't want to see you. And don't send me flowers. Just leave me alone.' I was surprised at how strong and confident my voice sounded.

He left, once again shattering my heart into little pieces.

Boris

People say that hope dies last. Is it true? I had lived, hoping for the past three years when I would visit her regularly at the hospital. At first, I was here every day. I sat by her bedside for days. I waited full of hope that this was the day she would wake up. I was sure that if I talked to her, read her books, told her what had happened in my life, she would come back to me. She would just open her eyes. That we would be able to be together again. That was the first stage of my journey. The second was anger, increasing gradually. It grew in me with each passing day. It was germinating, turning into rage. Oh, how angry I was at her! For what she had done to us. For what I hadn't done in time. I loved her so much. Maybe I told her that too rarely? Perhaps I didn't show it clearly enough? I probably did.

Natalie ended up at the residence by accident. A friend told her about the place when she needed a roof over her head. A scumbag that she called her father beat her, but she wouldn't tell me anything more. I tried so many times to talk to her. She refused to report it to the police.

She ran away from him and hid while the scumbag lived with impunity.

The first time I saw her, it was summer. I remember exactly what she was wearing. The white dress moved gently in the wind. She looked like an angel with her shiny blonde hair. I stood and stared at her, struck by her beauty. She looked sweet and innocent, and I liked to think of her that way. Of course, those were only appearances. The very fact that she was staying at the residence suggested the opposite.

My father ran the whole business, and he wanted to pass it on to me for several important reasons. The most important of these was the distance from home. He and my mother lived far away, and he was weary of the constant travel.

I visited the residence more and more often. I also saw Natalie on many occasions. I liked her, and she liked me too. She looked for the slightest excuse to talk to me. That's how the feelings between us were born. I told her about them. She moved in with me. I didn't want her to see the girls from the residence. She was going to start a new life just with me. And that's exactly what happened. At first, it was perfect. But as time passed, she began to fade before my eyes. She kept saying that she wasn't good enough for me. I knew her past. I couldn't say I wasn't jealous of all those men before me. The past couldn't be changed. I explained that to her. I begged her to let go of it. She grew sadder and sadder. She closed herself off. She became consumed by her past. She wouldn't let me talk her into seeing a specialist. Instead, she secretly took tranquilisers. She wouldn't admit it. I asked. I begged. She said over and over again that our relationship was a mistake. Then, she overdosed. Time stopped. My life had ground to a halt. I would do anything to turn back time. She was unconscious for several weeks. Fortunately, the doctors revived her. They said her body needed rest and recovery. I sat in the hospital all day. The nurses would drive me home to get some rest. My parents were very worried about me. They knew I had a girlfriend, but they didn't know anything about us getting married. She didn't want to tell anyone. The ceremony was modest. Just us and the witnesses. Alex was my witness. He knew the whole story and always supported me.

Then came the surrender. I was afraid to admit that I was losing hope for a happy ending. Despite this, I visited as often as I could. My parents were worried about me. I walked like a corpse for the first year. I had lost my old self. I started pretending in their presence. Sometimes it worked, sometimes it didn't. Most importantly, they no longer looked at me with pity. In solitude, I could return to my suffering. Alcohol helped, although I knew that getting drunk was not the right thing to do. I didn't want to have anything to do with the residence. Sue took over the running of the business. She had always helped my father. She turned out to be doing a great job. As time went on, Alex started helping her out.

I couldn't sleep at night, so I started running the club. I was also on sleeping pills. They worked, but I felt dull after taking them. In the meantime, I was dating Vivian. It wasn't a relationship but more like an attempt to satisfy a temporary sexual need. I was selfish. No hearts or flowers or chocolates. I always made myself clear. I never lied to her. We dated for company and for sex. I didn't stay the night; I didn't invite her to my apartment. I shared that place with Natalie. I didn't want to invite another woman there. After Natalie woke up, she was quiet, absent. She didn't talk much. She avoided my gaze. She quickly became hysterical. Then she was put back on strong medication that sedated her. She didn't want to come home with me. I asked her, begged her, but she would shut down even more. She wouldn't talk to me or answer my questions, so I stopped insisting. Days passed, months, as I waited for a breakthrough. I waited for her to come back. I waited for the old Natalie.

Then my life turned around. After the first night with Sarah, I fell asleep like a baby. I couldn't tell if it was because of her. Perhaps it was the explosive mix of whiskey and this woman. I longed to have her. I wanted peace. I was a selfish bastard. My head was buzzing with thoughts.

I sat in the hospital for another 24 hours. This was Natalie's second suicide attempt. The monitor showed her heart beating evenly. The only proof that she was alive. The staggering amount of equipment that monitored her vitals terrified me. Natalie lay between these devices, fragile and almost translucent. I felt like a traitor. I was leading a double life. One in which I waited for my wife to return, and out the other there; outside the hospital. Now, even that had been taken from me. I was losing those I cared about. I sent a huge bouquet of roses to Sarah with only one word, "sorry". That was all I could give her—an apology.

Sarah

Alan rushed into my room and turned off the music.

'I can't stand this anymore, please change the song.'

'Don't you like Million Reasons?' I looked at him, puzzled.

'I love Lady Gaga's songs. You know that. But you've been pounding it since this morning. I'm sick of it. Why don't you take a walk? You've been sitting at home all day.'

'I'm studying.'

'I doubt it.' He looked at me like a wayward little child. 'You have fifteen minutes, or I'll kick you out the door just as you are.'

I assessed whether or not he was serious. He looked very serious. I checked my phone one more time and texted Mick back about how I was feeling. I immediately got a return message. He wanted to meet up. I agreed to meet up with him at a nearby cafeteria. On my way out, I stuck my tongue out to Alan and ran quickly down the stairs in case he chased me.

A strong wind was blowing, tangling my hair even more than usual. I wrapped myself more tightly in my coat and sped up my stride. I looked everywhere in the cafeteria, but I was the first one there. I ordered a coffee and sat down at a table.

'Hello, beautiful,' Mick greeted me as usual. 'Do you want another coffee?' He looked at my cup.

'No, thanks.'

I saw the waitress smiling at him. I shouldn't have been surprised. He was a handsome man. Several women glanced in his direction as he headed for my table.

He took off his coat and hung it over a chair. He sat down across from me.

'I wanted to know how you were feeling.'

'As you can see. I'm doing okay.' I wasn't going to show how much pain I was in. He'd probably repeat everything to Boris. I wasn't going to give him the satisfaction, even though it was tough for me. I smiled charmingly.

He watched me for a while.

'I'm glad about that. Boris, on the other hand, is not doing so well. He's drinking more than usual.'

I focused my gaze on the coffee. He had hardly drunk anything.

'You want to make me feel guilty?' I looked at him.

'No. I'm just saying he's not coping with your breakup.'

'He's the one who has a wife!' I said it a little too loud. Several people looked in our direction, curious about my outburst.

'I know he has a wife, but their relationship is practically non-existent. That's what he told me. It's obvious that he is in pain. Look,' he hesitated, 'I didn't know he had a wife. He never mentioned her before, and I've known him a long time. I have witnessed his mood swings, sometimes he was depressed, but the wife? Who would have guessed?'

'I don't want to hear about it. He fooled me, not the other way around. Correction, he cheated on his wife, and he betrayed me. Can we talk about something else?' My attitude screamed that I wanted to change the subject. 'How's work?' I said without thinking. They work together. He'll start talking about Boris again. But no. Mick was considerate enough to leave out things about Boris. It turned out that Vivian had been questioned by the police. She was the one behind the previous destruction of the bar. She did it all out of jealousy. I felt sorry for her. She hadn't achieved anything, and now she was in trouble with the law. She got a hefty fine and was banned from entering or even going near the club.

Once we finished talking about Boris' complex issue, he started asking me about college. I told him what my plans were after graduation. There was a lab near the university, and I wanted to get a job there. Thanks to my high average, I had a good chance. I hadn't noticed how quickly the time passed. He walked me to my house.

'Call me if you need anything.'

'Yeah, sure. Thank you.' I walked away, and he walked toward his car. I thought fate was very capricious. If

I hadn't chickened out at the beginning with Mick, things might have turned out very differently.

Amy called me every day. I knew she was worried about me. Niko walked around me on eggshells too. They were all acting crazy. After all, I was fine. I was just heartbroken. I wasn't going to die of it. It will pass - I told myself every day. One day, I would stop checking my phone every now and again. Despite being adamant that I didn't want to have anything to do with Boris, I kept looking out for him. Sometimes I behaved like a masochist, or maybe I was just hopelessly in love?

Another month passed, and I tried to live my life as before. I spent every spare moment with my nose in my books.

Sometimes I saw Alex. I was kind to him, but I hadn't forgiven him for withholding the truth. He saw me at the residence one day and shoved his phone into my hand.

'Mum wants to speak to you,' he said briefly.

I didn't feel like talking, but Elizabeth was always kind to me. I thought I owed it to her.

'Hello?' I said into the receiver.

'Sarah, it's good to hear from you. Thank you for agreeing to talk.'

I had been put on the spot, but I kept that thought to myself.

'It's nice to hear from you,' I said.

'It's so good to hear your voice. I'm worried about you. I just wanted to tell you that we didn't know Boris had a wife.' I suspected she didn't use her name on purpose.

'How is that possible?' I interrupted her.

'He had always been secretive. From an early age, he disapproved of the operation of the residence. He was an idealist. He didn't tell us. We weren't even invited to the ceremony. Everything was done quietly. He never officially introduced her. When I saw you two together; I was rooting for you very much. Please don't be mad at us.'

'I'm not.' I couldn't stay mad at them.

'Thank you.' There was silence on the phone. 'If you need anything, Alex will give you my number. Please don't hesitate to call. Boris is my son, but it doesn't mean I'm always on his side. And talking to a woman sometimes helps.'

'I'll keep that in mind.'

'I hope to hear from you.' She hung up.

I got back to Alex and handed the phone back to him. During the conversation, I moved away from him. He didn't need to hear what we were talking about.

'I already sent you Mom's number.'

'Thanks.'

I walked away, leaving him standing in the middle of the hall.

In the evening, I noticed Boris' silhouette in the entrance again. I tried to concentrate on my work, but I couldn't, knowing he was so close. Moreover, at the end of the evening, he brazenly sat down in the lobby and ordered a whisky. He wanted to annoy me, so I tried to ignore him. I felt his gaze on me every time I glanced in his direction. To top it off, we had an extremely annoying customer today. Money and alcohol triggered the worst instincts in men. The combination made some of them feel capable of anything. I collected the empty glasses from the tables, once again purposefully skipping Boris' table. He already had five empty whisky glasses in front of him. I was walking across the room with the tray when the guy who had already paid me vulgar compliments pulled me by my elbow, making me land in his lap. The tray rolled toward the bar, and two glasses fell to the floor.

'Give me a kiss, sweetheart.' He kissed my bare shoulder with his lips. He smelled of expensive cologne mixed with the stench of alcohol. Pushy customers were usually put in a cab and driven home. I didn't have time to react when I felt strong arms around my waist. I stood up onto my feet. Then, I watched everything with panic in my eyes. Boris jerked the drunk guy and punched him centrally in the nose. Blood started pouring down the poor guy's shirt. He was harmless in reality. He was a regular customer. He often got drunk and grabbed girls by the ass, but he left large tips. Boris tried to take another swing, but Niko held him back.

'Dude, come on.' He tried to pull him away.

He broke free and punched the customer a second time until he landed on the ground.

'Boris! Get off him!' I yelled, as he struggled with Niko.

There was quite a stir, but he heard me and looked at me reproachfully. As if I was to blame for this. He walked towards me. He looked mad. The clenched fists at his sides did not promise anything good. What had I done? He grabbed my arm and pulled me towards the exit. I turned around, to see Amy applying tissues to the nose of the poor guy he'd beaten. My heels tapped on the floor as I tried to keep up with his quick stride. He dragged me into the conference room. Immediately, images and memories came flooding back. He closed the door from the inside and put the key in his pocket. Leaning against the wall, I was unable to catch my breath. Or escape.

'You didn't have to beat him up.'

'I did.'

'What do you want?'

He put his hands on either side of my head. We were only a short distance apart. I could smell his whiskey--scented breath.

'I want you.' Then, he threw himself at me.

It crossed my mind that this was wrong. His touch was effectively taking away the remnants of sanity. My pulse quickened. I clenched my thighs tighter. I didn't want to yearn for him, but my traitorous body was begging for his touch.

'You look so sexy in that miniskirt,' he whispered into my neck. I felt his warm breath, and I was lost. He lifted me up, pressing me further into the wall. I squealed in surprise, which only fuelled his action. He held me up, firmly. He pulled down my panties with one single pull, while he kissed me without restraint. I wrapped my legs around him. When he entered me, a moan of pleasure escaped my lips. It was wrong, primal, fast…and wonderful at the same time. Never before had I felt so filled and lost at the same time. My involuntary moans brought him to a quick orgasm. I came right after him, feeling his cum inside me. He rested his forehead against mine.

'Don't leave me.' He said it with such regret, that I wanted to listen to him.

'Boris, you can't do this. Put me down!' I demanded. My sanity had returned.

He hesitated for a moment but finally pressed the key into my hand. I ran out of there like the devil himself was chasing me. I waved at Amy, who measured my appearance with a silent question on her lips.

'I'm going home.'

'Okay. I'll say you felt unwell.'

'Thank you. You're wonderful.'

'And you're stupid.' Her words rang in my ears for a long time. She was one hundred per cent right. I was a moron.

After that incident, I became even more shattered. I heard that Natalie's condition had improved, and she was slowly recovering. When I thought of her, I thought of the pictures in her photo album. Her bright hair, her carefree smile and her guitar. I also heard that Boris was out of town for a while. I didn't have to worry about running into him at the residence. I hadn't seen him after our last meeting. Maybe he made his choice and finally left me alone? I was happy about that, but on the other, I wished with all my heart that he would have chosen me.

I felt sorry for myself once again. Amy and Alan decided that they would take me to the disco. My sceptical attitude didn't dampen their enthusiasm. They ignored my lack of interest for their plan. After two drinks, the idea of going out seemed pretty good to me. After another two, some of my problems disappeared. I was having more fun than I cared to admit. Amy had chosen a newly opened club for us. She did her best to make sure I didn't associate the outing with Boris. I, on the other hand, subconsciously compared this venue to his.

I got home in the morning, and if I had known beforehand what was ahead of me, I would not have put a single drop of alcohol in my mouth. Still not completely sober, I answered the phone. Amy was asleep in my bed. I remembered that she had been so drunk that she had fallen asleep before me.

I heard the worst news of my entire life. My world stopped for several long moments. My eyes went dark. My lungs ran out of air. The phone slipped out of my hand and fell to the floor. I could still hear the voice coming from the phone lying on the carpet. Amy woke up and, seeing me drenched in tears, hugged me straight away.

'Sarah? What the hell happened? What did that asshole do again?'

I wiped my nose, trying to swallow a torrent of tears. The words wouldn't come out of my mouth; it seemed like the longer I didn't say them out loud, the longer they wouldn't be real.

'Talk to me!' Amy shook me. Her concerned face was in front of me.

'My grandmother died.' I burst into tears once again until I got the hiccups.

Amy held me in her arms. She didn't try to calm me down. She just let me cry. Apparently, she knew that the pain of losing a loved one could not be soothed. They say time heals all wounds. At that moment, I felt my heart shatter into tiny pieces. Everything that had happened to me recently felt like a wound that was never going to heal. Alan pressed sedatives into my hand. They allowed me to sleep for several hours.

I dreamt that I was a child again. I didn't know how old I was. In any case, I was small.

'Are you going to eat your soup?' my grandmother asked me. She was standing by the stove in my family home with a plate in her hand. She was much younger, and her hair was a soft shade of brown. The warmth of her gaze shifted to the person behind me. I followed her gaze.

'Mom?' I pushed back my chair, almost knocking it over. I hugged her with all my strength. I barely reached her waist. How old could I have been? They died after my sixth birthday, so I assumed about five.

'Honey, what happened?' Mom was worried.

'I love you,' I said quickly. I had to tell her how much I missed her. I inhaled heavily, revelling in her scent. I wanted to remember as many details as possible.

'Where is my princess? Ready for a bike ride?' Dad was even more handsome than in the pictures. He looked at Mom and locked us in a strong hug.

'Don't leave me!' I asked pathetically.

'We will always be with you,' said grandma.

I woke up abruptly, gasping for air. I brushed wet strands of hair from my forehead. For a moment, I wondered how the dream could have been so realistic.

For the next few days, Amy was constantly with me. She helped me with all the paperwork and made decisions for me when I was short of strength. I refused to take the tranquilisers. I was sure I needed to cry to end this phase of my life, and come to terms with the loss of my only family.

Pale and completely without makeup, I dressed in black. At the funeral ceremony, I stood stiffly with my eyes fixed on the floor. I could not bear to look at the coffin standing in the middle of the altar. Nor could I stand the sympathetic gaze of the people gathered. To my surprise, quite a few people came. I saw neighbours from the neighbourhood where I lived with my grandmother, nurses from the facility where she was staying. The girls from the residence occupied the last rows in the pews. Elizabeth also showed up. She surprised me because she didn't know my grandmother personally. Right next to her stood Alex and Boris. I could feel his gaze on my back.

The priest spoke beautifully about eternal happiness in paradise. I wanted very much to believe that this was where my grandmother had ended up. After the ceremony, those gathered expressed their condolences to me. I tried not to cry as more people came up to me to offer encouragement. I was tired and wanted the day to be over. Amy and Alan bravely stood by me throughout the day. Finally, Elizabeth came up to me and hugged me tightly. I felt her warmth and the soft scent of her perfume. Once again, she assured me that I could call her at any time. She would always make time for me. Boris was the last to offer me his condolences. We both felt uncomfortable in this situation.

'I'm so sorry.' I heard the same words again. He may have wanted to add something else, but Amy pulled me firmly toward the car. I gave her a look that made her raise her eyebrow slightly. I didn't want to cry anymore, and Boris could only cause me more suffering.

I ended up with a handful of friends at a pub, where they served alcohol in the morning. I wanted to get drunk. I needed it. Amy placed the first shot in front of me. I cringed, my throat was burning, but then it went down somehow—one after another. Before the place closed, I got a message from Mick. Amy snatched my phone and sent him a message.

'You know you shouldn't do that, right?' I said in a bit of a gibberish tone.

'Someone has to drive you home. You can't count on Alan.'

In fact, he was sitting immersed in a conversation with Niko, and there was no indication that he would be coming home any time soon.

'I'll take a cab.' My sober thinking has returned.

'Someone should keep an eye on you. I'm leaving in the morning, and I still have a gigantic hangover ahead of me. But what's not to be done for friends? You can thank me later.' We had one last shot.

'Come on, princess. It's time to go home.' I heard Mick behind me.

'Go, sweetie.' Amy shoved her purse into my hand. I took my coat, and took unsteady steps out into the cold air. I realised; I didn't want to go home.

'Do you have a cigarette?' I mumbled.

'You smoke?'

'No.' I shook my head awkwardly and almost lost my balance.

Mick caught me firmly before I fell. He looked into my eyes, then at my lips. He swallowed hard on his saliva. 'Get in the car,' he said. He unlocked the vehicle door right behind me.

'I don't want to go home. I don't want to be alone,' I added, with a defeated look in my eyes.

'I thought you've had enough and wanted to go back. It's been a long day.'

I held on tighter to his jacket.

'Let's go to your place.' I decided.

'That is not a good idea.' His gaze rested on my hands clinging to his jacket and then moved to my lips.

'You wanted me to buy you a drink. Here's your chance.'

'That's not exactly what I meant.'

'No?' I was surprised.

'You've had enough alcohol for today,' he said in a serious tone and then added, 'Get in.' He opened the door, and I climbed into the front seat.

He was silent the whole way. He was probably fighting some kind of internal battle. I didn't care about anything that night.

He made me herbal tea at his house and wouldn't tell me where he kept the alcohol for anything in the world. All this time, he looked at me with a impenetrable gaze.

'You should go to bed. It's almost dawn.'

I got up unsteadily. I was about to raise my objection, but I trembled again. Mick grabbed me awkwardly by the elbow and held me in place. I looked meaningfully at his lips. I hadn't planned this. All I felt was that I needed to free myself from Boris' charm to move on. I pressed my lips to his mouth, surprising him with it. I put my arms around his neck and deepened the kiss. He was careful, gentle. So different to the kiss with Boris. His kiss was like a hurricane, leaving ashes and ruins in its wake. It burned me from the inside out and left me breathless. The kiss with Mick felt more like a gentle caress. It was as if he was afraid of hurting me. It started unexpectedly and ended just as abruptly. I protested with a quiet moan.

'Sarah, this isn't right. You're drunk. You'll regret it tomorrow. It's been a hard day. I will prepare a sofa for you to sleep on.' His saddened face was already telling me that he felt guilty. Maybe he was right. I turned around, marching directly to his bedroom. At least that's where I thought the bedroom was. He followed me.

'Or I'll go prepare the sofa for myself. Make yourself comfortable,' he added resignedly.

'Sleep with me,' I asked. 'I don't want to be alone.'

'I will stay until you fall asleep. I don't want you to regret your decision.' He took my hand and kissed the inside of it. 'If you change your mind tomorrow, we will think about it later. I'll leave you a towel and a new toothbrush on the sink.'

I felt pushed away and hurt, but at the same time, I was grateful that at least one of us was thinking soberly.

Boris

I stood on the sidewalk, watching Sarah getting into the car with Amy. I felt like I should be there for her. Not to leave her alone in a situation like this. She probably expected me to be supportive. Instead, I stood there like a peg, watching her drive away. I didn't tell her how I really felt, how sorry I was.

'Shall we get something to eat?' Mom looked at me suspiciously.

'I'm not hungry. I'm sorry.' I could see the disappointment in her eyes. My words must have hurt her. 'Are you going home tonight? Do you want keys to the apartment? Are you staying for long?' I was trying to get some enthusiasm out of myself. I knew very well that she wouldn't stay more than half a day. She didn't like this city. Or perhaps, she didn't want to run into Sue. Even at mass, they sat far apart. Their relationship has been a mystery to me to this day. They were sisters who wouldn't speak to each other unless it was absolutely necessary. They usually avoided each other or did everything possible to avoid being in the same room together.

One time, I decided to ask my mother about this. She brushed me off, gave no definite answer. Sue did the same. Even though she was my aunt, I had always called her by her first name.

'I don't want to bother you.' She stressed the last word bluntly. 'Alex will take me in for the night.' She smiled softly. She brushed the dust off my jacket.

'Promise me something. Don't drink too much. Again. I don't want to worry.'

'You don't have to.' I kissed her on the cheek and walked away to my Audi. Even the car reminded me of Sarah. It must have been an obsession because I could still smell her inside the car. I pulled up to a nearby store. I bought whiskey and car air freshener, the strongest they had. I needed to get rid of the smell that constantly reminded me of her. I drove around the neighbourhood aimlessly. The mundane activities helped clear my mind. I regained consciousness in front of the hospital where Natalie was staying. I sighed heavily. Seemingly, my subconscious had led me here. Since she had woken up after her last suicide attempt, it had been even more challenging to interact with her. She ate little, spoke little. I went into her room. Although it was a hospital, it looked more like a hotel. I paid a lot for it. I stopped at the doorway. Dressed in pyjamas and a bathrobe, she sat on the bed, reading a newspaper. She was quite underweight, but her face had taken on a rosy colour.

'Hey.' I walked up to her and kissed her forehead as I always did. I did this every time to say hello and goodbye. After her first suicide attempt, she told me not to kiss her on the mouth. At that time, I would have agreed to anything as long as she was happy. It had stayed that way. She put down the paper and looked at me cautiously.

'Coffee?' I went over to the kitchenette to keep my hands busy. I wasn't in the mood for coffee at all, definitely more in the mood for whisky.

'No, thank you.' There was a moment of silence. 'How is she feeling?'

The spoon fell out of my hand and bounced on the kitchen counter. I looked at her in surprise.

'Yes. I know you found someone.'

'Since when?' I mouthed.

'Since the beginning. I may be sick, but I'm not stupid. Besides, I've often smelled a women's perfume on you. You can't hide.'

'She…'

'I know everything. I pressed Alex. He told me about everything. He brought me my guitar.'

The fact that she wanted to play the guitar was a huge step forward. She hadn't touched it in the last two years. I glanced at the case standing in the corner. Why now?

'What is she like?' I heard another question.

'You said Alex told you about her.'

'I'd like to hear it from you.'

I decided to make myself some coffee. I poured hot water into the mug. Natalie waited patiently for me to start talking. I didn't know how to begin. She deserved honesty. I walked over to the window with my mug. The words began to flow from me on their own. I still stood with my back to her. I was too much of a coward to tell her the truth face-to-face.

'I met her by accident. She came with Alex for our parents' wedding anniversary. They pretended she was his girlfriend. I knew from the beginning there would be trouble with her. She was looking for a one-night stand, and it happened to be me. Then, I found out she was working at the residence and needed money for her grandmother's medical treatment.'

I paused for a moment as I heard Natalie suck in a loud breath. Clearly, Alex had given her a very truncated version.

'Should I go on, or is that enough?' I looked at her shocked face.

'Keep talking,' she urged me.

'I got myself an exclusive contract. And I became more and more attached to her. Then she found out about you. I treated her badly.' I took a sip of coffee to give myself time to collect my thoughts.

'Does she love you?' I heard a quiet question.

'I don't know. She's trying to be fair. As soon as she heard about your existence, she terminated her contract with me.'

'Boris, come here.'

I put my coffee down and sat on the edge of the bed.

'We had something wonderful.'

'Yes, that's right.' I smiled at the memory of our moments together. Suddenly a horrible thought came into my head. 'What happened last time... That failed attempt...' the rest didn't want to go through my throat, 'was it because of me?'

'No. It had nothing to do with you. The psychologist said that self-acceptance is key in this case. I try to listen to his advice. We had something beautiful, but it's no longer there. We each have to go our own way.'

'Don't say that. I will always be there for you.'

'Like you've been with me for the last six months? Out of obligation?'

'No, it's not like that.' I tried to deny it.

'It's okay. Believe me.' She took my hands and pressed her cheek into them. I saw unshed tears. 'Go to her. Explain. Both of us deserve to be happy.'

'I don't deserve you.'

'Maybe not. Now go, silly.'

I kissed her hard on the lips. I felt her warmth one last time.

'I'll come visit tomorrow.'

'You don't have to.'

'I'll come. And you'll play me something, so start practising right away.'

'Okay.' She smiled at me through her tears.

'I'll take care of you anyway. You know that.'

'I know,' she whispered again and chased me out of the room. She didn't want me to see her tears.

I was on a mission. I had to find Sarah and ask for her forgiveness.

Sarah

The pounding in my head didn't stop. It wasn't in my head. It was a banging on the door.

'Are you expecting someone?' I asked sleepily. It took me a moment to realise where I was. Mick had jumped out of bed. I got another flash of his bare butt before he put on his sweatpants. My head was pounding. I wasn't sure if anything had happened between us, and it would be difficult for me to face the consequences. I just didn't know that the consequences would fall on me so quickly. Mick was already opening the door in the other part of the apartment. At first, I heard some kind of rustling. I thought it was the letter carrier or a neighbour. Then I heard a familiar voice. My heart started pounding. My hands were shaking. Oh, fuck! What is he doing here? As quietly as I could, I got out of bed. I tried to eavesdrop as much as possible while hurriedly putting on my pants and blouse.

'Mick, I fucked up badly.' I could hear Boris's voice clearly. 'I've been calling her since yesterday. She's not answering my calls. I should be with her. Support her.

I've been everywhere, at her house, at the residence. No one's seen her. You were the last one to see her. Did you drive her home? Alan says she's not there. He was probably lying.' His voice came from different parts of the living room. Boris was pacing back and forth across the room.

I glanced at my phone. I had messages from all my friends and countless missed calls. I had muted my phone before the funeral ceremony. After that, I didn't turn on the sound again. Tears formed under my eyelids. Now, there was no time for grief. I turned up the volume on my phone and put it down on the coffee table. At that exact moment, it started ringing again. The music blasted across the room. The name *"Boris"* appeared on display. I declined the call the moment I saw Boris standing in the bedroom doorway. I only had time to fasten one shirt's button. He looked at me, then at the bed with its crumpled sheets. Then at me again. He shook his head with disbelief. I was standing in front of the man I loved, not fully dressed, my hair tousled. He had seen me so many times that he knew exactly what I looked like the morning after sex. I was afraid to speak up. Besides, what was there to say? Everything was clear. Mick walked up to me, separating me from Boris with his body. He only made it worse. I could see the grief and desire for murder in my beloved's eyes.

'My best friend. How could you?'

'Are you for real?' I stepped in front of Mick, poking my head up to look into the familiar honey eyes. 'You're a bit of a hypocrite, don't you think?'

'Did you sleep with him?' He asked in disbelief. It was as if he hadn't heard my plea. As if he wasn't the one with the wife. Fucking liar.

'Get out of here,' I demanded in a firm voice.

'I hope it was worth it.'

'Get out!' I said, my voice breaking. I didn't care that I wasn't at my place. I wanted him to leave so that he wouldn't look at me with such disappointment in his eyes anymore. At the same time, I wanted him to hug me and reassure me that everything would be okay. I wanted to feel his closeness again.

'It's time for you to go,' Mick urged him.

'I'll make my way out myself.' Boris turned and marched out of the room. Then we heard another loud slam of the door. I wanted to run after him. To shout for him to wait. Instead, I stood in the middle of the room and felt like I was going to pass out any second. I felt bad. I felt like a slut.

'Come here.' Mick extended his open arms toward me, and I accepted them. I snuggled into his bare chest, dampening it with tears. I cried for my grandmother, for love, for myself. When there were no more tears, I got the hiccups. I extricated myself from Mick's grasp.

'He's going to fire you.' The thought terrified me.

'He can't. I'm part-owner of the club. He'll probably want to buy my shares to get rid of me, but he can't fire me.'

I breathed heavily, the hiccups not going away.

'I need a drink of water.'

Mick quickly put on the T-shirt slung over the chair.

'Come on. I'll get breakfast ready.'

It crossed my mind that he was another man who could cook.

'Did we... You know... I can't remember anything from yesterday.'

He laughed.

'No, we didn't...' He shook his head playfully. 'I wasn't sure that was a good idea. You've been through too much. I was afraid you were driven by alcohol. But tonight, if you want....'

I shook my head negatively.

'That's what I thought. Come on, let's feed you. Then I'll drive you home, and we need to correct Boris' beliefs.'

I just nodded and followed him into the kitchen. I felt physically and emotionally defeated. On top of that, I thought I must have fallen on my head, suggesting sex to him last night. When did I become so frivolous? Where were my principles?

'Are you sure?' I looked at him suspiciously. 'You weren't wearing any briefs this morning.'

'I always sleep naked.' He shrugged his shoulders, amused by my behaviour.

He fed me and drove me home. I crawled into my bed and slept for the next two days. Amy checked in on me from time to time. It took me a while to allow myself to mourn, cry and grieve. On the third day, I realised that my grandmother wouldn't want to see me like this. She was always optimistic about life. She told me to take full grasp of it. The moment I realised this, I took a shower and got myself cleaned up. That same evening, I showed up at the residence. I surprised everyone with my presence. I finally felt, that I had fulfilled my grandmother's wish.

* * *

Alarmed by the strange news, I hurried to Mick's apartment. He wanted to see me immediately. He knew where I lived, but he insisted that I come to him. Even at the door, I could see the stress and guilt written all over his face.

'What's happened? Why the rush? Are you feeling okay?' I looked at his pale face once more.

'Someone wants to meet you.'

'Oh no! You will not play games with me.' I was already turning back to the door.

'It's not him.' We knew damn well who he was talking about. I stopped to see if he was lying to me.

I walked into the living room and soon regretted my decision. To my right by the window stood Alex. He nodded to me in greeting. On the left, Olivia was sitting on an armchair. She was holding a glass of wine in her hand. She raised it as a toast and drank some of the red liquid. What surprised me most was the figure standing in the centre of the room. A blonde with warm eyes was looking at me intently.

'You are so pretty,' she finally said.

'Thank you,' I asked rather than said. Her big eyes kept staring at me. Subconsciously I knew who she was. Besides, I had seen her photographs before. She looked much different, healthier in the photos. In reality, what I saw was a pretty but shabby blonde in oversized sweat-pants. She was without makeup, which accentuated the unhealthy tone of her skin. She looked sick.

'I'm Natalie,' she introduced herself. 'Olivia is my friend.' She hurried to explain as I glanced towards the other girl. Suddenly this information explained a lot to me. Since my arrival at the residence, I had always been the other girl, and that was the reason why Olivia had been so nasty to me. The pieces of the puzzle were finally falling into place.

'Can you please sit down?' Natalie patted the seat next to her with her skinny hand. 'Don't look at me like that. I'm going to live,' she laughed at her own joke.

I sat down next to her; I didn't want to look at her from a standing position. She immediately took my hand.

'I'm beginning to understand Boris' infatuation with you.'

I panicked when she said those words. She knew. I looked to Alex for support, but he stood like a statue facing the window. Mick wasn't there either. He had disappeared from the room. I couldn't even count on Olivia for support.

'I knew exactly when you started seeing each other,' she said calmly as if she was telling a story to a child, without anger or reproach. 'I began to see the light in him again, the spark that caused the flame—his will to live. So now I carry that spark in me, too. It turned out that I have a half-sister. I need to take care of her, but I need to recover first. What was I going to say again? Oh, yeah. Do you love him?'

'Why are you asking me that? Does it matter? You're his wife. I'm nobody.' She ignored me and went on.

'He loves you. Not like he loves me, it's a different kind of feeling. He's responsible for me, but that's not what he feels for you.'

'Stop it!' I pulled my hand out of her grasp.

At the same moment, Boris burst into the room, followed by Mick.

'The cherry on top of the cake.' Olivia laughed tartly.

'You left the centre?' Boris' worried gaze focused on Natalie.

'I'm well taken care of. Don't worry.' Boris looked at his brother.

I didn't know what this was about, but I shouldn't have been here. Seeing her and Boris in the same room was too painful. I got up to leave. Boris focused his attention on my face, and his gaze brightened slightly. It was starting to get to me what Natalie was talking about.

'That's what I mean,' Natalie added. 'That spark.'

A confused Boris wondered what was going on here.

'I have a gift for you.' Natalie handed me a folder resting on the sofa just behind her back. I looked at the item, puzzled.

'Should I open it?' I wanted to make sure. She nodded affirmatively.

I took the documents out on the table and started reading. Boris watched my reaction. I trembled. Suddenly, I felt weak. Boris grabbed me awkwardly to keep me from falling and sat me down on the sofa.

He knelt at my feet.

'Sarah, are you alright? Mick, get her some water.'

'Take care of him,' Natalie said. 'I'll see you later. Alex and Olivia will drive me back. Stay with her,' she turned to Boris. 'She needs you more than I do.' She left the room, taking her friends with her.

'Those papers…' I whispered once they left.

Boris broke off and read the papers.

'Divorce petition.' He uttered in disbelief.

I saw a whole range of emotions written across his face. He grabbed and kissed my hands. I was so shocked that at first, I didn't react at all and let him do it.

'We can,' he continued…

I slapped his face so hard that I felt the pain in my hand.

Shocked, he looked at me. He pressed his palm against my reddened cheek, and I took a step back.

'Don't you dare come near me.' I pointed a warning finger at him. 'We? Who are we? There is no us. We never were an us. All I had were lies. You think you snap your fingers, and I'm yours again? After everything I found out? After what you said in the car? The way you said it.' As the arguments continued, my tone of voice rose. 'How am I supposed to ever trust you again?'

'Sarah…' Boris raised his hand as if he wanted to touch me, but at the last moment, he changed his mind and lowered his hand along his body.

'Please get out of here.' My voice got quieter. I felt tired and defeated.

'I'll walk you to the exit.' Mick supported me and escorted his friend out of his own apartment, for which I was extremely grateful.

I sank heavily onto the sofa. I picked up the folder on the coffee table and ran my eyes over the text once more.

'What are you going to do now?'

Mick pulled me out of my reverie.

'I don't know. I really don't know.' I repeated helplessly, waiting for some clue.

'I wish you the best.'

He said, and I wondered how he could have used the word "*you*". After all, there were no us. I couldn't forgive him, or at least I shouldn't.

My reason told me exactly what I should do. Unfortunately, my heart had a different opinion on the subject.

Boris appeared everywhere I went. At first, I was furious that he was harassing me. Even though I said some unkind words to him, that did not discourage him. On the contrary, I saw the determination on his face. I ostentatiously turned my back on him, trying to ignore him. Later, however, when I was working at the residence and he didn't show up, my gaze kept running towards the door. I missed him more than I was ready to admit.

Amy had dragged me to Boris' club for a party. She probably wanted to reconcile us, but I had completely different plans. Besides, she was convinced that this time Mick was watching the club and Boris was away for the weekend. After a lot of persuasion, I gave in and we went dancing.

I danced with a random guy. The poor guy was unaware that he was on a losing streak. He was doomed from the start. Subconsciously I was thinking of Boris, even though he wasn't at the club, or was he? I saw him leaning against the railing on the higher level. He wouldn't take his eyes off me and was not happy. I enjoyed the grimace of rage on his face as the man tried to kiss me. I didn't have to wait long for his reaction. He disappeared from my sight only for a moment before he appeared right behind me.

'Sarah!' He admonished me in an icy tone, and the man dancing with me quickly backed away, appraising his opponent.

'Coward,' I muttered under my breath.

I saw Amy smiling from ear to ear. She was dancing near me. The cheeky girl had planned this and didn't even pretend to be sorry. Instead, she showed me two thumbs up.

'Are you going to tease me like this for long?'

'Tease? I'm not teasing you.'

'Come on.' He grabbed my hand and pulled me toward his office.

When he closed the door behind us, there was an awkward silence for a moment. I couldn't remember the last time we were alone in one room. He turned back to the door and pounded on it with his fist. Then, he slowly turned to face me, as I moved back as far away from him as possible. He looked at me. I couldn't see an arrogant and confident man anymore. He had an uncertain look in his eyes.

'Sarah,' he spoke quietly, 'What can I do? How to prove to you that you are not just my toy.' He ran his hand through his hair. 'Say something,' he asked. 'I'm sorry. I should have told you everything at the beginning, but I didn't think that I would develop feelings for you. It wasn't part of my plan.'

He took two big steps and was already beside me. 'I love you, Sarah. Are you able to forgive me? Be with me. I'm going crazy without you.'

'Okay.' I agreed quietly.

'I can't sleep, eat, please....' He looked at me, puzzled. 'You said, okay?'

I nodded affirmatively, and he plunged his hands into my hair, then kissed me. I missed him so much, his taste, his smell, all of him. We talked for a long time.

It wasn't easy. Oh no. The disbelief and shock continued for some time. Boris was patient but firm.

He did not allow me to hesitate. I had to come to terms with the idea that I had broken someone else's marriage. Natalie turned out to be a warm, compassionate person. I met with her on several other occasions. She left the clinic to fight for custody of her half-sister. It turned out that she had inherited quite a substantial estate from her father.

After three months, the long-awaited decision about divorce came. We celebrated that evening with champagne in bed and a night full of passion. The next evening, Boris took me to our favourite restaurant.

'Your parents are here!' I ran up to them, overjoyed to greet them. I also spotted Amy, Alex, Niko and the rest of the familiar faces.

'Boris, what is all this?' I asked the man I loved.

He smiled at me, as he got down on one knee in front of me. He pulled out a ring box from his pocket. I was breathless with emotion.

'Sarah, you are my light. I want to belong only to you. Will you marry me?'

In his warm honey eyes, I found enough love to warm the two of us.

'Yes,' I whispered.

The guests around us went wild with joy. Natalie, who was standing nearby, hugged me and congratulated me first. She said a few words to Boris and kissed him on the cheek. She wasn't so skinny anymore. She tried very hard to get back to good health. I looked at this amazing woman who had given me happiness. She approached her younger sister, who smiled radiantly at her. I was drawn into a whirlwind of congratulations and good wishes. I caught a glimpse of my man's eyes staring at me with adoration.

I caught Amy's pleased look and thought to myself that she would be next in line. I would make sure of that…

The End

Author's note

Acknowledgement - Appreciation - Saying Thank You

First of all, thank you, my Reader, for reaching out and reading my book. I'm genuinely curious about your opinion on the story you just read, and I encourage you to share it at www.goodreads.com, on Amazon, or any other site devoted to my work. I also invite you to share your opinion about the book on my Instagram and Facebook accounts under @Sandra Robins. The upcoming books in this series are Price of Truth, and Price of Lies, which I hope to release in English soon.

I would also like to thank Magdalena Wiacek for taking on the task of translating the text from Polish into English and Michalina Surynt for proofreading and Izabela Surdykowska-Jurek for the stunning book covers. I want to thank my husband for his support throughout our life together, not only with writing the book but also with each new crazy idea. There have been quite a few and probably more to come.

Thank you to every single person who asks about my next books. It really motivates me to keep writing.

Table of contents

Printed in Great Britain
by Amazon

31201504R00169